God
and the Others

God
and the Others

M. M. Costantin

Houghton Mifflin Company Boston

1972

First Printing c

ISBN: 0-395-13952-X
Library of Congress Catalog Card Number: 72-513
Printed in the United States of America

To Lee, on the joyous occasion
of his thirty-seventh birthday

I

Detroit: 1938–April 1941

OH OH OH her mother's voice went up up up then oh oh oh it came down again there's shootin' at the carworks the toffs are killin' the men your father your father and up and down up and down the words went killin' he's dead I know it Mother Mary I know it and another babby on the way and I know it himself dead somewhere mute-tilated the curs the dogs killin' decent men who only want a decent wage for their wives and babbies Mother of God Mother of God Ireland was bad but Deetroit is Hell itself wake up child wake up child and be a comfort to your grievin' mam

and the lights in her face and it so cold outside of bed even in her mother's lap with the oh oh oh coming through her mother's dress soft front and she could not get her head to stick up straight and her mother's hand on her chin shaking shaking her head and she tried to keep her eyes open

and this little child only three years old and already now dear God an orphan and the one on its way will never know its brave dad its brave dad shot down by Henry Ford himself just to save a few pennies to con-serve a fortune them in their fancy clothes aytin' and drinkin' God knows what while the men have nothin' but God is just listen to me MaryCatherine wake up now child it is a lesson you must learn that God is just and the good must suffer oh oh oh God allows the good to suffer to show the evil of men's ways and now we must pray for your dear father's soul oh oh oh down came the voice and she did not know the thing prayer her mother was through her dress saying Hail Mary Hail Mary was all she knew to say

ach the nuns will teach you all your prayers and how to endure sufferin' when you are old enough I will take you to school with them each day and I will myself stop in church all in black to pray myself for your murthered dad unless unless unless unless Henry Ford and the toffs and their gunmen come for us too we must be brave we must face them with never a tear though they murther us in cold blood for gain for proffit spill the blood of a preg-nant woman spill the blood of a tiny child without pity stop that cryin' child stop that bawlin' that howlin' you must be strong it is our lot our way the good suffer God allows the good to suffer stop that yellin'

and suddenly she was sliding out of her mother's lap hitting the floor trying to keep her head up eyes open

Rory my God Rory you're alive are you hurt they're shootin' at the works it was on the rad-dio they're shootin' are they not the voice up up up up

"I'm tired. Give me a drink of whiskey."

❦

she was flying up up into the air and it was cold not warm and her mam had her and was shaking her in the lights

this time for sure they've killed him all those other times God spared him your dear dad your darlin' dad now it's true they've killed him there was violence at the works where he was today doin' the biddin' of that Reuther that Reuther followin' him all over the state of Mishi-gan mark my words oh God in Heaven spare the life of my husband give this child not five yet her dad so she may copy his ways he is a saint on earth riskin' his life as he does for others without a thought for his own cares his young wife his little daughter and this time for sure I'm preg-nant and the poor infant will never know its brave dad

again and again and again sleeping then the lights and the cold and the screaming and "I'm tired. Give me a drink of whiskey."

II

Freshkill, New York

1. May 1941–December 1941

HER MIDDLE HAD GONE AWAY from all the throwing up into the paper bags. She pressed her cheek against the bus window and tried to look out at what was going by but it made her feel sick again. She was not the only one, even big people on the bus had thrown up. She lay back in her mother's lap and listened to her mother's voice.

I'm tellin' you Rory that baloney was off it's a con-spiracy they only stop the bus at the greasy spoons they own and then they sell food that's rotten and rob the poor poison them as well it's a con-spiracy and you an of-ficial of the C-I-O should look into it my stomach will never be right again and the kid thinner now even than when we started

Her father's face all puckered up in the seat next to them and he rubbed his hand on his hair, gray.

"Ah, Maureen! She's a picky eater is our Mary Catherine because you spoil her, that and a little unseasonal heat, that's the only reason she's sick. It's all in her mind."

high-strung the child is and I admit it my father was just such a person high-strung well-beloved by all the pride of the village who could have been king if he liked he had the right bloodlines ex-cept that the Protestants the Eng-glish and their plots blood of kings it's in the registry books even written

down in Dublin records for anyone who cares to see and now
another one of us undone poisoned somewheres between
Deetroit and Albany by the connivins of

"Do shut up, woman, with your rattling on and on. She'll
be all right once we get off at Freshkill. It may be a mill town,
that's true, but it's on the river, almost like a country town, on
the Hudson River. So it can't be bad, being on such a big river,
and you'll like it and her stomach will settle once she's rid of
the motion of the bus."

He was talking about getting off the around and around
feeling of the bus so she looked at her father but he had already
shut his eyes the way he did when her mam talked. She
couldn't help it, she yawned, without putting her hand over
it.

why tell me why stop those bad manners kid just tell me
why did you have to leave all that good money behind a Ford
worker you could have been yourself only a month it's just
the middle of May not later than just a month since His
Majesty Ford gave in signed the paper agreed to pay decent
wages I'll tell you why you have enemies within the la-bour
movement because of your followin' that Reuther fellow and
his silly brothers as well it's true it's true them just adventurers
and that Walter him with his Jew wife and his red hair and not
even Irish with that red hair and not even Catholic God knows
with that red hair not so fine a color as mine of course and you
made enemies because of him

Her father was getting mad, she could see.

and never stoppin' at home for weeks on end and off to Flint
and Dear-born and such places with shootin' and beatin' and
tear-gassin' and me never knowin' from one minute to the next
whether you was alive or

"Will you, will you shut up?" But he wasn't hollering. "I was the one wanted this job, who took it, plain and simple, for the peace and quiet of it. And keep your silly mouth off Reuther. He and I disagree on a lot of things, just like the President and I disagree on a lot of things, but he's, the both of them are after good for the workers with which I can't disagree. And you understand none of it. And it's not your place to understand any of it. Your place is to get the kid up and to get the bundles together because we'll be stopping soon and I don't want any trouble or delay. The Albany–New York City bus isn't supposed to make any stops. But I told the driver who I was and who my friends are and any minute now he's going to make a special stop for us because he's just given me the wave. Just do your job and let me alone to do my job. My wages," he was whispering, mad, "are better than most so you have no cause to complain. Get the kid up now, she looks half-asleep."

count all the suitcases and bundles they are sure to try and keep some of them locked up from us because we ordered baloney in their places instead of the costly stuff can you imagine plain Jell-O at five cents a tiny cup they will

She tried to walk along the aisle of the bus but her mother was pushing so hard along behind her that she kept stumbling almost fell and then there was fresh air hot and the sidewalk so she sat down.

get up kid have you no pride get up off the pavement this instance immediately pay attention to your mam I've had a hard journey you in my lap the whole time count the baggage Rory there should be five pieces that driver is in their pay you know that

"Shut up, woman, will you? I know you're tired out, but

this is the wrong time for you to be cross and complaining."

Her stomach jumped at the sound of each of the five pieces of baggage hitting the sidewalk. She wished her mam would stop being what her dad said and start being pretty again.

get his name his number will you in case there's anything broken arrogant he is and a bad driver as well

"Maureen, shut up. For once and for all, kindly shut up!"

Before they finished talking, she sat down on the sidewalk among the suitcases and boxes and threw up some more.

"Not here, don't do that here, kid! There are people! This is the Main Street! Five years old, nearly six, and puking on the sidewalk! Stop her, Maureen! She's too old for that, too old!"

Her mother pulled her up by one of her arms.

stop it stop it I say you're makin' fools of all of us

The bus pulled away leaping and bounding as she finished throwing up.

"Yes, ma'am," she said and then she heaved again but there was nothing more to come up.

you said there'd be somebody to meet us I told you that union is tryin' to gyp you out of all you've earned there's no one here so far as I can see

"The flat's just down the street. I have the address. Over that empty store is my guess. And the diner fellow has the key. You stay here, I'm going to take what I can carry down to the flat. Stay with the rest of the stuff. Kid, you go into that diner place there and tell them your name and tell them you've come for the key, they know about it, then bring it to me. Get up. Get up." He patted her cheek. "You can do that for your old dad, can't you?"

She hauled herself to her feet. She was so tired and it was so hot and the door to the diner place would not open.

Her mother shouted, red face, red hair.

slide it anybody can see it's a slidin' door are you daft or somethin' if I have to leave this stuff to open a simple door for you somebody is sure to rob us blind in this town as if we hadn't suffered enough already

Her mother sitting there on a suitcase with all the people standing around, looking.

The fat man in the white hat stopped wiping the table to help her as she tripped on the door thing and began to cry.

"Hey. Little girl," he said, "what's the matter?"

"My name is MaryCatherineMulligan and I've come for the key."

It smelled like food in here but she didn't have anything left to throw up.

"Listen, kid, sit down for a minute. You don't look so hot to me."

He lifted her up into the booth where he had been cleaning the table.

"Wipe your face with this. All right, hold still. I'll do it. Hold still. You feel better? You okay?"

"Please, my name is MaryCatherineMulligan and I've come for the key."

"I know about it. I got it. Listen, you want a drink of water? Would that make you feel better? Nice cold water? Or some ice cream?"

"Please, my name is MaryCath — "

"How about some ice cream? Nice and cold. On the house."

She cried out loud.

"Okay. Okay. Just a minute."

He went to the cash register and made it ring.

"Here you are. Here's the key. Where are your folks? Do they know you're sick?"

She grabbed the key and ran for the door, which wouldn't open.

"I'll do it. Here, I'll do it. Take it easy."

He slid open the door.

"Thankyouverymuch," she said without looking.

She brought the key to her mam.

you fool it's your father wants the key and it took you long enough what were you doin' in there playin' around as usual while I sat out here in the sun guardin' all these value-ables me out here bakin' in the sun surrounded by oh God oh dear God just look at this town it was their wives did it that's who hatin' me because I'm only twenty-three it was all of them old and withered up got their husbands to push him out to a place like this

"Ah, woman, do be still," her father yelled from down the street. "You're collecting a crowd. Come on, Mary Catherine, child. Bring me the key."

get on with it you lazy thing makin' us wait and wait

"All right," her dad said and the two of them went through the big brown door and then up the stairs to the landing. Her father looked at all the doors and then bent down and unlocked the door straight in front of them at the top of the stairs.

The door opened right into a kitchen and it was hot, hot.

"Christ, let me get some windows open in here. This place must have been shut up for months."

"It smells like kitty. Is there a kitty?"

"Open up that back door, kid. Just turn the key in the lock there and open the door so we can get a breeze started."

There were a million steps going to the ground from the back door of the kitchen. It made her dizzy to look but she didn't have anything left to throw up.

"Well, kid," her dad said from another room, "what do you think of your new home?"

She turned around. The front door came right into the kitchen at the other end of the room. Next to her, where she stood, was an empty door going into another room. Straight in front of her there was another door, right next to the front door, and it was through that door she could hear her father. Maybe he had the kitty in there with him. She went to see.

"This room isn't bad," her dad said, standing in the middle of the room in the front of the flat.

It had two windows in one end of it and it had two windows touching each other on one side of it, too, where you could see the wall of the building next door and they had a window over there, too. She looked out of one of the front windows and she could see cars going by and she could see her mam sitting on the sidewalk with all the stuff but less people now.

"In there's the bathroom," her father said. "You gotta go?"

The bathroom door was right over by the windows of the side wall of this room.

"I don't think so," she said, but she peeked into the bathroom anyway to see if maybe there was a kitty in there. There wasn't one unless he was hiding under the bathtub, which had tall straight legs. How would she ever be able to get up into it?

"Well, it's no palace," her father said, "but it would never do for me to come here and set myself up in some showy place. It'd destroy the confidence of the workers in me, it would. Christ, though, it could do with a coat of paint.

"Well, once your mother's had a hand at it, given it the woman's touch, it'll look just like home. And I'll get some furniture off the local merchants, spread a little cash and good will there, that'll set right with them, the storekeepers. They'll agree to what may come later. They're the ones'll profit from the workers getting fatter pay envelopes, even if it should mean a strike or two and the necessity of credit being advanced, temporarily. You'll see. You'll see. It'll all work out fine. This is a good move I've made, you'll see.

"All right, then, Mary Catherine, my love," her dad said to her, "I'm going off now to get the rest of the stuff and your mother. Stay here, now. Don't wander off."

As soon as her father went through the kitchen front door, she ran into the bathroom and looked under the bathtub.

There was no kitty there. No kitty. He must have gone away with the child who lived here before.

She went back into the room with the windows. The ceiling was way high and it was brownish like the walls and the floor and the woodwork. The woodwork was her job to keep dusted and washed. It was a job she liked, but at home it was white and hard to do just right and the places she missed always showed. Brownish wouldn't be so hard.

She looked down out of one of the front windows to see if her father was with her mother yet, he was and they were getting the stuff, and then she went and looked out of one of the side windows at the window next door and there was a lady sitting there with very big dark eyes looking back at her who hadn't been there before and Mary Catherine screamed and ran back into the kitchen, far away, and sat down in a corner, waiting.

There was a noise on the stairs, *the lady*, and then another one, and she was all alone, all alone.

"Look, I *know* you're all worn out but it's just there, just at the top of the stairs. Give me that bundle. The door's unlocked."

The door opened and there was her mam, bright, bright, blue eyes, not dark, dark, black eyes.

will you look at that now will you just look at that sittin' on the floor like that wrinklin' up her dress like that do you mean to tell me the front door opens up right into the kitchen what kind of place is it you've landed us in what kind of place is this

"The priest got it for me, you know that. I got his name and wrote off to him, Father Michael Rafferty, and told him our needs and how much we could spend and he found as best he could."

well all I can say is that no man with a fa-mily would have picked out a place like this get up child get up I can see from the posters there's soon to be a grocery downstairs an Eye talian grocery what does that mean tell me what does that mean does that mean this town is filled up with Eye talians you never told me will I be safe on the streets they like fair women you know like them with red hair.

"Shut up, will you, with talk like that in front of the kid! You knew when we got married that I might have to do some moving around with the organizing. You should have stayed in Ireland if you can't stand anything but Irish around you.

Just get it out of your head right away that being young and
pretty and the wife of an official is any excuse for being rude
and bigot-ty. Get it?"

it's dif-ferent you born here your father before you born
here in this meltin' pot place but I'm just a greenhorn not used
to well I'm not the complainin' kind never was nor will be but
what room is this, her mother said going through the empty
door into the room right next to the kitchen.

"Well, we have to arrange things," her dad said.

I don't ask much, her mother said, but a woman likes to be
safe and the kid too tell me there is a bathroom isn't there or is
that a little sur-prise you've been savin'

"In there."

Her mam went into the room with the windows and they
heard a door shut and a minute later they heard the toilet flush.

"There's a good view of Main Street, Maureen," her father
called, "and windows enough for a good cross-ventilation."

just imagine the stink of it all all that traffic comin' up here
with its fumes into this room which will have to be our bedroom because of the toilet openin' off it it'll be hard im-possible
to keep clean of course with all the stink from the traffic and
hard to sleep at night as well but what can you do just pray
to God that's

And then her mother screamed and ran into the room where
they were, the kitchen. Mary Catherine stayed pressed up in
her corner. Under the stove, which had high long legs like the
bathtub, she could see balls of dust and a crust of bread.

there's one of them an Eye one of them a witch lookin' right
into our windows where we will be sleepin' Mother of

Her father went into the window room.

"Will you please stop looking in?" she heard him say. Her
mother was looking around the kitchen and she looked mad,
not scared.

"Please, lady, stop looking in. I know it's interesting having
new neighbors but you're disturbing my wife who's just had a
long, trying journey."

Then he didn't talk, but she could hear him moving around.

"Listen, it's nothing to worry about," her father said, coming
back. "I got a good look at her and she's an old lady and blind,
it's my guess, and deef as well. Just pay her no mind."

just look at that, her mother said, just look at that is an icebox an *ice*box did I give up my Frigidaire for an icebox and a
lot of Eye foreigners that union that union it's doin' you dirty

"See if the gas is turned on and I'll go get some food." Her
dad's Stop That! voice was talking.

after that harrowin' trip you expect me to cook let's get a
bite out it's

"Bites Out Cost Money," her dad said and lit up the stove
with the burning part of his cigarette. "It works. Open up
the bundle with the pans and such. I'll get some bacon and
eggs. That'll do. And dig out the sheets as well. We'll have
to bunk on the floor. You'll survive."

He looked at them with a mad look and then went out the
kitchen front door.

Her mother walked up and down and up and down the
kitchen. Then she went through the empty door into the room
right next to the kitchen.

did you ever see such a place it's a closet that's what this
room here is it's a closet just big enough to hold all the
diamonds and jewels and furs and silken frocks me and Carole

Lombard wear what I have done to come to that I should have to live in a place like this when even my widowed man's humble cottage that I had to leave and go far away from in Ireland dear place because times were hard would be better than this and I could have married the son of the squire or the squire himself widowed he was who had an eye for me and who's to wonder under God's sky because you should have seen me at sixteen Mary Catherine you should have seen me I'm still in pretty good shape for twenty-three but worryin' movin' around it shows it shows and we'll just have to sleep in this room back here because a wop witch is a wop witch blind or deef or not I don't want any evil eye on me oh dear God in heaven dear God

And then her mam gave her a hard spanking because she was still sitting on the floor in the corner.

It was the day of the parade, it was the day of the parade and she had been waiting and waiting for it, even more than she had waited for her birthday, July 30, she was six! They had their telephone now as well as beds and chairs and things and her father had been on the telephone talking almost all the time he was home from the office for days and days about the parade and all. He was making it. They usually didn't have a parade to end the summer in this town but her dad said Labor Must Have Its Day.

And there was going to be a pitnit, too, and a ball game and then a band concert and then fireworks (a surprise, so don't you say a word to anyone, kid) and everybody in the whole town was invited, regardless. And her father did it. He was the boss for a change, her mam said, and the mill bosses could like it or lump it take it or leave it put it in their pipes and smoke it and more and more like that, almost like singing because her mam was happy as happy about the parade and pitnit and all, too. Even before breakfast, her mam had been up and about and singing, and all they did, her mam and her dad and her, too, was to laugh all the way through breakfast.

And then the phone kept ringing and ringing for her dad and her dad had to tell them to stop making so much noise because happy noise was still noise and he couldn't hear a damned thing.

come on then Mary Catherine let's me and you get dressed it'll take some time because we want your dad to be proud of us the whole town'll be lookin' at us for sure and here's your dress all pressed and ready come on then

Mary Catherine put on her clean underwear and her petticoat as fast as fast because she could hardly wait to get on the dress, a sailor dress!

"Ouch ouch ouch ouch," she said, as a joke, while her mother was braiding her hair. It really hurt, so it felt better to say ouch, but she didn't want to make her mam mad so she wasn't going to do one single thing to spoil today.

well then go and show your dad how nice you look while I do up my hair it takes a while

Her dad was still talking on the phone.

"Yes, Larry . . . of course, why not, Larry?" to Larry, who was the mayor of the whole town, so she didn't make a noise, only stood there until he saw her and then she did a little dance around in a circle so he could see her back where the sailor collar was as well as her front where the red tie was.

He kept listening and talking but he smiled at her and pulled her up on his lap, just the way he did with her mam.

"Mary Catherine, you look like a dream walking," he said as soon as he hung up Larry, but the phone rang again before he could say anything else. He gave her a kiss on the cheek and she decided she would go off and watch her mam do up her hair.

Her mam was sitting in front of the bureau mirror in the little room off the kitchen which was their bedroom. She had on her dress already, but she had on her bathrobe over it.

okay watch if you want but this is com-plicated business so no talkin' you'll see what a hard job it is to do when it's your time to do it

Her mam called her dad Black Irish you Black Irish devil because he had huge black eyes and his hair used to be all black instead of only in streaks, so that must make her mam Red Irish, even though only her hair, not her eyes, was red.

Sometimes Mary Catherine wanted to laugh when she saw her dad and mam standing next to each other. Her dad dark and tall, looking like the priest, and her mam, bright and small, looking like a funny little devil. Sometimes, as a joke, her dad would sweep her up in one arm and her mam in the other arm and hold them, both at the same time, high off the floor, and they would both scream because it was nice to be high up but scary, too. And then he would lift them up even higher!

silly silly silly, her mam would keep saying, laughing.

Mary Catherine sat on the edge of her mother's bed and watched her combing and brushing her long and soft red hair, pinning it up into a fat roll all around her head. This was the way she liked her mam the best, busy at something, humming to herself, quiet. So she kept very still, so she wouldn't spoil it.

Finally, her mam was finished and she stood up and took off her bathrobe so that you could see her dress that had all little blue and white and red flowers all over it, and her mam leaned closer up to the mirror to brush at her eyebrows with a finger and then she looked at Mary Catherine and said

how's that then

"You look like a movie lady. The prettiest movie lady!" She did, too.

clear to see you've got the gift of your dad's blarney but I do look nice don't I let's go and see your dad *if* he's off that in-fernal oh but wait I almost forgot what a witless creature I am sure it's all the pre-parin' almost put it out of my and what do you think I have right here in this closet my little missy

Mary Catherine thought and thought.

"*I* don't know."

well, her mam said and drew a little American flag off the shelf.

"Oh, boy!"

who on earth said this little banner had anythin' to do with you may I ask this is my American flag for wavin' at the parade

"Oh."

but this one is yours, and the other flag was in her hands almost before her mother could say the words.

you're a grand old flag, her mam was singing, come on let's go see your dad you're a high flyin' flag

"Oh, Jesus," her dad said into the phone. "Well, it's hardly unexpected. Christ, it'd hardly be Labor Day without them, would it?"

Her mam stopped singing and put her hand on Mary Catherine's shoulder to show her she should stop singing, too. And Mary Catherine could see why. Her dad's face didn't look happy anymore. It didn't look mad or worried or anything, it just looked very serious, and, then, so did her mother's face.

"Any idea of how many of them? Uh-huh. Are they arm — hell, *you* know what I mean. I don't have to spell it out. Not with an audience here, I don't."

what is it Rory tell me this instance what

Her dad waved his hand at her.

"One thing, for sure, they won't try anything on Main Street. Sure I'm sure. Too many cops around. If they make a move, it'll be at Mem — right, yeah. Don't worry about it, Larry. It won't do a damned bit of good to worry . . . yes, I've got some of my lads on the lookout already."

Then her dad listened to Larry for a while.

"To *you* they may seem respectable men, but to me they're mill owners and it's been my experience that where profit is involved, where a union is coming into being is involved . . . Look, I'll see you in a few minutes. It'll all keep till then. Right. Thanks for calling back. Good-bye."

it's that same Deetroit business startin' up all over again isn't it all that vio-lent

"Not now, Maureen. Not in front of the kid. Everything's in hand, take my word for it. Just sit back and enjoy the parade and all, okay? There's no reason to . . ."

every reason in the world to worry you think I've lost my memory every reason in the

"There won't be a better-looking pair of girls than you two

in the whole town today, mark my words. You're going to watch the parade from up here in the flat, aren't you? You'll get a good lookout from up here and not have to worry about the crowds."

What! What? *Up*stairs? She couldn't help it. She began to cry. She didn't want to watch it from up *here*, she didn't know *that* was the plan, she wanted to watch it from down there where all the people were going to be.

"And what's your problem, young lady?"

"I wanna be downstairs."

She felt better as soon as she said it, but she kept on bawling in case they didn't think she really meant it about being downstairs.

no up here I can't possibly sit all those hours of the parade down there watchin' the sun'll burn me to a crisp can I help I got this fair skin of

Mary Catherine cried some more.

"All right, all right. You can go downstairs to watch but you stay all of the time just where your mam can see you, okay?"

She gave her dad a big hug, poking him with her flag.

"Ooh, you little devil! I just hope that's the heaviest stick laid on me today!"

oh Rory you're keepin' somethin' back from me I know I can tell what do you mean the heaviest stick

"A joke, a bad joke, that's all. You oughta know by now there's those don't like the idea of anything but company unions. Hate especially industrial unions, and that as long as they're around and I'm around . . ."

when is it ever goin' to end when is

"Stop before you start, Maureen. Got me? It won't do anybody any good to have you all up in the air. People will be watching you today, you know, just because you're Mrs. Rory Mulligan, which reminds me. I'll be riding in the open Buick with the mayor and when we get as far as here, I'll point up to you in the window and you smile and wave, so everybody can see where we live and understand we're plain folks just like them. Got it? You smile and wave, if it kills you, I don't care what you think about the mayor being Dutch Reformed. I've got to keep the town officials as well as the workers of this town happy and, if you haven't tumbled to it already, I'm telling you. Good will is ninety-nine percent of my job."

and gettin beat over the

"Stop."

And her mam did, at least while her dad was still there. But once he went, she was all changed from the singing way she had been.

it's just as well you're goin' to be downstairs it would only con-fuse matters if people had to look at two windows not one because both of us can't fit with any comfort in one and will you look at these curtains grimy already only three months up just like I said that first day and you missed a lot of places here on the woodwork you've already messed up your braids hard enough they were to do with that limp hair of yours and your dress what did you do to the front of it I'll bet your Cousin Deirdre never let it get into such a con-dition when she had it and look at that I can already see worn marks beginning here on the sofa bed you're supposed to sleep on it not jump on it like an el-ephant it is the sofa you know and only part of the time your bed and my only hope is that an

ugly ducklin' like you can turn into a beautiful swan like
rooned rooned gang-sters here too like Deetroit in this little
town gang-sters too ah me what

Mary Catherine went down the stairs with her flag. Shut
up, shut up, shut up, she said the whole way down, but to herself so nobody could hear. Shut up, she said out loud while
she banged the downstairs door to. If you didn't bang it, it
didn't catch and then it hung open like a slum, her mam said.
Her mam always and always and always said *some*thing!

The tiny little bit of feeling good she had left stopped feeling good right away and she knew why. She had gone against
Honor Thy Father and Thy Mother, that thing! That thing
was one of the things the nuns, her mother had showed them
to her in church, a lot of ladies in funny clothes, don't say
funny, you heathen, her mother said, the nuns will teach you
all you need to know but all you need to know right now is
Honor Thy Father and Thy Mother which means God Will
Get You if you talk back you silly faggot

And He *would* get her, too, because she had said Shut up,
shut up.

She sat down on the curb and, because nobody was around,
she pressed with her hands at the front of her dress. But the
wrinkles had been there when she put the dress on this morning and it was her favorite dress and she wouldn't do anything
to spoil it her mother should know. And why was it her mam
had to go and get all crabby when it was such a good day. It
made her head ache, all that talking of her mam's, and even if
she shut her eyes the way her dad did, the headache didn't go
away. Especially how her voice got all screeching when she
talked about the babby that was un-doubtedly comin'. When-

ever would that baby get here so she wouldn't have to be the only one to hear all it was her mother said when her dad was at the office? When ever!

An old man and an old lady came next to her carrying fold-up chairs and little flags and a thermos jug. And then a fat boy and then a mother and father and a baby and then more and more people until finally both sides of Main Street were jam-filled with people and none of them, not one of them, even the fat boy, tried to make her move from her place. They must know who her dad was.

She held up her flag and, every once in a while, waved up to her mother so her mother wouldn't yell MaryCatherine! MaryCatherine! in that way she could. Her mother yelling her name like that would make all these people think she was a baby when she wasn't and could already read some words when they were printed big in the newspapers which it was her job to go and buy just down the street at Van Dine's each day for her dad. She would get away from all that talking soon and go to school, not long now, and then that old babby, if it ever did come, would be the one that had to listen to her mam.

MaryCatherine MaryCatherine

Shut up, she said without even looking over her shoulder and I don't care about Honor Thy Father and Honor Thy Mother because those ladies in their funny clothes, don't say funny you heathen, those ladies haven't told me yet about Honor Thy so It Doesn't Count!

She had heard the sirens coming from far away but still it surprised her when the parade came to where she was sitting on the curb.

First, policemen on their motorcycles and then a policeman all by himself on a horse that looked tired. Then MissFreshkill in an open car in a long dress, it looked long even though she couldn't see its bottom, with crisscross straps and blond hair and a crown, her father had talked about all of that for MissFreshkill on the telephone.

And then, right away, a band dressed all in white with navy blue collars and red ties, just like hers, playing "Starsandstriesfevver," her favorite song. And then more people marching and then a band all in kelly green, emerald green, Irish, and her mother's voice hurrah! hurrah! and then more people marching with caps and then a fire truck, going very slow, with all its lights flashing and its sireen going *oohway, oohway,* slow so that no one would think there was really a fire and then a whole lot of men in clothes just the color of gum before you chewed it and then some more in costumes just the same color only they were a band and they were playing a song she had heard once in the movies and which was much better even than "Starsandstries."

"Listen, Mother," the old man said, "they've made a march out of 'Alexander's Ragtime Band.'" And the old lady said, "It sounds nice, but it's hardly decent, is it, Father?"

Decent, that was like Honor Thy, all that.

And more people marching, more than she had thought, and bands and bands and then, and then!

Her father! Her father! And everybody, the old lady and the old man and the mother and father, even the baby, even the fat boy, shouting and clapping, her father! There he was in the car with no top with Larry and they were waving and she screamed Dad! Dad! And he pointed at her and the mayor, Dutch whatever he was, looked where her dad was pointing his finger and he smiled at her, just at her, and waved, and then when they were almost gone by, her father pointed up to where her mother was, but nobody seemed to see and she could hear her mother, she hoped nobody else could hear her mother, you rooned it Mary Catherine you mean devil you rooned it

She tried to think of a way not to have to go upstairs again where she was supposed to go before they walked across town to Memorial Field where the pitnit and all of it was.

"Yer the Mulligan kid ainchu," the man in the pickup said. He came at the end of the parade, after the bands, and after the kids with red and white and blue through their bicycle wheels and off their handlebars.

"Yes," she said because he looked very strong.

"Tell your old lady I'm waiting for the food she's fixed for the pitnit."

She ran up the stairs and struggled with the door her mam had locked against robbers.

"The food! The food! The man's here!"

carry, her mother said and shoved the big bowl with cole-slaw into her arms Rory Rory I will never de-file po-tatoes in the way you're askin' cabbage salad is as far as I'll go and bake a ham and that's well enough

Her mother was carrying the ham.

here it is here it is, her mother sang out to the dark man in the pickup and he looked all different, smiles, than he had when he told her to get upstairs.

Some of the people in the street stopped in their business of folding up their chairs and folding up the newspapers they

had put on their heads against the sun to watch the man in the
pickup adding the baked ham and the coleslaw to the treasures
he already had in the back of his truck.

"It'd be my pleasure to give you a lift," the man said to her
mother.

how kind of you how kind of you but I've promised to walk
along with friends and you know how friends are I'm sure

"My bad luck," the man said, "my very bad luck. See you
at the pitnit."

Her mother smiled and waved as the truck drove away.

in a pig's eye you greaseball, she said, in a pig's eye get on
with you child go on up to the toilet I want to close up the
windows in case of rain hurry hurry hurry hurry

And Mary Catherine did and, finally, they began to walk
with all the other people across Freshkill to Memorial Field.

Nobody was hurrying, Mary Catherine saw. Not like a
regular day with everybody rushing off in a lot of different
directions, being busy, stopping to talk to each other only for
a minute. They were all just walking slowly, all in the same
direction underneath the trees which had more leaves than
anybody could count.

Deetroit had trees, too, but not so many of them on each
street and not streets and streets full of them. Her dad had
gotten them a nice town, Freshkill, to live in and it had lots
of gardens, too, almost one for every house and a river with
boats in it and even a mountain, Mount Freshkill, with a
funiculee, funiculah going up the side of it, and a creek and
trains and a liberry. And here all around her were all the
people of this whole town, all going to her dad's pitnit.

Everybody was invited but they were supposed to bring

their own knives and forks and spoons and plates and glasses and such things, so each mother, even her mother, and some of the fathers and big kids, too, were carrying baskets or paper bags with the stuff. And some of the mothers, like her mam, were carrying opened-up umbrellas of all sorts of colors to keep the sun off them. The pretty umbrellas made it all look like a big dance with a lot of people in it in the movies. Just like a dance, with no pushing or shoving to get there first. And that was because there was going to be Enough for All, her dad said.

mark my words us that did all that hot cookin' will end up with nothin' to eat and all those as brought nothin' will

"I have wheedled and cajoled enough food out of everybody in this town's got it to sell or buy, there'll be enough to feed an army and a half, you mark *my* words. This town is so worn down and beat up by hard times that what it needs is the biggest blowout it's seen in years, which is exactly what I have organized, and once the workers have had a good time, for a change, they'll listen a little closer to talk of *labor* organizing, especially organizing along industrial lines. Now, what do you think of that?"

faith now listen to all of that what would my dear old mother rest her soul think of me the youngest married to a gray-haired old man of forty-one who turns out to be an in-tellec-tual as well for the love of God what would she

"I'll give you gray-haired old man, you vixen! It wasn't my gray hairs you were making eyes at up there in South Boston, was it? Come here, just get here in my reach!"

And her mam laughing, that day, in that funny silly way and even though they were in the next room and she couldn't see them, she knew they were kissing each other and doing that stuff they chased her away from watching. Why couldn't it be that if her mam had to do one thing more than another thing, that it was the laughing, even the silly laughing, she did, instead of all the talking. Even right now, her mam was laughing, talking with her lady friends and every one of them was telling her how pretty she looked, and it was true, and maybe she would forget the talking into the telephone with Larry that had made her stop being cheery and start being mean and crabby.

"Look at that," she heard a lady walking along say, "Doctor Revere's roses are still making a good show," as they passed the place where one of the Prot-estant priests lived.

"Well, *Em!* How are you? I haven't seen you in a hound's age!" "Oh, *I'm* fine, but Arthur is ailing. Had to leave him behind today." "That's too bad, too bad."

". . . wet summer?" It was one man with big hands talking to another man with big hands. "Good for crops, though. Just right." "Yes, you're right. You'd think I'd get used to it but I still miss the farm, even after all this time." "Yes, yes, me, too. Mill work just can't compare . . ."

"Ey, Tiziano!" A little round fat lady with black clothes, carrying a shopping bag in each hand almost down to the ground. "Tiziano! Vuol aiutarmi . . ." "Speak English, Mama," the big boy said, "it won't kill you." "TSK!"

"Gotcha, gotcha," a boy on a bike called to his friend as he whizzed by him. "Cheat, cheat," the friend yelled. Then he laughed and worked his legs hard to catch up.

Millions of people walking from Main Street, carrying blankets and babies and chairs and blankets and baskets and jugs of cool stuff to drink.

Mary Catherine caught up with the kids who didn't have

bikes and they ran along under the thick trees of the streets, even if they didn't know each other's names, playing tag and imitating the bands and getting all excited about what was going to happen at Memorial Field, which even had a playground.

Even though the sun was hot, it didn't seem to bother anybody, even those without umbrellas, because they were thinking, just like her, about all that was going to happen at Memorial Field which her dad had fixed and she hadn't told anybody, even these kids she was getting to be friends with, about the fireworks, a surprise.

⚘

Memorial Field was a very big place because it had the park with all the trees, the playground, the tennis court, and way on one end of it, the field where the high school kids played football and there next to the football place were board seats going up the side of the hill. And right in front of those seats there was a big platform made out of boards and covered all over with red, white, and blue puffy flag stuff. That was where her dad and the nobs were going to sit and then get up and make speeches. Her dad said. Right at the end of the football field, where the fence was, she could see big curtain-stretcher-looking things made out of thin boards.

"What is that?" she asked her mother.

Her mother was busy talking to somebody, another lady.

"Ma, ma, what *is* that?"

hush now can't you see I'm talkin' with Mrs. Wilkerson then child

And she went on talking some more.

"Please, ma'am, what is that?"

"Aw, isn't that cute?" Mrs. Wilkerson said. "She looks fit to bust."

well then what is it Mary Catherine child that is so important you can't wait even half a minute

"What is that, please?" she said, pointing again.

it's rude to point you know that the frames for the fireworks

"But it's supposed to be a surprise! Everybody can see!"

Her mother and Mrs. Wilkerson laughed. It wasn't funny.

you silly silly child they couldn't wait until the last minute to build such com-plicated things now could they get off then and play until it's time for the speeches only a few minutes more I'll be joinin' you up there in the seats get away with you now

Well, Mary Catherine thought as she ran the long distance which was mostly in the sun to the seats, it will still be a surprise, nobody will know just what the fireworks look like until *boom! boom! powie!*

"Yippee!" she yelled out loud and began to run even faster.

Even now there were people beginning to come along behind her, coming to where the speeches, her dad, would be, but they were still just taking their own sweet time and talking and chatting together.

She sat right down in the front row of the board seats. It was hot in the sun but not too hot and there was a good little breeze blowing and it smelled like leaves and grass. She spread her skirt out to save a place big enough for her mam. What she wanted to do was not to sit still on the board seat but to get up and dance around and around.

It was the most beautiful and the best day in the whole world and there wasn't a cloud, not even a little white one, in the whole sky, which was even bluer than the stuff her mam put in the water to make the white clothes very white. The trees and the grass looked so green she could hardly bear to look at them. And far away down in the other end of the park where her mam still was, she could see the little dots of people under the trees, making all sorts of colors with their clothes and blankets and umbrellas and tablecloths. Like flowers. Like a garden. Better than Dr. Revere's roses. The pickup was down there and so was the ice truck, Mr. Machin's truck who brought them ice three times a week for their icebox which she liked better than the Frigidaire which she couldn't exactly remember. And ladies, tiny dots of ladies, maybe even her mother, putting food from the pickup onto the long tables and also, it looked like, putting some of the food into the back of Mr. Machin's truck who always gave her a little chip of ice to suck on because she never grabbed or even asked for one.

She got a happy, burning feeling in her chest, looking at all of it. She didn't tell her dad or mam then, but she had been scared when they went away from the upstairs house in Deetroit where her bed was, and then got on that bus for all those days and nights. Even when she got here she had been scared with all the throwing up and with Mrs. Governelli looking at her from the other window with her blind eyes.

But almost as soon as they got here to Freshkill, her dad had started taking her on the walks with him around the town which he called Getting to Know This Town, and she had stopped being scared after a while. In between talking to big people, he showed her this Memorial Field where the playground was and showed her where verysoon she would go to school and he got ice cream for her at Pappas', the ice cream place, the man gave it FREE, and everybody spoke to her in a nice way and shook hands with her dad. No matter how serious the people looked that her dad talked to, after a little bit her dad got them to laugh which made them feel good, she could see it. And, today, they would look happier than they had ever looked.

And here they were, lots of them, beginning to sit down in the seats around and behind her.

A big fat lady with white hair stood right in front of her and said, "Get up, girlie, you got no respect for yer elders?" and Mary Catherine did not know what to do because her voice suddenly stopped working just when she tried to say something.

"Come on, Aunt Grace, I'll find you a seat somewheres," a man said to the lady. "That little girl's father is going to make the most important speech of them all today. Let her sit, just this once."

"Well," the old lady said, "I don't know what things are coming to these days. No respect a-tall."

"Come on, Aunt Grace," the man said, and he made another kid in the front row get up and then another and another because Aunt Grace was very wide.

And then she could see the cars coming, in a line, all the way from Branck Avenue, driving right across the park on the grass and then closer and closer and then in a row behind the platform with all the flag stuff on it. There was quiet for a minute and then, one after the other, the men popped up onto the platform from the back of it where the stairs were and there was her father, smiling and waving and

whew kid shove over I'm half-boiled from that walk in the heat

And all in a flash, Mary Catherine knew she just couldn't stand to have to sit still so she whispered, "I'm going where the kids are" as fast as possible and shot away before she could hear if her mam had said yes or no. Where the kids were was on the grass and you didn't have to sit all still and quiet. From there, easy as anything, she could see her dad and he was waving right at her and all the kids around her were saying, "Is that your father? Is that your father?" and her saying yes, even forgetting to mention he had made this whole day and look at things set up for . . . fireworks!

"If there is somebody . . . you all ought to thank . . . for this glorious outing — " it was the mayor talking and he was wearing his eyeglasses — "this grand day . . . the likes of which . . . this town has not seen in many a year . . . and the concerted effort of all of you . . . which this grand day represents . . . that man is sitting here . . . right next to me . . . and too modest, yes, too modest . . . to take credit . . . where credit is due!"

The crowds of people began to yell and clap and whistle.

"I give you . . . *Mr. Rory Mulligan!*" the mayor shouted, "and let's hear it for him. Hip, Hip — "

"Hooray!" the crowd yelled.

"Hip, Hip — "

"Hooray!"

"Hip, Hip — "

"HOOOORRAAAAAAAAAAAAAAAAY!"

Her dad stood up while they were still clapping and smiled and looked as if somebody had made a mistake. And all the kids kept poking her and yelling.

"Thank you, folks. Thank you."

But they were still yelling. The only people not yelling were some of her dad's friends, she knew one was named Jerry, and they were standing around the bottom of the platform with their arms folded looking around and looking around. They looked very silly just standing there when everybody else was jumping up and down and she wondered what kinds of friends were they, anyway?

But anyway, her dad had started up his speech about Hard Times and Labor Day and the Hudson man who found Freshkill and the Rev-olution soldiers, ill-fed, ill-clad, she knew it by heart, he had tried it out so many times on her and her mam.

He was a good talker, her dad was. She had already seen that herself, walking with him and people listened to him, just like now. Only there were still some dummies making some noise somewhere, making it hard to hear him.

"These last few years have been hard on Freshkill. Mills laying off, even closing up, management squeezing the workers for all . . ."

There was such a loud bunch of noise that her dad stopped talking and looked behind him because that was where it was coming from.

"Just a minute, folks," her dad said, nodding at the crowd just the way he did to her when he was straightening out something between her and her mam. He started to walk between the men, including Dr. Revere, sitting on the platform, back toward the back, when suddenly, it looked like he was flying, a huge man with a red face popped up from the stairs part and went right for her dad, swinging his arm and his fist. Her dad quick stepped to one side but the man got him anyway and shoved him very hard right up against the railings at the front of the platform and she could hear ladies screaming and she was screaming, too.

"Dad! Dad!"

Pushing and shoving toward him where the man was pounding on him and the flag stuff was getting ripped and people were all running around, she kept her eyes on her dad and tried to get to him. And just as she got near, she saw it, her dad got an arm free and he gave the man a big punch on the top of his head and the man stopped hitting him and then her dad just grabbed the man and sailed him over the edge of the platform, not even looking to see where he was going to land, which was in a space in the crowd which opened up like a shot.

The whole platform was filled up with fighting men and some of them had baseball bats and some of them had blood on them and she was scared and she wanted to run away but you couldn't run away when someone was trying to hurt your father! She got right up to the bottom of the platform when suddenly she felt somebody grab her from behind, hard! and she was too scared out of her wits even to yell and then whiz! she was flying into the dark underneath the platform where there were other kids and she heard her mam hollering to her

for God's sake stay under there MaryCatherine it's the only safe place I'll get you later

But it didn't sound safe at all under there with all the thumping and banging over her head so she started to crawl out but before she could get out there was a terrific crash as two men wrapped up in flag stuff and fighting and punching landed just on the spot she was trying to get to and a whole lot of wood came down with them, too, so she thought she had better stay with the other kids.

There were a lot of them under there and the little ones were crying and crying and the big ones looked scared but when they heard that the fighting over their heads had at last stopped or gone someplace else the big ones like her went over to the edge of the platform and watched.

It was like in the movies when three or four men ganged up on one man to punch him and kick him and knock him down. Only it wasn't just like the movies because the kids, one after another, were screaming, You let my dad alone! You let my dad alone! And then she was screaming it, too, because a crowd of men with baseball bats were chasing her dad and the sireens weren't going *oohway* anymore, they were going SCREE! SCREE! which made her cry even more and all the kids holding onto each other. Deetroit, Deetroit, she kept thinking and remembering all the dreams about her mam crying about the gunmen in the night and it was all happening all over again and that was why her mam had started to be cranky today and now the gunmen had changed to baseball bats and they were getting him, one of them was right up to him!

Her dad stopped dead still, turned around, grabbed the man's bat with one hand and the man's front with the other hand, yanked him forward very hard, then shoved him sideways into the bunch of men with the baseball bats and they all fell over backwards and on top of each other and people began to cheer and to stop standing around, even ladies, and just pitched in and kept those baseball bat men on the ground.

All the kids began to laugh and cry together and pound her on the back, only she was sure of it, she could hear her mam yelling like anything, screeching worse than about the babby and, sure enough, around the corner of the platform came her mother's shoes and skirt and her shoes were kicking at a pair of black pants so she didn't care, she just jumped out and grabbed the black pants and got a good kick for it which landed her half under the platform again but not before she saw that the man was pulling her mam's hair and he was fifty times bigger than her mam so she didn't care again, she grabbed the legs . . .

hold him kid hold him

. . . and her mam got the man on the cheek with the shiny knob on her umbrella handle and he let go of her hair but he looked like he was hauling off to hit her only suddenly there was a policeman there and he had his hand on the gun in his belt and the man just stopped and stood still.

"Gus Dingman, you goddam fool, you just made yourself a lot of enemies in this town. Countin' me, so just stand still. Whatever they paid you, it wasn't worth it."

"Ahhh, go to hell."

"I don't advise insulting an officer of the law on top of what I just saw. You okay, Mrs. Mulligan?"

Dingman is it I can hardly think of a better name for such a jackass come on child we'll

"No! Come under!" and Mary Catherine dragged her mam under the platform and they stayed there until all the fighting quieted down and it was safe to go out and see about her dad.

"Maureen! Maureen!" They could hear him roaring like a lion over by the board seats.

here and here and here we are, her mam was crying and try
ing to talk all at the same time.

"Thank God, oh, thank God!"

Her mam pushed Mary Catherine out in front of her who
was crying, too, she couldn't help it.

here's the bravest little union man you ever saw Rory the
bravest

⚜

It took a long time to get everybody still and sitting down
again because families had to find each other and the doctors
had a lot of people to bandage up and some of the baseball bat
men tried to get away but in the end everybody sort of sat
down where they had been sitting before it all started.

Her dad was standing right at the front of the platform,
even though there wasn't much railing left and all the flag
stuff was gone and the chairs the men had been sitting on were
broken to pieces all over the grass.

"As I was saying before I was so rudely interrupted . . ."

All the people began to laugh, not too loudly at first, but
finally so loudly that Mary Catherine had to put her hands
over her ears and lean against her mother's side where they
were sitting on the grass. Nobody seemed to mind that her
dad was standing up there, right in front of all of them, looking a mess. His coat and shirt were all ripped up and his neck-
tie was pointing in the wrong direction and there was a big
red mark under one eye and his hair was going every which
way.

And her poor mam. Her hair was all pulled out of its lovely
mountains and was falling down her back because of that Ding
Man! And the shoulder of her dress was ripped, but she was

laughing and laughing and rocking Mary Catherine in her arms.

Her dad held up his hand and finally the people stopped.

"Police Chief Ed McAndrew has asked me to announce that the baseball game, scheduled for next, is canceled, owing to lack of equipment . . ."

And there they were, the whole crowd, and some of them looked more beaten up and messy even than her mam and dad, there they were, laughing like crazy all over again.

His dad cupped his hands around his mouth.

"Let's EAT!" he hollered and the whole lot of them, still laughing, began walking slowly down toward the tables under the trees.

⁂

After supper, when it got to be twilight and all the big people were lying around on blankets on the grass from eating too much, the kids all got together to play except, at first, the brown kids. They stood around watching.

There was something about being brown that made you scared. Again and again she had gone down Ferry Street with her dad which was where all the brown people lived but they wouldn't talk to him for a very long time, just turned their heads away and made their eyes very white. It made her feel scary to be where everybody was a different color from her dad and her, but finally they talked to him and to her, too, so it wasn't so bad.

"Come on, you nigs!" a big boy shouted. "Get in this line! We want this to be the biggest Red Rover in the worrrld!" The brown kids came then and the two Red Rover lines *were* the biggest Mary Catherine had ever seen.

But even before they could finish it, they could hear the ladies at the tables calling out, in different voices, "Come on, folks," or "Come-and-GET-it," or "Seconds and thirds," or "We don't want a single leftover!"

Mary Catherine came back from the tables with her plate filled up with potato salad and the veal and peppers stuff and ice cream and chocolate cake and a weenie with some sauerkraut on it which was all right because her mam wasn't right there to say call that a nourishin' meal. She was *starving* from playing.

"Come on, come on," her friends said. "Take your plate up to where your dad talked. If we get up there right now, we'll have the best seats for the band stuff and the fireworks!"

And when they all got up there they were pushing each other to sit next to her because they said, and it was true, her dad was a Hero.

⚜

"You want to come up here, kid?" her father called to her softly in the dark. "You'll get a better view from up here on the stand and I'd hold you so you wouldn't have to worry about falling off." He was sitting up there with her mam and some other people and the band, which had stopped playing.

She pulled her shoulders up to show him where she wanted to sit.

"Okay, I know. It's better with your pals."

Her dad, he knew everything.

⚜

It was the best night in the whole world, too. Even if the noise from the fireworks was very scary and made the ground

shake sometimes, the colors were so good and so magic she
didn't care.

And the people, all together, saying Ooh! and Aah! made
the fireworks even better.

"I hope all you folks will remember to thank the members
of the Saint Rocco Society for providing this display."

Her father was talking, not too loud, but everybody, looking at all that was happening in the sky, could hear him, she
knew, because they were saying to each other how nice it was
about Saint Rocco. And about the band concert, the town
band, about how it was the best they had ever played.

Mary Catherine looked at the colors winging and zinging
in the sky and she could still hear inside her — even with the
boom! boom! powie! — the sound of the band playing.

They had played such good music that everybody had
started to sing with them about the Grand Old Flag and Over
There and Kit Bag and Hi-Hi-Hee in the Field Ar-tiller-ee.

Then there was one song which they played a long time a
whole lot of different ways called "Zanders Ragtime Band"
and people even started to dance even though it was the song
the old lady on Main Street had said wasn't decent.

That was a good song about Zanders and now there was a
big American flag waving with lots of noise on the curtain-
stretcher frames. The flag waved which was really a lot of
fireworks because you could hear them going off and everybody was quiet looking at it but she could hear her father's
soft, nice voice and so could everybody:

"The summer's over, folks. The summer's over. And now
the work begins. And now the work begins."

❦

whoosh child you gave me a start whatever are you doin'
up at this hour it's barely five your dad isn't even up yet there
now thanks for the hug but go on back to bed for heaven's
sake

"Ma! Ma! It's the first day of school!"

Her mother laughed and she stopped putting all the coffee
stuff into the coffeepot for a minute.

it is prac-tically the night before the first day of school
that's what it is

"I don't want to be late! I don't want to miss about learning how to read!"

faith you are goin' to sleep through the whole lot of it if
you don't get back to bed go on then I'll wake you up at seven
in plenty of time oh for heaven's sake don't start to cry now
come on Mary Catherine I can't cope with both break-fast
and a weepin' kid do me a favor why don't you go in wake up
your dad but gentle be gentle he's a bear in the mornin'

Mary Catherine ran into their bedroom and jumped on her
dad's bed.

"What, what," he said.

"Dad, Dad," she said, bouncing up and down, "it's the first
day of school!"

"Jesus! What's the matter, what's going on?" Her dad
opened one eye. "Mary Catherine, what is it?"

"It's time to get up. It's the first day of school!"

Her dad snorted into his pillow, then he lifted up one arm.

"Come on in with me," he said. "Let's just let the day sneak
up on us."

It was warm in there with him and she started to tell him
about how it was for sure that some of the kids she had gotten
friends with at the pitnit would be in first grade, too, when

suddenly her mam was shaking her shoulder and her dad had gone away and it was bright daylight.

    ach child there's piles and piles of French toast in there gettin' cold as stone and you're some bugler you are Mary Catherine

❦

    Her mam helped her with her first-day-of-school dress, special, which was very pretty, dark red, which had come in a box from Auntie Kathleen in South Boston who was her dad's big sister who she had never seen who had this girl called Deirdre who used to wear this red dress but you couldn't even tell.

    just look at that just look at that a perfect fit and what a savin' hold still now while I do up your braids Mary Catherine will you please please hold still

    Her mother stopped doing her hair and looked at her.

    whatever is that poor sister goin' to do with you she'll have to lash you down to get any work at all done she will with all your jiggin'

    "What's a poor sister?"

    the nun I showed her to you in church who is goin' to teach you and you must remember at all times to be re-spectful to her because she is a bride of Christ who is God's only Son and she doesn't need any back chat from the likes of you you understand

    Mary Catherine shook her head yes.

    sit quiet then

    From where she was sitting on the edge of her mam's bed she could see herself in the huge big mirror over the bureau and how beautiful the soft dark stuff of her dress, velvet it was called, looked with its white lace trimmings. And even though her hair was plain brown and not nice and red like her mother's, her braids coming out of her mam's hands looked thick and pretty. And even though her nose went down, instead of up like her mam's, and even though her eyes were a darkish gray color instead of bright blue like her mam's, she didn't mind because she looked all right and even nice and she wished her dad could see her now. She would keep her dress on until he came home from the office tonight and she would tell him about everything in school and maybe even read something for him, right on the spot.

And when she grew up, she knew it, her hair would get red and her eyes would get blue and she would look just like her mam and she would be as smart as her dad and know even *hard* reading.

here now this'll do just fine

Her mam was cutting in half a string of lace from out of her bureau drawer and she was tying one piece each on the end of Mary Catherine's braids.

Mary Catherine jumped up and gave her mother a big hug.

ach Mary Catherine I hope you live through the day push off now so's I can get dressed and then we'll go

&⋈&

But her mam couldn't come after all with her because her silken stockings when she went to put them on were all full of holes and ladders.

that Rory that Rory I told him to leave off doin' the polka at the K of C dance with his hard shoes there isn't even Polish to speak of in Freshkill you have to im-press I told him but he said oh no he says dance woman the music's playin' them are workers lookin' on and why didn't I pay atten-tion when I was washin' up these stockins but then there are always a million and one inter-ruptions in this wretched small place with all of us on top of each other they'll laugh you and me outa Holy Redeemer if I show up with such raggle-taggle stockins

If they laughed her and her mam out, she wouldn't be able to be in first grade. "Don't come, don't come! I'll go! I'll go!"

what what are you sayin' just for that you can go on your very own your lonesome you little smarty aleck

But Holy Redeemer was on the other side of Main Street with all its cars.

"Ma, please! I can't get across Main Street by myself. The cars'll kill me and I'll never get on Sycamore Street!"

hush hush hush, her mam said, not looking mad at all now. of course you can child they put a traffic cop on special just to get the school kids across safe you know what a cop looks like well you just go up to Van Dine's which is where he'll be and wait for him to stop the cars and don't you dare go across on your own or I'll find out and you'll get the spankin' of your life

"Yes, ma'am."

and at Holy Redeemer tell the first sister you see your name and that you're signed up for first grade and if they want to know where I am tell 'em I got sick that's only a white lie and when the stores open up I'll get some stockins and I'll walk over to school and get you at lunchtime okay

"Okay."

give us a smile then that's better all right you'd better get
movin' it's five to eight a little early but you don't want to be
late today of all days good luck good luck don't lose the pencil your dad gave you from the office

Mary Catherine didn't wait one second more. She gave her
mam a kiss and ran like anything out of the flat.

☙

The traffic cop wasn't there even though she waited and
waited with all the cars and trucks and buses going by and it
must be getting late, late!

A lady in the bus line said, "Why are you crying, little girl?
What's the matter? Can I help you?" But she didn't answer
her, just backed up and backed up against the window of Van
Dine's because her mother said Never Talk to Strangers I
Don't Care How Kind They Look They're the Worst Kind,
and all of school would go by and she would still be standing
here when school was finished up and, she tried not to, but she
started crying some more.

"Here, here," the traffic cop said to her. He was leaning
down and he smelled like coffee, she could smell it. "What's
the trouble now?"

"I'm late for school," she bawled.

"You're *early* for school. Why, you got here even before
me! Are you the early bird?"

"What."

"The early bird that catches the worm."

"What."

"Give me your hand. I can see there's nothing to it but to

get you across the street. You know where to go once you're across?"

"To Holy Redeemer School in the first grade."

"Okay then. Let's go!"

She stuck her hand in his and he blew his whistle and then he raised his other hand and all of it, all of the cars and trucks and buses, just stopped right away, leaving a big space open to get across.

"Thank you very much," she said to him.

"You're welcome very much," he said and laughed some more. "Hurry up now, old-timer. You look like you're going to explode!"

And she ran right around the corner onto Sycamore Street and she could see lots of kids and their mothers, too, and nobody was hurrying at all but, she couldn't help it, even though it couldn't be late, she just couldn't stop running.

❦

Her mam was right, the sister lady in the hall showed her the first grade room which already had some mothers and children in it and she got a seat right in the front row. When she got used to it, Mary Catherine began to look around the room to see where the reading books were and there was a whole big bookcase full of them, even bigger than the bookcase in her dad's room. And there *were* some kids from the pitnit in here. One of them, his name was Joey, waved a little wave to her and she made a little wave back just as the first grade sister who had been shooing out the mothers came in front of the room and said,

"Good morning, class. Welcome to Holy Redeemer School

and the first grade. My name is Sister Mary Angelique, which I know is a hard name for you to remember, but you will after a while and we'll get along just fine. Now. We seat according to height here, so I think since you're tall," Sister said, pointing to a boy, "you should sit back there. And you — " she pointed at another boy — "and you, too. And you — " another boy — "too."

All those boys got up from where they were sitting and went to the back part of the room, waiting for somebody to get up so they could sit down. Nobody got up. Mary Catherine watched. It must be very bad for those boys to have to go away from the angel sister.

"And you, too." Sister was talking again.

"You, sleepyhead." Sister's voice sounded very close but still Mary Catherine was looking to see if the boys got a seat.

"*You*, the one with the lace on her pigtails." The whole class, Mary Catherine, too, laughed at the silly word pigtails.

Suddenly Mary Catherine felt the sister's hand on her shoulder, and she turned around to the front of the room like a shot.

"The first thing you," Sister said to her, "and all the rest of you must learn," she said, looking at all the rest of them, "is that first grade is a place where you have to pay attention, no matter what."

She kept her hand on Mary Catherine's shoulder the whole time she was talking and Mary Catherine stared hard at her dad's pencil sticking up out of her fist and she wished she could be invisible like The Shadow Knows.

"There now." Sister gave her arm a pat. "Find a seat at the back because you're one of the tall ones, too."

The boys had gotten places to sit down but nobody got up to give her a seat.

"You, with the . . . earrings," Sister said, "get up. You're too short to be sitting in the back row. Get up and give this girl your seat."

The short girl got up and, as Mary Catherine went toward her seat, the girl said, "Snot!" and made a scary face.

"That's enough of that," Sister said. The girl sat down hard in Mary Catherine's old seat. Sister looked at her until the girl finally said, "Excuse me, Sister."

✠

They each had to get up, one after the other, and say their name and something about themselves. Mary Catherine couldn't make up her mind whether to say about how she came on the bus for days and nights from Deetroit or about how her dad made the pitnit.

When it was her turn, she got up and said "My name is Mary Catherine Mulligan and I . . ."

"Oh, so *you're* the Mulligan child. Father Rafferty spoke to me about you. Children, Mary Catherine has come halfway across the country with her mother and father because her father is a famous union man who is going to keep the Reds out of the mills of this town," Sister said. "The Reds are people who hate God and want to kill all Catholics in their beds while they lie asleep."

Mary Catherine listened to what Sister was saying, just like the other kids.

"You all ought to be very, very thankful that Freshkill will have such a fine Catholic gentleman as Mr. Mulligan looking after your fathers and mothers who work in the mills in these dangerous and difficult times," Sister said, folding her hands and looking just like a saint's statue.

"You may sit down, Mary Catherine."

"Thank you, ma'am."

"Thank you, *Sister*."

"Thank you, Sister."

She sat down, and the next kid, in front of her, began to talk. She didn't know all that about her father. That was why she said thank you.

❦

here I am here I am, her mam yelled from the sidewalk to her as she came out of the front door of Holy Redeemer. did you learn your readin' yet

"No, but . . ."

well I got your favorite chicken noodle soup for lunch maybe that was what Sister was waitin' for for you to come back all strong from hot chicken noodle soup to learn readin'

"Oh, ma! We do *other* things besides reading in the first grade."

❦

They called up from school and her mam came and got her. She didn't feel good and when she coughed she had to stand still for a minute because she got all dizzy and it was so slippery walking in the snow even though she had her arctics on. It had started to snow again right after they got in school and it was cold, too. Her face was hot as fire. She didn't feel good.

hurry up now kid it's freezin' that cough sounded bad to

me why-ever did you say you felt okay this mornin' no matter how much you like school you're supposed to tell your mam when you're feelin' odd that's what mams are for God knows the worry of it and I'm feelin' a bit fever-ish myself now who needs that

While they were crossing Main Street the coughing started up again and she tried to walk and the next thing she knew her mother was sitting her up in the sofa bed and she didn't re-member but she had her nightie on.

drink this up now it's the best thing for you will ease that coughin' just a drop of whiskey and lemon in hot water

It tasted terrible but she drank it up and she fell asleep and she had mixed-up dreams. She woke up once and there was a man putting this cold silver thing on her chest and she yelled because she didn't know him so he must be one of the ones who would hurt you and he said, "Whooping cough," and she just went back to sleep again.

❧

She woke up and her eyes felt as if they had dried up in her head. Her mother and father were yelling in their room and it was dark, except for the light coming from their room.

"You stupid bitch, how could you let her go to school in such a condition? Mike Rafferty himself told me she fainted dead away at her desk from the coughing."

I didn't know I didn't know be-lieve me you know her she'd go to school with an un-mended broken leg if

"Oh, shut up, Maureen. That's no excuse. She may be a kid but you're a grown woman with eyes in your head! The simple fact of the matter is you sent a dangerously ill child to

school, contagious as well, contagious as well, with never a
thought for her or for what people would think. I have a
position in this community to keep up, you know, and how
does it look if my own kid falls down from being sick in
school? It looks like neglect, that's what it does, you lazy
pig, you lazy young idler, spending half your life looking in
the mirror to see if you're as pretty as you were the minute
before, and how does my kid fainting from sickness in a public
place affect my position, tell me that!"

well well is that all the gratitude I get for all I've done
workin' my fingers to the bone and you gone day and night
here's no better than Deetroit not even less dangerous you
worryin' about other folks gaddin' about to the Elks and the
Lions and the Moose and that whole damned men-agerie God
knows with never a thought for your own hyp-ocrisy that's
what I call it hyp

There was a loud noise like when her dad smacked her bare
behind for being a bad child and then her mother's voice going
up and up and up and then *smack!* again, and then her mam
was pushing at the covers and getting into bed with her.

you hear him callin' me a pig the pig himself God I feel
awful the dirty old pig himself old enough to be my father
al-most only no such gentleman as my dad and I could have
married the squire himself I'll never get into his bed again and
I'm preg-nant that's sure that's why I'm burnin' up can't keep
a mor-sel of food down oh whatever is goin' to happen to me

Mary Catherine rolled over and put her arm around her
mam because her mam was crying and crying. Hot tears,
hot skin.

She woke up for a minute when her dad came in but he

didn't talk to her the way, before in the night, he had. He was talking to her mother.

"Maureen, can you ever forgive me? Please, forgive me. I love that little kid like my own life. You know that. I was worried. It's no excuse for me being so mean, but I was worried. I didn't mean, I never meant all those bad words."

hush Rory hush now

"You're sick yourself. Can you get up? What a bastard I am. You're right; I do give more time to the workers than to . . ."

can you give me a hand dizzy I'm a bit dizzy

Mary Catherine opened her eyes to say good-night and what she saw was her dad picking up her mam in his arms, right up in his arms, as if she were a tiny baby. And then she forgot to do anything for a long, long time, but to sleep.

❧

It was Sunday and the radio was on, playing the music from New York City that her father liked but that her mother just put up with, she said, all that longhaired stuff it's enough to drive you batty all that squeakin' and squawkin'

But he always put it on on Sunday afternoons while he read the thick Sunday papers which he had to buy for himself at Van Dine's since she wasn't allowed out of the house until next week. She still had a cough but now it just went bark! bark! without taking all her breath away and her dad called her Puppy, my little Puppy.

She lay back on her pillow, a little tired, and watched her mam and dad looking at all the papers. She had read all the funnies and she still had lots of books to read because her dad had gotten them for her from the Freshkill library right near his office because Sister Angelique had said Your Mary Catherine has read the first grade bookcase out of house and home. Which — Bark! Bark! — made her dad laugh like anything. She took in a breath slowly to get rid of the cough. In a minute she would get the book about the princess and the pea she was reading but right now she would just listen to the music and maybe close her eyes a . . .

"We interrupt this broadcast to bring you a special news bulletin."

"Turn it up, Maureen," her dad said right away and her mother turned the wrong knob.

"Stupid!" her father said and, when he fixed it, the radio said ". . . Pearl Harbor. The attack came at . . ."

"Bark! BARK! Bark-bark-bark-bark!"

"Shut up, kid! Will you shut up? This is important!"

"Bark! Bark-bark-bark!" She was trying to stop, sitting up and swallowing and swallowing and trying to stop.

"Shut her up, will you, Maureen? For God's sake, shut her up! It's something about the Japs. Pearl Harbor, that's a Regular Army base. Get her out of here!"

Her mother got her on her feet and the floor was like rubber and icy so she had a little trouble walking and the bark! bark! got louder. The phone began ringing.

"Oh, Christ! Oh, Christ!" her father yelled. "Something terrible is happening and I am afflicted with a noisy child and the telephone. Christ's eyes!" he yelled.

"Hello, yes, what is it?" he said into the telephone. She could hear him from the kitchen where her mam had brought her, all wrapped up in a blanket. "Ah, ah," her father said in a terrible way. "Can it be true?" he said into the telephone. "It was that Hitler I was worrying about with his peculiar brand of socialism when all the time it should have been those deceitful Orientals. The mills will have to gear up, that's all. It's just as I said. They'll have to take on, double quick, all the men still laid off, that's all. Full employment! Full employment, though it's a hell of a way to have to get it. All right, Jerry," he said into the phone, "I'm going to stick by the radio for now because the President's sure to come on soon and give us the word. All right, then. Yes. Okay. I'll call you back later. Where are you, anyway? What crowd is that I hear behind you? Well get the hell out of that saloon, man! What the hell are you doing there, anyway, on a Sunday! This is a time when you should be home with your wife and kids. I'll call you at home as soon as I hear what they have to say on the radio. I DON'T CARE if Ricatelli owes you a drink, you hear! Get home, will you!"

He slammed down the telephone.

"And you now," he said, looking at her and her mam, who were still standing in the kitchen. "You get her in the bathroom and shut the door because I don't want any of that damned coughing drownding out the news reports. This country may be at war, there may be bombers over our heads at any minute, and I want to know what's going on!"

when I was a babeinarms there was shootin' and killin' even in the village the Black and Tans and here it is all over again oh whatever shall I do

Her mother sat down on the toilet lid and began to cry.

Mary Catherine took drinks of water and drinks of water to stop her bark. It was bad to cough now when it was happening. Whatever it was.

2. Grade Three, Holy Redeemer School

MARY CATHERINE SAT, tired and fidgety, in the back corner of the third grade. She had finished this afternoon's assignment of fifty arithmetic problems and what she wanted to do was to reach, without anybody seeing, into the bookcase right behind her back, not even a foot away, if somebody wanted a book she had to stand up to get out of their way, and get a book to read.

Sister Flavia was way over on the other side of the room teaching the fourth grade English. But she knew if she tried to get a book out of the bookcase without asking, and it was not allowed to interrupt Sister while she was teaching the other class, Sister would see her and holler. Sister saw *everything*. You wouldn't think she would be able to with so many of them squashed together in such a big room, but she almost always did.

It was a *big* room, too, with wood walls painted syrup color up as far as the windowsills, which were higher than even Sister's head, and the top part of the wall was painted tan. And to open the windows, you had to use a long pole with a hook on the end of it and try and hook it in the loop thing on the window and then kind of lean on the end of the pole until the window started raising up. It was hard to do and you were always scared the pole was going to slip out of the loop and shoot up and break the window and then your father would have to pay for it.

The other bad thing about the room, besides the windows, was that it was so stuffed full of kids you could hardly move around or even breathe, it got so stuffy and stinky sometimes. To make all sixty kids fit, they had to make double rows with their desks, which meant you always had somebody sitting practically on top of you, maybe getting you into trouble by whispering to you or trying to copy. Her partner was Ralphie Sisco but, since his best friend Richie sat right across the aisle from him (how did Sister Flavia ever let *that* happen?), she hardly ever saw anything of Ralph but the back of his head so she was lucky in one way. But in another way she wasn't lucky because she always had to keep an eye on Sister so she could warn Ralph so he would stop fooling around so Sister would not stand up there in the front and yell at their corner.

And the other thing about the windows was that they went down the third grade side of the room and around her corner. It was cold sitting under them and it seemed no matter what grade she was in, she was a tall kid and always sat in the back in the draft and the radiator was always next to somebody else. The fourth grade walls were all covered over with radiators and with blackboards, too. But the really best thing that made the fourth grade better than the third grade was they had ink in their inkwells.

Mary Catherine shifted in her seat, restlessly, then, just to be safe, picked up her pencil again so in case Sister looked she would think she was checking over all these dumb baby arithmetic problems. What she would really be doing, though, she decided, would be making up a story in her head, like the ones her mam and dad listened to on the radio which were either as funny as anything or full of murders.

Once upon a time, in a great city, there lived a crusading newspaper editor and his beautiful assistant . . .

What was a good name for a beautiful assistant besides Margo?

It was hard to think of beautiful names, though, because Sister was really screaming at the fourth grade about how they didn't get diagramming even though she had taught them it yesterday, too, and had given them a lot of sentences for homework to diagram. *She* had learned to do diagramming yesterday just from listening to Sister in the empty time she had when she finished yesterday's arithmetic which was also a million baby subtraction problems. They must be real dummies over there not to get diagramming fast just to keep her from hollering and hollering at them which she was doing right now.

She slid a clean piece of paper on top of her arithmetic and started to diagram the sentences Sister had put on the fourth grade board. To make it interesting, she added in a lot of adjectives and adverbs and compound objects and prepositional phrases. Sister had taught the fourth grade all that stuff before, too, but they were still on simple declarative sentences and Rosemary Watson, whose father was a town officer, couldn't even read the word "traffic" off the board when it was her turn. It was enough to make a cat laugh, which was what her mother said sometimes.

Well, Mary Catherine thought, putting her arithmetic paper back on top of the diagrammed sentences, when I get upstairs to the fifth and sixth grade room with Sister Marissa, there will be really hard sentences to diagram and long division with bi- and trinomials and fractions. Up there, it'll be lots of fun!

But she didn't have anything left to do and there was still a lot of time left before Sister Flavia finished up with that old fourth grade and then taught both classes at once catechism. Which, even though it had a lot of big words, was not too interesting.

She looked out of the windows at the tops of the trees, but just for a minute because Sister would see her if she looked longer and yell, yell a whole lot because she had to stop teaching to do it. Oh, why couldn't she just have a book! There wasn't anything to see out of the windows, anyway. The trees were all shriveled up with the cold and it was too soon to look for snow.

She bent her head over her arithmetic. She couldn't remember about Deetroit, she only knew what her mother said, that it was better than Freshkill, but it was nice when the snow came here. It came around Thanksgiving and stayed and stayed even past Easter sometimes. All through the winter, there was always a place in town where you could sleigh-ride and she would go there with her friends and she would watch and sometimes someone would give her a turn on their sleigh. Her mam and dad said sleighs were dangerous and her father told her that his best friend in Rhode Ireland Island when he was a boy had been killed when his sleigh went under the wheels of an ice wagon, and it was disobedient to ride down the hill on her friend's sleigh but it was like flying! especially on the Rombout Street hill, which was the best hill in town and closed off most of the winter as a play street. No cars came on Rombout Street, not even the cars of the people who lived there, because of the snow and ice, no ice wagons,

either, because these days there were ice *trucks*, and the hill
flattened out long before Mattewan Avenue, which crossed
at the bottom, and the sleigh stopped long before Mattewan
Avenue at the bottom so there was no danger of getting killed
so it wasn't really disobedient. She told herself.

It *was* disobedient, though, to keep writing to Santa Claus
about a sleigh, stop doin' it her mam said. If only she could
talk to God about getting a sleigh, but He would know she
was being disobedient because He knew everything and then
she would be in real trouble. God was her friend she could
talk to and she wouldn't want to hurt Him by disobeying her
parents, the Fourth Commandment. That old Fourth Commandment!

Even if He *knew* she would never take the sleigh anywhere
but Rombout Street or the Asylum grounds, which had a big
fence at the bottom which kept you from sliding into Asylum
Avenue, she couldn't ask Him. He had had enough trouble
with the Jews killing His Belov-ed Son. So she couldn't go
around hurting Him some more by not doing Exactly What
You Are Told, even if, inside, she felt that getting a sleigh and
sleigh-riding weren't bad things.

She folded her hands inside her desk and said a little silent
prayer to God to ask for help to be a good child. "Stop me
from being wicked," she said.

And still Sister was yelling away at the fourth grade.

Maybe I could ask my dad to get Father Rafferty to get me
into the fourth grade right now, Mary Catherine thought, so
it wouldn't take so long to get upstairs to Sister Marissa's room
where they made topographical maps of Africa on cardboard . . .

The radiators began to knock pleasantly with the heat.

. . . out of real thick flour paste and then they painted them with poster paint to show the jungles and the rivers and where the . . .

Mary Catherine yawned.

"Open some windows in here," Sister said all of a sudden. "You're all asleep, all of you. Open some windows. Get some fresh air in here to wake you all up. Vincent, get the window pole!"

"Vin-cent's ab-sent," the fourth grade said together in a tired voice.

"Don't you sing-song at me. It shows a real lack of respect. All right, who's the next tallest? Mary Catherine! Get the pole. Get some fresh air in here. I'm not going to have you all asleep while I'm teaching catechism."

She hated to open the windows in winter. If she opened them wide enough for Sister, everybody else hated her and she didn't blame them. And if she didn't open them wide enough for Sister, Sister yelled.

"Please, Sister? My hand hurts from writing?"

"Never mind. Get those windows open. If Father Rafferty comes in, he's in school this afternoon, and finds you all asleep while I'm teaching you about grace, there'll be a lot of trouble!"

"It really hurts, Sister?" Let Frannie have the job, he was the next-tallest kid after her. Vinnie was probably staying home sick on purpose so he wouldn't have to open the windows.

"Offer it up, Mary Catherine!"

"Yes, Sister."

Offer it up yourself, Mary Catherine thought, getting down the window pole. Offer-it-up didn't have anything to do with

God. It was just something the nuns said to get you to do something *they* didn't want to do.

Sure enough, when she turned around from the windows everybody was already hunched up with the cold.

"I'll get you after school," Jackie Slensky said through his teeth at her as she sat down. He was a fat short kid and she didn't care. The only reason he was back here with the tall kids was because he told lies. She could knock him over with one hand if she had to and she was just a bag of bones, her dad said so, plain as paper, a long drink of water, my own little bag of bones.

"Shut up, you fat stupid!"

"Spare ribs! Spare ribs!"

"Is there something you have to say to all of us, John Slensky?" Sister asked.

"She called me a name!"

"I sincerely doubt it. Liars burn in the hottest part of Hell, young man, so you had better watch out or you'll end up there."

Mary Catherine sat up very straight in her seat and looked ahead of her at the back of Billy McCarthy's neck. You are a good girl, a smart girl, Father Rafferty had said to her in confession, but you have to be twice as good as ordinary children to make your dad happy who is suffering like a saint with his sickness. Well, *any*body could be better than Jackie but maybe . . . maybe there was another place in Hell for people, even if they were good, who kept wanting something they weren't supposed to have, like a sleigh. "I didn't mean it," she said to God. But saying it after, like that, did that count?

"Very well, then. Third grade, pass up your arithmetic papers and I hope they are very much better than they were yesterday. And fourth grade, you will do pages seventy through seventy-nine in your English book for homework, that means page seventy-nine, too. And I will not put up with any more laziness from any of you, understand?"

"Yes, Sis-ter," both classes said.

"Catechisms, now. Page fifty-eight. Grace. Hurry *up*, third grade! And, Philomena, put them in a tidier stack on my desk than you did yesterday."

The back of Philly's neck got all red and she whispered "Yes, Sister." *Any*body could make a better stack than old Philly who had pierced ears and was practically a midget. She had holes in her ears and earrings because she was Italian and her mam said Eye talians! that's what's wrong with Freshkill that's why the mills aren't doin' good even with the War Production what can you expect of people who eat pi-zuz who-ever on God's earth ever heard of such a thing as a tomahto pie just the sort of thing as rots their brains and makes their beautiful girls fat and bowlegged and here I am over twenty-six years old and better-lookin' than any twenty-year Eye talian girl you can name because Irish eat proper and don't run to fat and bowlegs no matter what

Still, it wasn't old Philly's fault she didn't know anything about stacking papers. She only got the job because she was short and had to sit in the front row practically on top of Sister Flavia's desk.

Grace, there it was, page fifty-eight. Had they had it for homework? She shivered. She could not remember. An assignment book, it only cost a nickel and it lasted all year, but she had lost hers and her mam said they did not have any more nickels for such things these days when she had a perfectly good memory perfectly good. She could remember, she would *have* to remember because nickels were important when her father had been off sick from work, his breathing wasn't working right, for four weeks and her dad had said to her mam to watch the pennies and be thrifty in case he was sick a while longer because the union couldn't be expected to keep him on a full wage, listen, her mam said, will you just listen to him talkin' like that no matter how hard he's worked for that union enemies enemies

"This is your soul." Sister was drawing on the blackboard. There was white dust all over the ends of her big black sleeves. "Nobody knows what a soul looks like, of course, so I am going to make it look like a paper bag for the moment."

The classes laughed. And stopped when Sister turned around. It was even harder to stay stopped because she had some chalk dust on the end of her nose. Mary Catherine stared hard at her catechism to keep from laughing like an ordinary child.

"I'm glad you all find this so funny. It's just a matter of your *im*mortal soul, that's all. Go right ahead and laugh and then tell God when you face Him when you die that you thought what Sister Flavia had to say was so funny."

Everybody looked very hard into their catechisms.

"Pay attention now. Your soul is there, you see, and it works beautifully — " Sister rubbed at the end of her nose — "just so long as you don't commit a sin. You do a good work, let us say you work extra hard over your spelling homework, and you earn some sanctifying grace as a result. And it falls on your soul — " she turned the chalk on its side and made a shady line falling into the paper bag she had drawn — "and your soul catches it. You empty the wastebasket, let us say, at the right time and without being asked and some more grace — " the chalk moved again — "is caught by your soul and all this grace is counting up against the time when you die and come before God to be judged. But . . ."

She stopped talking and all of them watched her. She looked back at them, her eyes like slits. She slowly shook a finger at them as she began to talk again, but this time in a whispery voice.

"But, suppose you have committed a *sin*, even a *venial* sin, a tiny one, even though *no* sin is tiny in the eyes of God, mind you, *each* sin you commit hurts God as much as the *spear* and the sponge soaked in *vinegar* pained our crucified Christ, only some more than others. *Which* more than others?"

Nobody raised their hand. Sister jerked up straight and used her regular voice.

"*Which* sins hurt God more than which *other* sins? Come on, we had that lesson just a couple of weeks ago."

Mary Catherine put up her hand. She was scared not to, because if nobody at all raised their hand, Sister might . . .

"Put your hand down, Mary Catherine. I know *you* know it. What's the matter with the rest of you? We just had this lesson and you even had it back in second grade when you were preparing to make your First Holy Communion because you have to know about sin for *that*. Come on, now. You know I'm already displeased with you and there'll be punish . . ."

The classroom door opened and Father Rafferty came in. The head priest of Holy Redeemer Church and School. Her dad's good pal.

The classes stood up without being told.

"Good after-*noon*, Fa-ther Ra-ffer-ty."

"Very good, children. You may sit down. Well, Sister Flamia, how are the third and fourth grade doing this afternoon? Let's have the windows closed, shall we? The parish can hardly afford to heat the great out-of-doors now, can it?"

"No, Fa-ther Ra-ffer-ty."

"Mary Catherine?" Sister was smiling and smiling and Mary Catherine ran to close the windows.

"A job well done, Mary Catherine," Father Rafferty said. He was wearing his cassock, his long black dress. It had some spots on the front of it, she noticed. He always wore a suit, a black suit, when he came to see her father now he was sick in bed and it never had any spots of any kind on it or dust or hairs. Father Rafferty and her dad had long talks together. It was an honor.

"I visited with your father earlier today, Mary Catherine, and he's feeling better, although he's not out of the woods yet."

The way he said it made it sound as if her dad were in Freshkill Hospital or the Asylum, instead of at home in the flat in his own bed, talking to one after another of his union helpers.

"Let us all stop for just a moment in our busy day and say a prayer for Mr. Mulligan's speedy recovery."

The kids looked at each other sideways. "Our Father . . ." some of them said. "Hail Mary . . ." others said. Mary Catherine could feel her cheeks getting hotter and hotter. They would all hate her, even her friends would hate her, for this.

"No! A *silent* prayer! Each of you say a *silent* prayer for Mr. Mulligan."

Father Rafferty's face turned red and so did Sister's. (Why

did he always say her name wrong? Why did he always call her Sister Flamia? It made her mad and today she had been mad even before he had said it the wrong way; she would really kill them when he left.) The lights were reflecting off Father's glasses blink! blink! blink! because he was shaking his head very fast. Between the two of them and the kids, Mary Catherine wished she were dead, except that was not allowed.

"All right, children," Father Rafferty said to end the silent prayer. "Very soon, Mary Catherine, you'll have your dad as good as new. He's one of God's hard workers, you know, an example to us all, an example to us all — " it was his sermon voice — "helping in the parish as well as fulfilling his commitments to the many working people of this community. All *your* fathers, you know."

Grades three and four kept silent. Oh, they were hating her, she could feel it.

"Now, Sister Flamia. Just go on with the lesson you were teaching, just pretend I'm not here. I'm just an ordinary visitor, and you're not to notice I'm here."

He sat down at Sister's desk, smack in the middle of the front of the room.

"Well, now, where was I?" Sister looked at the drawing she had made on the board.

"Ah, yes. Mary Catherine? You were just about to tell us what sins hurt God more than what other sins?"

NO! Mary Catherine almost said out loud as she stood up. You said you *didn't* want *me* . . .

"Now, Sister," Father Rafferty said, smiling in that terrible way he did, she didn't know anybody else in the world who had a *scary* smile when he wasn't trying to be scary. He had gray hair and a bright pink face and eyeglasses with silvery frames, and when he smiled, his teeth looked shiny and not friendly. His smile, it scared them all, she could tell, she was not the only one.

"Now, Sister. Any sin, *every* sin, no matter how big or how small, gives God pain because out of the goodness of His heart, He has given us weak mortals free will and we use it to hurt Him again and again."

Sister made a little bow to Father.

"Just exactly what I was telling them, Father, before you came in. The spear in His divine side and the sponge dipped in gall."

"Good. Very good. Mary Catherine?"

She couldn't remember it, she couldn't remember any of the catechism words now that she *had* to answer!

"Mortal sin," she said, thinking very hard. "Mortal sin hurts God much more than venial sin. Which isn't nice, either."

"What exactly is a mortal sin?"

Some hands went up.

"No," Father said. "It is still Mary Catherine's turn."

"Well, a mortal sin is when you do something you know is very bad but you do it anyway."

"Very bad?"

"Very very bad. Like robbing a bank. That it will give God a whole lot of pain, like missing Mass on Sunday, on *purpose*."

Father said, "I suppose that will do." He turned his head stiffly on his neck to look at Sister. Her cheeks each had a bright red dot which was something to worry about.

He wants the book words and I can't remember them and I'm the smartest! We *are* going to get it when he goes!

She squeezed her eyes together to try to push the exact right words into her mind so she could see them and say them because she could see him getting ready to ask the other question.

"And venial sin, Mary Catherine? What is a venial sin?"

"It's not so bad, Father, and sometimes you do it before you think."

But they weren't the right words, either, ver batum, like Sister said.

"I suppose so," Father said. He looked at Sister again.

"Go on with your lesson, Sister. You may sit down, Mary Catherine."

"Thank you . . ."

But Sister had already started to talk. "Well," she said and her voice sounded funny.

"Well," she said, "you commit a venial sin, like disobeying your mother . . ."

"I would hardly consider *that* a venial sin."

"Oh, I agree, Father. Let me think for a minute."

She looked at the floor.

"Like forgetting to make your bed or set the table or quarreling with your brothers and sisters."

"Very good."

"Then — " she rubbed here and there at the outline of the bag she had drawn — "some of the grace you have earned for *good* deeds leaks out of these holes, each made by a venial sin, and so long as these sins go unconfessed to Father . . ."

"To a priest, now. I'm not the only priest in the world, children, you must remember that."

His teeth opened in the middle of his face and he laughed.

"Just so," Sister Flavia said. "So long as the sin goes unconfessed to a priest . . ."

"And you are truly contrite . . ."

"Yes, and say the penance the priest gives you . . ." Sister paused and looked over at Father Rafferty but he was smiling at Philomena right in front of him. Mary Catherine was very glad, after all, that she was not a kid sitting up in the front.

"Well, then, you're going to get all these little leaks plugged up until the next time you commit a venial sin.

"Now. When you entertain some serious wrong and then deliberately, with full consent, go ahead and do it, you commit a mortal sin and this is what happens."

Sister took up an eraser and rubbed off the bottom edge of the paper bag she had drawn.

"There," she said. "Now what have we got? You have committed this mortal sin and you have not confessed it, truly penitent, and said your penance which the priest gives, but you go right ahead and do a good deed in this state. Well. It doesn't do you a bit of good. Not one little bit. Because this is what happens."

The broad chalk line went from the middle of the blackboard down, down into the paper bag and right through its bottom to the bottom edge of the blackboard.

"And another good act that is rewarded with grace. And another and another."

All the lines ended up nearly in the chalk tray, far away from the paper bag soul, and the room was so still and quiet you could hear the sound the chalk made drawing the falling-down lines.

Mary Catherine, moving her head just the littlest bit, looked around. Lots of the kids, even some of the fourth graders who had had this lesson last year, they looked afraid. Very, very afraid. And Father Rafferty had his mouth in a thin line and another line was coming down between his eyes and he was glaring at them, it was so serious. It was serious about mortal sin, she could tell.

All this time she had only been worrying about venial sins because she thought *mortal* sins were things big people did, not people in the third and fourth grade, not people like her. Didn't even *Jesus* say A little child shall lead them? He did say that, she was sure, but maybe that didn't mean that another little child couldn't be a bad sinner. So maybe even a little child, even a big child in the third grade, could end up in Hell, *burning*, which hurt like anything, and not even be as bad as Jackie Slensky and then God wouldn't be able to lift her up out of Purgatory when she died up to Him in Heaven (only real saints went straight to Heaven without waiting first in Purgatory and saints lived in the olden days when they were eaten by lions or stretched on the rack or roasted on the grid-iron — turn me over, please, St. Lawrence had said, it was right in the book, I am done on this side, and he never even cried out from the pain of the flames) and He wouldn't be able to lift her up to Him because she would be down there in Hell with Jackie Slensky where she never meant to be.

3. May 1947

SHE SAT IN THE KITCHEN, right next to their bedroom
door, while Dr. Kennedy gave her dad his checkup. All
Saturday morning, waiting for the doctor, his pal, her father
had talked of nothing else: "I know it, I feel it in my bones,
Jim's going to give me my walking papers and, before long,
I'll be outa this bed, back onta the streets of this town again,
feeling the pulse of the people, getting matters in tiptop shape
again. I did it before, whipped them into shape, and I can do
it again." And he kept humming that song "We did it before
and we can do it again," that had been on the Hit Parade during the war.

When Dr. Kennedy finally came, looking as usual as if he
had just eaten rocks for lunch, her dad was so cheerful and
talky the checkup could hardly be done.

Dr. Kennedy tried to listen to her dad's chest and sides and
back and he finally said, "For God's sake, Rory, shut up! I
can't hear a thing!"

So her dad stopped saying Listen to that Jim I sound clear as
a bell Jim what do you think of that Jim? and was satisfied
with just sitting there and grinning for God's sake, her mam
said, Rory you look like an organ grinder's monkey. KEEP
STILL MAUREEN, Dr. Kennedy thundered.

Mary Catherine marveled to herself that grownups could be as rude to each other as the sixth graders were among themselves. Still, it was nice that the reason they were all hollering at each other was that her dad was so cheerful. Six months in bed had made him thin and flabby and less and less cheerful.

When the checkup was done and her dad had finished buttoning up his pajama jacket, he said to Dr. Kennedy: "Well, Jim? What do you say? How soon before I'm back at my desk?"

Dr. Kennedy didn't say anything for a minute while he was putting the examining stuff back into his little black bag. Her father, sitting up in his bed, just waited because Dr. Kennedy, they all knew, was not a man who liked to be rushed.

But, finally, impatiently, her dad said again: "Well, Jim?"

Dr. Kennedy slowly straightened up his six feet four and said, "Well *what*, Rory?"

Her father laughed. "I meant just what I said, Jim. You getting deef in your old age? How soon before I'm back to work?"

The doctor looked at her dad just the way her dad looked at her mam when he had explained something to her a hundred times and she still didn't get it.

"My God, man, do I even need *tell* you that any thought of your going back to work is just out of the question?"

Her dad nodded his head.

"I understand I can't go back tomorrow or the next day but I've improved. I'm feeling better." He tapped his chest. "It must sound better in here, too."

"It sounds better, all right, there's no denying that . . ."

"What did I tell you?" Her dad beamed at the three of them.

"I've heard dying men who sounded better," Dr. Kennedy barked.

"What a hell of a thing to say!"

"Well, it's the truth and you know it, you stubborn mick. The last time you were seriously ill I told you what could happen. It's *emphysema* you've got, Rory, not just some little touch of the bronchitis. Not just some cold you can shrug off with a few days in bed. *Emphysema*. That's serious business."

"I know that, I know that," her dad said impatiently. "Didn't I give up smokes right away with that first attack? And, damn it, dropped right after that, from out of a sickbed, into that trouble with — the government inspectors — over at Serco Rubber — " his breath was getting short — "which could have meant — the canceling of contracts. And I never sneaked — even one smoke then, or from that day to this. From two and three packs a day, to zero!"

"All right, all right, but you went right on getting only three or four hours of sleep and out in all kinds of weather and under constant strain from that day to this. As those lungs of yours are now testifying."

"Well, this is no nursery — school I'm running! I've got eleven different — locals to watch over — and they need to be watched — every goddam minute!"

"*And* wrecking yourself with that temper of yours."

The phone between the beds rang. Her dad looked tired.

"You answer that, Maureen," he said, "tell 'em I'll call back later."

Her mother lifted the phone off the little table and sat down with it on the far side of her bed, talking into it in a low voice.

Dr. Kennedy turned his head away from her dad, looking in the direction of her in the kitchen. He didn't seem to see her at all. But she could see him. He looked as if he couldn't believe what was going on. Then he looked back at her dad, who was halfway watching her mam.

"It's just that sort of thing I'm talking about, Rory Mulligan," he said, pointing at the phone. "Doing business from a sickbed. What's the matter with you? You're supposed to be resting, not listening to the complaints of any goddam ninny in this town who has a nickel to call you up!"

"I had the phone — moved in here — and it cost something — I'll tell you — so I could rest — while I was . . ."

"I ought to walk right out of this flat and never come back. You never pay a goddam bit of attention to anything I tell you."

"Well, your oath says . . ."

"I'm a physician, not a *veterinarian*. There's nothing in my oath says I have to treat a goddam jackass!"

It was because he was her dad's friend that Dr. Kennedy yelled at him. Usually doctors didn't yell like that, except Dr. Swanson, who was the school doctor, but everybody said that was because he hated children and only took the job because he was too old to be a regular doctor.

"All right, Jim. Simmer down. Simmer down." Her dad wasn't smiling now. "I know I'm not — the easiest patient — in the . . . who was it, Maureen?"

Jerry and he says the men in Department Four at Sylvester's are threatenin' to take a walk because they're bein' timed how

long they're in the toilets and he says the time and motion men
are in the pay of

"Never mind what he says, Maureen," Dr. Kennedy said.
"Just the both of you listen to me, right now. I want your
undivided attention and that phone can just go to hell if it
rings again. Understand!"

"Okay, okay," her dad said. "No need to — get your . . ."

"Shut up. And listen. Pay close attention. Whether you
like it or not, Rory, you have got yourself a disease that hasn't
got a cure. The best I can do for you is to give you sulfa
if you come down with a secondary infection, which isn't a
hell of a lot. There just isn't enough working lung in that
chest of yours to run a grown man's body at the pace you're
set on running yours. Suppose I did let you go back to
your office . . ."

"Jerry'd give me a ride — I wouldn't move — out from
behind my de — "

"I don't give a good goddam if Jerry carries you there in
his arms and stands over you with a palm fan. All that has
to happen is a rubber worker comes in to see you right after
work. Why, just the stink off his skin and clothes'd be enough
to cause your lungs an acute embarrassment. You'd be half-
dead after one breath!"

Her dad looked upset. He was turning his head this way
and that.

"Two, three years ago you spent eight weeks in this bed.
This time it's over six months and you couldn't walk to that
door without having to sit down once or twice, and you know
it. Not if your life depended on it. And here you are asking
me when you can go back to work. Christ Almighty! Well!

I'm telling you. Keep on the way you're going and you won't live to see the inside of your front room again, much less any shit-ass union office."

The quiet was like ice when he finished yelling. Her dad seemed to be holding his breath the way she was holding hers. She looked hard at her dad's red face as she tried to blot out the *Dies irae, dies illa* which was going through her head and which was what they sang in the choir at funeral masses. She never liked to sing funeral masses, even though it meant they were let out of school to do it, because funerals meant somebody was dead.

"Okay, Jim, okay," her dad said, so softly she could barely hear from her kitchen perch.

"But let me — explain something — to you," he said. "Then maybe — you'll understand — what's up — with me."

"Lie back down, take a few deep breaths if you can, then tell me." The doctor sat down on the near edge of her mam's bed. It must be terrible to be a doctor when it was your best friend who was sick, really sick. Almost sick enough to d —

"Well, you know the troubles, with the reconversion."

"I've heard as much."

"The mill owners don't want — to sink money into reconvertin' — mills left over — from the Industrial — Revolution — when the pool of workers — is diminishing. All the kids — want white collars — these days — her probably included."

Mary Catherine was startled by the three pairs of eyes fastened on her for the moment.

"And the workers — well — they got used to — overtime with war — production — so — now — they're spinning out — what little comes their way — trying to push it — into

overtime — and all those cost sheets — the owners keep —
all they say is — lack of productivity. Jesus."

"Rory, I'm sure you could get somebody from the CIO to
help out."

"A stranger. How much good — you think *he'd* — be able
to do?"

Dr. Kennedy shook his big bald head.

"So," her dad said, "I thought — if I could just get back —
into circulation — no more than — just being available — at
the office — for just a coupla weeks — I could make — a
show of strength — might make — all the difference — in the
world."

"Stop talking for a minute, Rory. And the rest of you keep
quiet, too," Dr. Kennedy said. "Just listen."

They didn't have to keep still to hear it. His breathing
sounded like the whistle on the hot dog wagon that
came around the mills at lunchtime. She knew it, people
weren't supposed to sound like whistles.

"Jim," her dad said, "you know I've *got* — to work.
Things are going — downhill very fast. Unless I can turn it
— around — you can see — what's going to — happen."

"Yes," the doctor said, shaking his head again, "yes, I can see
exactly what's going to happen."

"Well, at least tell me — the earliest possible — date . . ."

Dr. Kennedy stood up.

"I've told you everything there is to tell. The rest is up to
you." He picked up his bag and came out into the
kitchen without looking at her dad again.

"Mary Catherine," he said, "you're more of a beauty each
time I see you."

But he was hardly even looking at her when he said it and she knew he was just saying it to try to make *some*body feel good. She wished she could think of something to say to make him feel good. Sister Marissa, who was the best teacher in the world and her teacher, often said that God chose the exact, perfect cross for any child of His to bear and she was right: her dad sick when he knew the workers needed him, and Dr. Kennedy angry and sad because her dad was making himself sicker trying to get well.

Her mam was hurrying out of the bedroom.

there's this I'll see you out Doctor there's this pain in me shoulder I wanted to ask you about and

It was her dad she wanted to ask about because she always used the same excuse about her shoulder to talk alone with the doctor when he came.

And it was then, when he heard the kitchen front door shut, that her father turned over in his bed and his shoulders shook and she heard him start to cry.

Her heart began to pound as she looked around, frantically, for some escape from the sound of her dad's choking sobs. She grabbed up the package of swill tied up to be taken downstairs to the big can and ran with it out the back door and halfway down the outside steps. Then, hopeless and miserable, she stopped and sat down on the stairs, keeping her tears inside of her because at any minute somebody might come walking along the alley.

She was the reason her dad wasn't getting better. She was always filling up the million prayers and novenas and First Fridays she did to get him better with little thoughts about how if he *did* get better they all could live in a house and eat something besides the specials at the A&P and how she could have clothes of her own, instead of Deirdre's weird hand-me-downs. Her prayers weren't prayers at all; they were selfish, greedy dreams and she should be confessing them in confession instead of always thinking about what a good girl she was and what good marks she got without even trying. She was the reason her dad was crying with so much pain in his voice, for sure, because the only other time in her life she had seen her dad cry was when President Roosevelt died. That day, he had sat by the radio with tears running out of his eyes, but he hadn't made any noise crying.

Please, PLEASE, God, forgive me. Punish *me* good and hard but don't hurt my dad any more. Please don't hurt my dad any more.

She didn't care if the whole world saw her crying.

4. Spring 1948

THE FIRST THING you always heard when you came through the front door of Annette D'Artaglia's house, who was her best friend in seventh grade, was either music playing or somebody laughing. It was always that way. The D'Artaglia house was never stiff and quiet the way her flat was. That was probably because there were nine D'Artaglias and some of them, the children, were as old as twenty-three. And today, Mary Catherine could smell it, Mrs. D'Artaglia was cooking something wonderful. Something all full of tomatoes and garlic.

"Oh, P.U.!" Annette said. "Trippa *again!* It's my dad's favorite," she explained.

"What is it, whatever you said?"

"You think *I'm* going to say? It makes me want to throw up just thinking about it. I practically die when I'm eating it."

"But it smells so good."

"A lot you know, Irish! Come on, let's get upstairs before she catches us, and see if we can find out if Terry and Gina have hidden anything new."

They charged up the stairs at the same moment Mrs. D'Artaglia trotted out of the kitchen yelling, "Ey! Ey!" over the sound of the opera-singing on the radio.

Annette's room was huge, full of windows and sun and

closets and beds. She shared it with her sisters in Fresh
kill High, Teresa and Regina, who spent every cent they got
on clothes and on movie magazines and, and on *love* comics!

Quick as a flash, Annette climbed up on one of the beds
near a window and felt around in the chintz-covered val-
ance over the window.

Mary Catherine watched, crossing her fingers.

"Nothing!"

"Try the hatboxes."

"Ahh, they just used them last week."

"Try anyway."

Annette pushed open the sliding doors of the closets that
took up a whole wall.

"See, I told you," she said, standing up on a chair as she
rummaged through one hatbox after another. "There's nothing he — JACKPOT!"

"What! What!"

"*Modern Screen, Photoplay,* and *Romantic Life!* Which
one do you want?"

"Oh . . . *you* take the love comic." It was the most you
could say to your best friend. "Give me one of the
movie ones."

"Here!"

Annette flopped down on a bed with the comic.

Mary Catherine held the movie magazine in her hands for a
minute before she opened it. It felt heavy and full of exciting
things. Even if you didn't count all the pages used up for ads,
there were still lots of pages filled up with pictures and
stories and gossip about the Hollywood stars. What must it
be like to do a job where you got *photographed* all the time,
so you could see exactly what you looked like and not just have

to guess? And where, even in your private life, you had to get all dressed up and go around in fancy clothes or jewels because, even then, there were people taking your picture. Well, if nothing else came out of it, you were sure at least of how the world saw you, and that would be enough for her, any day!

Annette was reading the love comic so hard it was all right for her to do what she liked to do best when she came up here. She could see herself in one of the three full-length mirrors as she sat in the turquoise boudoir chair with the thick magazine in her hands.

You look a little squinched up, the director said to her. Don't be nervous now.

Quietly, silently, she drew one leg out into a long graceful line. Like a dancer. Then she lifted up her chin, just a shade. That was all right. Yes, it was all right. She looked just like a ballet dancer in the movies taking a moment's rest. Well, almost. Her hands and fingers, holding the movie magazine, looked long and tapered, like a concert pianist's, also in the movies, and that wasn't her imagination, they *were*.

She could see how good she looked in that wonderful mirror; why couldn't anybody else see it?

She let the pages of the magazine turn slowly, in case Annette was halfway paying attention to her.

She knew why nobody else liked what she saw.

Her hair was plain dark brown instead of red, or blond, or raven black like Annette's and, instead of being all curly or wavy, it was thick and straight and she got it cut short, like a boy's, otherwise she would have to live in curlers.

And so *what* if she had the smallest waist-measure of all the seventh grade girls? It was because she was skinny as a rail.

She didn't have any interesting curves above or below that Scarlett O'Hara waist.

And her face seemed to have a permanent serious expression. Big dark gray eyes, almost as black as her dad's, brown . . . wings for eyebrows, a straight nose, a nicely shaped mouth, everything orderly except her chin wasn't as pointed as she might have liked. Her face looked practically grown-up which, although she didn't mind it, made her look like nothing else but a real old seventh grader. What you needed when you were twelve was dimples or blue eyes or a blond pageboy if you had to wear your hair straight. Even though she looked a lot more like the pictures in the movie magazines than Annette or the others did, it was all wrong because you weren't supposed to look like that. Yet. And being five feet seven didn't help when everybody else, boys included, was around five-four.

Well, what could you do about it anyway? These days her father said, when he said anything at all, "You gotta take what life hands you. No use crying over spilt milk."

Life had handed her not looking the way she *should* look.

She opened up a movie magazine to a story about a messy divorce. It was probably a sin even to read it. She would just have to take a chance, but then the page turned over on its own and she was facing a picture of Farley Granger, the actor she liked the very best. There was something about his face she liked an awful lot. It wasn't just that he was handsome . . .

"Ey, Annette!" Mrs. D'Artaglia hollered from downstairs. "You gonna practice you music or not, that's what I'd like to know!"

"Yeah, Ma. I'm coming. Be right down.

"Quick!" she said to Mary Catherine. "Let's get these back where they were."

Annette climbed back up on the chair and stuffed the magazines and comic into the hatbox.

"No!" Mary Catherine whispered urgently. "Put the hatbox so the picture on the front's half turned around. That's the way it was. Otherwise they'll know for sure!"

"Boy," Annette laughed. "You'd make some spy."

"Ah, skinny little Mary Catherine," Mrs. D'Artaglia called out of the kitchen when they got downstairs. "Taste this for me, see if it's okay." She was holding a cooking spoon full of the tomato stuff out in the air to cool it off.

"Oh, don't taste that . . ." Annette said.

"Hush you mouth," her mother said. "Here, little Mary Catherine, you taste."

"Ey," Mary Catherine said to Mrs. D'Artaglia, "you're the one who's little."

"Taste."

"Oh, it's scrumptious!"

"Sit down. I give you some. I got good bread to go with it. You dunk it in the sauce. Annette, you shut up and go eat you Ostess cupcake junk."

Mary Catherine ate up the whole bowl and wiped the last of the sauce away with the good bread.

"You wanna know what you just ate?" Annette said.

"What?"

"Trippa! *Tripe*, Irish! You just ate a cow's stomach. Even all cooked up with vegetables, it's still a cow's stomach. Blah!"

Mary Catherine didn't know exactly what to say.

Finally she said, "Well, I tell you what. The next time we have lamb stew, I'll save you mine if you save me your tripe."

"No-o-o thanks."

"You want some more?" Mrs. D'Artaglia was already carrying her bowl over to the big pot.

"Oh, no! I have to eat dinner at my house, too, you know. My mother'd kill me if I came home already filled up."

"You're a good girl. And —" her mother turned to Annette — "she knows good food when she sees it, nah like some people I know. Practice, now!"

"You gonna stay?"

"No, I better go home. In case my dad needs something. Otherwise I'd love to stay. I just love that new Chopin piece you're learning."

Annette grunted. Her mother grunted even louder and pointed in the direction of the living room, where the piano was.

"Listen," Mrs. D'Artaglia said, "I hope you dad is better soon. It's no good for such a young man to be sick."

"Thank you," Mary Catherine said. "And thank you for the tripe, too."

"You wanna take some home? I got plenty."

"Ma!"

"Well . . ." Mrs. D'Artaglia said, shaking her head testily.

"I really have to go. Bye," she called as she went out the front door.

"See ya."

"Practice!"

Running along Sycamore Street from Annette's house, she had a sudden thought. All the times she had gone home with Annette, like today. Well. She had never had Annette home. You were supposed to do that. That was manners. You were supposed to . . . *entertain* people who had entertained you, even if it was your best friend who didn't expect something like that. After all, Annette sort of knew how things were at the flat, but maybe . . .

She had a dollar still saved up from her birthday last summer. She could buy some love comics and a bag of potato chips and two bottles of Coke . . . it wouldn't be the same as everything at the D'Artaglias', but it would be *something*. *Something* to give back in return, something to say thank you, to say I like you best, too.

The problem was her mother had never let her bring anybody home, not even before her dad got really sick and her mam had to go to work in the town clerk's office to make ends meet. outadoors is meant for kids to play in not in here with all the breakables

But that was when she had been little. Her mam would understand now that she and Annette would be as quiet as mice, because of her dad. That they wouldn't tip over the furniture or anything, like three-year-olds.

Yes, yes. She would do it! She would ask Annette over, and they would have a ton of fun together. Yes, yes!

And then she had another sudden thought. Young. Mrs. D'Artaglia had called her dad *young*. He was forty-eight. Forty-eight! That wasn't young. Even her mam wasn't young anymore. On her birthday she had cried right into the thirty-one candles Mary Catherine had so carefully stuck in the frosting, instead of blowing them out. a proper bonfire that's what it looks like a proper bonfire But they had made her laugh finally. Maybe getting old was what made her crabby almost all of the time now. And being sick had made her dad crabby.

If she ever got old and sick and crabby, she would just go someplace and live by herself and just try to be patient, instead of hanging around and grouching.

Oh, what did she care anyway? She was going to have Annette over!

⚘

The very next day after school, Mary Catherine told Annette her plan. She hadn't mentioned it to her mam yet, because her mam had come home from work yesterday all tired out and not in a good mood.

"Anyway," she said to Annette — they were standing on Annette's front walk — "I'll ask her and see what she says. *She* wouldn't be home anyway, she'd still be at work, and I'll tell her we'd be very quiet, okay? Because of my father. In case he's sleeping. You know."

"Okay," Annette said with a little smile and a shrug of her shoulders.

She wasn't doing this right. Mary Catherine just knew she wasn't doing this right and it didn't help a bit to think she was messing it up because she hadn't had any practice doing it. All she wanted to do was have her best friend over, that's all. Annette would understand.

"Anyway, I'll ask her, and then, on the day you come, on the way home we'll stop at Van Dine's and pick out two or three love comics, okay?"

"Great!" Annette said. "Listen, I forgot to tell you. Last

night I found another one they had hidden. In the leg of Terry's new green slacks, for crying all night! And there's a story in it about how this girl is going with this boy, I had to read it in the john, and he keeps her out one night after twelve o'clock and this girl, she doesn't know anything about *anything*, see? Well, she thinks, just because of *that*, even though *nothing* happened, all he did was kiss her, she thinks she's In Trouble — " Annette giggled and stretched her mouth so it was just the shape of a downward boomerang — "and then she's going to kill herself and . . . it's the best one yet and it's all full of kissing!"

"Oh, it sounds eeEEee!" Mary Catherine giggled and stretched her mouth, too, like a boomerang. She didn't really know what being In Trouble meant, except the kids always said it in a whisper which couldn't mean anything good, and she was ashamed to ask. So she just acted as if she did know and read the love comics like crazy hoping that, one day, one of them would just come right out and explain it.

"Anyway," Mary Catherine said again, "I'd better go now because I have to go to the A&P for my mother, and my father probably has something for me to do because it's the last day of the month."

"Come over when you're done? I'm dying for you to see this comic and Terry and Gina have Glee Club practice so they won't be home until supper."

"Well, if I'm not back by four, it means I can't come. I'll try to call you up if I can't, okay?"

"Okay. If the line's busy, try again. I promised Philly I'd call her up if I had time."

"Sure," Mary Catherine said, her heart sinking. Philly was

trying to get to be best friends with Annette. She didn't blame
her because Annette was pretty and nice and fair and the
seventh grade girl the whole class, even some of the boys, liked
best. It was like a miracle she had picked Mary Catherine for
her best friend. But it was getting late!

"See ya, Annette Annette, fulla spaghett!"

"See ya, choochie Maryoochie!"

She ran down the street toward home. She could blam in
and out of the A&P in no time and get supper started, too, it
was just meat loaf and boiled stuff, and be back at Annette's,
maybe even before four. That would even give her time to
get out of this dumb dress of Deirdre's that had Yo Te Amo
printed all over it, which made her dad laugh but which would
have caused the whole seventh grade to break out in hysterics
if *they* knew, out of it and into her dungarees and sweat shirt,
like a normal person.

Dummy! She had forgotten about her dad.

꧁

What she always did when she got home after school was
to pop into her dad's room and give him a kiss on the cheek.
He liked it, most times, she could see.

But not today.

"Cut that out, will you?" he snapped, holding up a little
brown paper bag in his hand. "I got work for you to do and
it's important, so pay attention."

She didn't have to pay attention, though, because she knew
the routine by heart, hadn't she been doing the exact same things every month for months? Trot *way* down
Main Street to the post office to her dad's box, the one he had

kept from his office days even though there was no more office, open it up with his key, slip out his "confidential mail"
into the brown bag, run back home with it, then, tomorrow,
gulp down her lunch, run to the bank with the bag, now
stapled shut, then back home to him with the bag restapled
by the teller, and all of that before ten of one when she had
to be back at school. It was enough to give you a nervous
breakdown, and he never had a kind word for all that harried
running around, he just said what took you so damned long?

"And I don't want any diddely-daddeling, coming or going,
get it? I don't care if you meet the Prince of Wales on parade,
get it?"

"My mam wants me to get some stuff at the A&P for her.
For supper tonight. It's right on the way to the post office and
it wouldn't take a minute."

"Oh, Jesus," her dad said.

"It's all right, dad. I'll make two trips."

"No, no," he said. "Get the stuff but do it before you go to
the post office. I don't want you leaving the confidential mail
in the A&P."

"Oh, thank you!" She wouldn't be able to get over to Annette's, but maybe she could get on the phone to Annette so
Annette wouldn't have time to call up Philly. Her dad was
sure to give her a lecture about Kids Using Telephones but
since she hardly ever did and since she would run both ways
and get his "confidential mail" back to him before he even expected it, he would probably let her call up Annette. Of
course, the phone being in his room now, instead of in the living room the way it used to be, might be tricky . . . "I have
to change, but it'll take just a minute."

"Go as you are," her dad said impatiently.

"My mam says I have to change out of my school clothes as soon as I get home." That wasn't exactly true but she wasn't going to wear this thing all the way down Main Street.

"Oh, Jesus," her dad said. "Get on with it then."

Mary Catherine got her dungarees and sweat shirt off the hook in the living room closet, and changed as fast as she could. She would wait until she got home to ask her dad if she could call up Annette. It would make him mad if she asked now. And it would probably make him mad if she asked him when she got home because he liked to look at the "confidential mail" before her mam got home from work, but she would just have to take the chance.

She looked around the living room for a second as she was putting Deirdre's dress on its hanger. It really was an ugly room. None of the colors matched and there was linoleum on the floor and the sofa bed where she slept was beginning to look very worn out. She hoped Annette, whose living room got done over practically every year, would understand. It would be different if she had a room of her own. Your own room was *allowed* to look crummy.

☙

By ten of five, the meat loaf was baking and the potatoes and the rutabaga were on the simmer. Mary Catherine sat quietly on the sofa, her dad was asleep. Keep outa here I wanta take a pee in my jar, he had yelled, just before he went to sleep. He hadn't let her call up Annette.

"The phone has to be kept clear for union business!" in a scream. "Damned kids have no business using the phone!"

What he said wasn't true. There was no more union business. Most of the regular mills had closed down. The men took whatever wages they could get at whatever jobs they could get. Even Jerry had moved to Long Island where his brother-in-law had a garage.

Philly had talked to Annette on the phone, though, without doubt. And probably about *her*, too. On the playground she had overheard some of the nasty things Philly was always saying about her but she hadn't known how to answer back, short of hitting Philly in her mean mouth, which would be dumb to do.

"She *never* has anybody over to her place, Annette, and when you try to call her up either her crabby mother or her crabby father answers and tells you to go to H-E-L-L and you *know* how she says she can never go to Pappas' or on the ferry to Westburgh with us because she *says* she's sorry but she doesn't get an allowance in that *stupid* way and when we go to the movies she never buys candy or popcorn so we have to share *ours* and she thinks she's so smart because she always gets the highest marks . . ."

(I can't help that, Mary Catherine thought, defending herself from her own imagination, I don't even study much!)

" . . . thinks she's too *good* for us with those fancy grown-up clothes she's always wearing and you just wait and see. When it comes time to buy the club jackets with GRANGER GIRLS done on their backs, she'll say she can't *afford* it and try to borrow one of ours."

The jackets cost $8.95 without the lettering, $9.95 with. They might as well cost a million dollars. And even though she couldn't buy one, she really wanted one because, of all the seventh grade girls, she was Farley Granger's most devoted fan.

Oh, she had done the only thing she could do: she had asked God for help in getting a jacket but without much hope right after she had asked Him, for the trillionth time, to find a cure for emphysema, which Dr. Kennedy had said was incurable.

Sister Marguerite, who was the seventh grade nun and mostly unpleasant, had talked about scientists (who were the men in the world who found cures for incurable diseases) one day in class and she said they were all atheists, which was the same as Communists, especially that old Alfred Ein-Stein at Protestant Princeton, whatever that was. And then, practically in the same breath, she had told them how busy God was, these days, dealing with the Communists because of the elections in Italy ("We'll have a day of prayer on Italian election day," Father Rafferty had said in church off the pulpit) and how, because of the way the Reds were taking over this country, mark my words, blood will be running, Catholic Christian blood, will be running in the streets of Milwaukee not later than 1949. Milwaukee was where the motherhouse was.

She had said a prayer to God asking him to convert one of the atheist, Communist scientists so he would have grace enough to cure emphysema. All the time, though, she felt she had been wishing on a rainbow.

There was one thing she could do, though, that might catch God's attention. Give up the thing in the world she liked the best, which was going to the movies on Saturday afternoon with the kids.

She hadn't yet been able to figure out how to do it. Her dad was the one who wanted her to go. He said two pictures and assorted short subjects for twenty cents was value for money, sometimes educational, and kept her and her long legs and her bit noisy feet outa the flat for a peaceful three hours of the weekend. He also sometimes, depending on his mood, liked to have her tell him the stories of the movies she had just seen . . .

She heard her mother coming up the stairs. She began to breathe hard as she struggled to remember the exact words she had figured out for asking her mother. She just had to let Annette come, she just had to because it was true, Annette might get tired of always having her over and then when she couldn't get a jacket she wouldn't have any friends left except for Rowena or Mickey or Ardelle, all of whom acted sneaky as anything for Catholic kids.

She had to chance it.

"Ma," she said as her mother came into the living room, "can I may I have Annette over and we would be very quiet and not make any noise I like her so much she's my best friend and I'm hers and she would only stay to four o'clock because she has to practice her piano and her mother expects her home!"

how is your father it's a horrid day more like July than the end of April this weather is un-natural for April anyone will agree is he asleep

"Yes, ma'am. *May* I have Annette over one day after school? I haven't promised her or anything."

Annette which Annette

"Annette D'Artaglia in my class who is my best friend."

D'Artaglia what can you be thinkin' of that wog even among Eye talians there is a sense of honor even they won't

have anythin' to do with Black Hand Si-cilians like a D'Artaglia

Her mam kept on and on while Mary Catherine's insides
filled with pain.

common nuisance here child put this next to your dad's bed
I'm too bushed to get up again ole lady Eustice was a sore trial
today so old she for-gets everythin' too proud to re-tire and
me doin' her work plus mine but not gettin' a wake up
Mary Catherine I'm ad-dressin' you or do I need an en-graved
in-vitation here's your dad's Luckies put them on the bed table
and I hope he has the de-cency not to smoke 'em while
Father Rafferty is here the lecture I got last time

Annette wouldn't have liked it here anyway, Mary
Catherine thought as she carried the cigarettes into her parents'
bedroom. It's ugly and I couldn't have given her anything
really good to eat and dad would have probably yelled.

Her dad was sleeping on his back, his mouth open, one arm
thrown across his eyes, the front of his pants open so she could
see It, even though she didn't want to see it. Pink and soft it
was, and she didn't want to see It even though she looked and
looked. Mortal sin, it was a mortal sin for sure and she was
the only one that day on the playground who wouldn't look
at the playing cards with the dirty pictures Jackie Slensky brought and now she was in worse trouble than any of
them because seeing the real thing was worse than looking
at any picture. And they had made fun of her, too.

"Gee," she whispered to Annette the next day. They were
on line in the church vestibule waiting to go to confession,
which today scared her very much and there was no way to

get out of it, even though she still wasn't sure if only *looking* was a mortal sin or not, because during the school year the school kids always went to confession on Friday afternoons so they wouldn't crowd up regular confession on Saturdays, no exceptions whatsoever. And she should be trying to think of the best way to tell whichever priest she got exactly what had happened, that she hadn't *planned* to see it, his Thing, but she had to try to tell Annette again that she was sorry she couldn't have her over so Annette wouldn't make that little shrug of her shoulders over again.

"Gee, Annette," she whispered, "she said you sounded like such a nice girl that she was sure you would understand that just having company in the flat would make my father sort of uneasy and then he couldn't get his rest right. He couldn't sleep . . ."

The soft pink thing flashed before her eyes, stopping her words, he had one, she didn't, maybe that was the only reason she had looked and looked, and maybe it *wasn't* really a mortal sin because she didn't think she had had an impure thought about It. It was just that she had never seen It before and when they all whispered together sometimes it was about a boy's Thing and she didn't even know what that was until . . .

God, I love You, she said, but that didn't help now.

"I mean," she whispered, but Annette had turned around and was talking to Philly who was in line behind her about Farley Granger and how she just loved him and how she could hardly wait until tomorrow afternoon because he was in the movie tomorrow afternoon and she hoped it was a good gooshy love picture and she would just die if he ever kissed her. And Philly whispered something to Annette that Mary Catherine couldn't hear and when she moved closer to be in on it, Annette turned her back.

Well, that's all right, Mary Catherine thought as she made a quick little move that made it look as if she had been turning to look at the bulletin board which was about the missions, instead of turning to hear.

She didn't know I was right there, that's all. She doesn't do mean things. Philly might, but . . . and anyway, even if we are only in the vestibule, God is right in there where the red lamp is burning to signify His Presence and His picture is on the ceiling, too, and they shouldn't be whispering on line. Especially about kissing.

Kissing was practically like an impure thought and that was how you got babies, Ardelle said. And she knew because her big sister had got a baby just because some bus driver had kissed her one night and she didn't even like it. But there must be something more to it than that because the kids did whisper about boys' Things and she had seen the boys' bathroom one day at school and it didn't even look like the girls' bathroom.

And there was a joke Rowena, who always said "call me Weenie" but nobody did except the boys, had told one day on the playground when Sister wasn't looking about the farmer's daughter and this traveling salesman who took her out in the field and he got her underpants off and she kept yelling, "Father! Father!" and finally he said, "What the hell do you think I am, a flagpole?" She didn't get it and they all laughed at her the way they had the day with Jackie's dirty pictures.

Looking at the red lamp burning inside the dim church, she

still didn't get it and she wished there was somebody who she could ask about it who wouldn't laugh at her. It wasn't just the joke. There was something going on she didn't know about, something that people talked about only in whispers so that meant it wasn't anything she could ask her mother or father about, even if her dad had still been like when she was little and she could ask him anything in the world and he would be patient. And even though she knew she should ask her confessor, who mustn't tell anything he heard in confession, not even if he was threatened with torture-and-death, she was afraid to ask Father Rafferty about it, in case she got him in confession today, because he was famous for yelling out loud at people in confession. But maybe if it was Father Cassidy, the assistant pastor, in the other confessional and not some visiting priest, she could ask him. Father Cassidy was a nice priest who gave you a chance and he only gave a few Hail Marys for penance while Father Rafferty, well, he had been known to give whole rosaries, which held up the classes going back to school and really showed everybody who the sinners were.

She could just tell Father Cassidy that she hadn't meant to see her father's . . . it was an accident like the boys' bathroom when she had been emptying the wastebasket and the janitor had put the big trash can right over next to the door of the boys' bathroom.

But she kept thinking about . . . It and thinking about It. She was doing it right now here practically inside God's house and that was much worse than talking on line about kissing.

Sister wasn't looking so she leaned her head back against the bulletin board. That way she could see what was going on be-

hind her in the line without really looking as if she were looking.

Annette was still talking to Philly and to Carol Devine,
too. Carol had on a dress that was beautiful. It was pale blue
with tucks all up and down the front and it had a white collar
almost like a priest's. And Annette had on the pink plaid
broomstick skirt Gina had made for her with a pink blouse
to match. And Philly had the best dress of all. A red dress
with a big white piqué bertha collar trimmed with navy blue
rickrack.

And she had on the same dress she had worn every day
this week. Deirdre's. It was lime green rayon gabardine,
two piece, with a peplum and felt flowers sewed on the
pockets. Only her mother had washed it, instead of dry-clean-
ing it like it said on the label, so the felt flowers, red, yellow
and purple, had run and each left a little blob of color on
the pocket. Times-were-hard-she-should-be-grateful-she-had-
any-clothes-at-all. She knew it, but she wasn't.

Maybe she should just ask Father Cassidy about *all* of
it. About the . . . the . . . the . . . It . . . and about
how she kept wishing she had red dresses with rickrack and
about why was it she kept wishing she had a little turned-up
nose and curly hair, too.

Or, maybe, if she could just once get back one of the
brown-covered Examination of Conscience booklets they had
used when they were preparing to make their First Holy
Communion in second grade, she could see laid out, for once
and for all, what exactly was allowed and what exactly was
not allowed. Whether it *was* a sin to want to look the way
other people expected you to look, vanity, vanity, Sister
would have said. And whether when something like yester-

day happened . . . The catechism was no help because it seemed to take it for granted there were a lot of things you knew that weren't even mentioned straight out in *any* of the catechisms they had used.

The seventh grade line, girls first, moved into church toward the confessionals as the eighth grade passed them going out of church. That class had some tall boys, but the seventh grade still didn't. It was awful to be taller than the boys in your class because then, how could one of them want you for a girl friend? You never married a boy who was shorter or younger than you, the kids had decided one afternoon when they were sitting around Annette's, talking.

If she couldn't get an Examination of Conscience booklet, maybe she could find a book in the library. Books were very good ways of finding out things without anybody knowing and asking you questions. If the book was in the Freshkill Library or in school, it was okay to read because they only kept good books in the library and, for sure, knowing Miss Verplanck, the librarian, nothing that might be on the Index. You were instantly excommunicated on the spot if you ever read a book on the Index.

So, if she could just find the right book, she could then find out the right page and read it and if she kept her hand tipped over what she was reading, she could find out about "Father! Father!" and all of that and nobody would know and she wouldn't have to ask anybody and then if somebody told a dirty joke and she didn't laugh (it was a sin to laugh) they couldn't laugh at her for not knowing because she could say, "Oh, yeah?" and they would know she knew.

"What do you mean, you talked back to your mother TEN times?" she heard Father Rafferty shout. But she couldn't tell which confessional his voice came out of and the line was divided up so she wasn't sure yet even which confessional she would get anyway but she prayed to get Father Cassidy. Father Rafferty knew her and if she even asked him about a little of what was bothering her or what was a book she could read and was it a mortal sin seeing . . . well, he could probably tell her mam and her dad and it wouldn't be like really breaking the seal of confession.

As the line ahead of her grew shorter, she tried to think of what to say if she got Father Cassidy and what to say if she got Father Rafferty and, as it grew even shorter, she suddenly decided that she would just say what came into her head, no matter what, no matter who was in the confessional and then she wouldn't have to worry about all of it any, any more.

When it was her turn, she went through the curtain into her side of the confessional and knelt down. She said a prayer to the Holy Ghost, Who was the brains of the Holy Trinity, to ask Him for help while she waited for the priest.

The little door slid open and, through the netting like a cane-bottom chair, she could see Father Rafferty's teeth. He was even making them click that way he did when he had food stuck between them.

"All right. What are you waiting for?" he said.

"Bless me Father for I have sinned. It has been one week since my last worthy confession. I confess that I have neglected my work once, that I have been disobedient twice and that I have . . . I have . . ."

"Well?"

"Let my library book get overdue which cost a penny." A lie!

"Mary Catherine . . . It is Mary Catherine, isn't it?"

"Yes, Father."

"Mary Catherine, you forgetful child. You know how hard life is for your parents and that even a penny means a lot to them. You're a good girl, even if you do seem to be given to dreaming. You must try hard to root that bad habit out of your character and do as much as you can to help your mother and father through this hard time in their lives. You are their consolation and you must not do anything to hurt them because they are good souls who don't really understand evil."

"Yes, Father."

"All right. For your penance say one Our Father, one Hail Mary, and one Glory Be. And will you tell your father, please, that I'll stop around this evening to see him after I've finished with the Dinner Committee of the Holy Name, which may be after nine. They're insisting on wanting to hold the fund-raiser dinner at the Regatta Hotel in Pough-keepsie, and that's such an expensive place, they'll never make any money out of it, even if the dinner is fully subscribed, which is doubtful, these days."

"Yes, Father."

"You're a good girl, Mary Catherine. Very dependable. Now let me hear your Act of Contrition."

"Yes, Father. Oh my God I am heartily sorry for having offended Thee and I . . ."

As the curtains closed behind her, she tried to forget she had not confessed what might be the mortal sin of seeing . . . what she had seen. She loved God, she had not tried to hurt Him willfully. Thinking about It just came into her mind; she didn't make it come; she didn't ask it to come and stay.

She went and said her penance at the altar rail in front of

the side altar with St Joseph's statue on it. The confessionals were on the side of the church where the side altar was to the Blessed Virgin, so that was where all the kids went to say their penance.

But she was feeling lonely and maybe St. Joseph was, too, with all his gray hair. So she knelt down in front of him and said her penance and then she tried to have a little talk with God but so many other things kept coming into her head. Like she knew that pretty soon Philly would be Annette's best friend. Especially when they all got their GRANGER GIRLS jackets. She tried not to think about Farley Granger and about seeing him in the movie tomorrow, and about how his lips looked. She said her penance all over again but even during it she kept seeing that new picture of him in one of Terry's magazines.

It was just of his face with all that curly, curly dark hair of his and showed his sideburns, which were longish, which wasn't supposed to be nice, but they were. The thing was, in the picture, he wasn't really smiling. His eyes looked far away and his mouth had a tiny crooked smile on it. He looked the way she felt inside sometimes — every, everything in the world was all mixed up and wrong but maybe there was a place somewhere else where it would all be different. Where there was someone you could just talk to and say even your most secret thoughts and dreams and ambitions to and they would understand.

And in the movies when he was angry, he clenched his jaw just the way she did when she was angry. And there would be someplace, like on the deck of an ocean liner at night, where they would meet for the first time and they would both be

hurt and angry but not with each other and he would
be clenching his jaw and she would be clenching hers only
she would start to cry and without even saying a word he
would put his arms around her and she would just cry and cry
with him holding her like that and finally he would lift her
chin up with his hand and he would look right into her eyes
for a minute and then those lips of his would come closer and
closer . . .

Somebody tapped her on the shoulder and she jumped a
foot.

"Sister says it's time to go back, if you're finished with your
penance."

It was Annette. Mary Catherine got up, all embarrassed.
Annette would think it was hilarious that there she was
dreaming about Farley Granger right there at the altar rail,
but, before she could tell her, Annette said, "Boy! What did
you do?"

And she remembered all of it again, and it was all back with
her again, so she just shook her head like a dummy. And everybody looked at her, even Sister, when she got in line.

❧

The kids always called for her for the movies on Saturdays
at a little past 12:30 because, even though the movie didn't
start until 1:10, it took time to get the tickets and then, inside,
to buy popcorn and candy and then, lots more time to pick
just the right seats by seeing who else was there. That meant
seeing if the boys were sitting anywhere near. Already twice,
Kenny Damone had walked Annette home from the movies

and everybody said that Billy McCarthy was talking about maybe walking Carol Devine home one of these days. And Philly said that Ralphie Sisco was always riding his bike up and down her street, which was not near his street, and it was true because they had all seen him one evening when they went to call Philly to sing novena. There he was, with the snow still on the ground except right in the middle of the street, riding his bike and Richie, his best friend, nowhere to be seen. "You coming to novena, Ralphie?" Bobbie Covetti, who already had bosoms and Vinnie Bertoni in the eighth grade had begun hanging around her, had yelled, and Ralphie had zoomed away and they had all giggled and felt dangerous.

It must be wonderful to have a boy walk you home or hang around in front of your house, just wonderful . . .

It was already past 12:35 and she hadn't heard the bell. There was so much noise, though, the traffic on Main Street, the radio turned up loud so her mam and dad could hear every word of the story they were listening to, a truck backing up in the alleyway to the grocery downstairs, that maybe she just hadn't heard the bell. They always gave it just one little tap because her mam had gone downstairs and yelled at them the day they gave it a dump-dumpy-dump-dump, dump-DUMP, so she had told them, after she had apologized about her mother, to just give it one short push because she would be listening.

Maybe the kids were a little late. That happened sometimes when one of them got her lunch late and the rest of them had to wait. She was always the last one to be called because she lived on Main Street and, even though it meant doubling back from the houses of the kids who lived nearer to the Freshkill Theater than she did (but not on Main Street), they always did it because that meant they could get a nice long walk down Main Street, which let them see who was around and what new dresses there were in the store windows.

So she waited until quarter of one and then she was afraid. They had never been so late before. Something must be wrong. They would never be late for Farley!

She didn't know what to do but, finally, at ten of one, she hollered "Seeya!" to her mother and father and thundered down the stairs to the street. She could hear her mother yelling something as she banged the downstairs door to, but she kept on going as if she hadn't, and didn't slow down until a block later. She stopped at the bus stop in front of the Palatine Hotel and looked back up the street to see if the kids were coming.

They weren't. And she couldn't see them ahead of her on Main Street, either. What could have happened?

Whatever had happened, it meant she had to walk all the way down Main Street on her own. Once she hadn't minded doing that, but now she did because she knew she might run into boys and boys looked at girls her age and she was a total flop so far as they were concerned and right now she didn't even have library books or dirty laundry for the laundromat to hold in front of her to hide her skinniness. And, all on her own, she would have to pass the CYO, where every Catholic boy in town of every age went to play pool or basketball. Oh, she'd *never* make it. But she had to! It was *Farley* at the Freshkill. Maybe the kids would let her in the club if she embroidered GRANGER GIRLS on the front and back of her plain white sweat shirt.

Oh, this wasn't the time to be worrying about *that!*

She ran all the way down Main Street as far as the post office, then she cut through Halvorsen's gas station to the alley behind the CYO. The alley was a weedy, overgrown place that only the mail trucks used to get to the back part of the post office and sometimes, at night, drunks went there to sleep, everybody said. It made her nervous to be all alone in such a lonely place even in the daytime, but it was a whole lot better than having to go past the gang of boys in front of the CYO because they did things like yell, "Hey, streamline!" at you and, if you even *looked* like you were going to turn around, they yelled, "Not you, boxcar!"

At the end of the alley she came out onto Howard Avenue, which went at right angles to Main Street, and she ran up to where the traffic lights were where the two streets met. There was a lot of traffic today on both streets because it was a shopping day, and the light turned red, against her, just as she got to the corner.

Across Howard Avenue she saw the kids going down the last long block of Main Street before the movies, and she yelled to them and waved her arms. They didn't seem to hear her so she yelled again, trying to be louder than the noise of the traffic passing in front of her. For a second, she thought she saw the flash of somebody's face turning around, but the kids kept going. Just before the light changed, she saw the face again for a second. It was Philly.

She crossed Howard Avenue slowly, dodging the turning cars, trying to figure out what to do. Philly had seen her all right but she just mustn't have told the others. Probably Philly was the one who had volunteered to ring the doorbell today but she *hadn't!* She had just pretended to. Philly really did want to be Annette's best friend.

Mary Catherine hurried up, but she didn't call to the kids again because she was going past the firehouse where there were a lot of men sitting on the sidewalk out in front because of the warm weather and she felt shy passing them. She broke into a hurried walk once she got past them and then, all of a sudden, she had the thought that maybe Philly *had* told them she was trying to catch up, and they hadn't cared. She stopped altogether when she thought of that. She had made a fool of herself two times yesterday: first, trying to explain to Annette, over and over, why she couldn't have her home; then, daydreaming about Farley in front of St. Joseph so long that she had ended up looking like a bad sinner.

She started to cry even before she knew it, so she ducked into the space between the abandoned bowling alley and the telephone building, and then she went all the way to the back of the bowling alley in case somebody could see her all gone to pieces. It was getting so hard to be alive.

But she didn't cry anymore when she got there. She just leaned against the building and felt sick and sad. From now on, probably, she would be lumped in with Rowena and Mickey and Ardelle, even if she didn't come from a bad home. To get kicked out of the kids, it was enough just not to be like the kids.

When she was sure the line in front of the Freshkill had gotten inside, she came out and walked the half-block to the theater. She saw with a shock that it was 1:30.

Oh God, she said to Him, please don't let it be Farley I'm missing. I just have to see all of him and his sad smile. Let it be Roy Rogers I'm missing.

🍀

In the space between Roy Rogers and the Previews of Coming Attractions, Mary Catherine stood up for a half a second in front of her seat way over on the right aisle next to the wall to see if the kids were, as usual, sitting down front just to the left of the center aisle. They were. It would be simple as simple just to go down to them and say, "Hey, you guys! Don't you even know how to ring a doorbell?" as if nothing had happened. That would wreck any scheming plans of Philly's, for sure. The thing was . . .

The thing was, maybe they might hate it if she just came and sat down with them. They might just ignore her, the way they did when Rowena or Mickey, one of Them, came and sat down without being invited.

She had never gone to the movies before all on her own. It didn't exactly spoil things not to have somebody to talk to or poke when the movie got good, but it wasn't the same, either. For instance, every time Farley kissed a girl in a movie, Bobbie Covetti would drum her fists in her lap and beat her feet against the floor and wiggle her behind in her seat, which was just exactly the way the rest of them felt. He was so gentle, but so strong, the way he sneaked up on the girl he was going to kiss. The way he did it made it twice as good. Even when it was Ann Blyth, who was a Catholic as well as a movie star. She'd be shy with him because he had this big reputation in the public high for being a wild kid, but that was because

when he was born his mother died so his father hated him and
he just didn't know how to put up with it all. And he would
keep getting closer and closer to her in her simple white formal
and she, Ann Blyth, would keep saying kind things to him,
soothing things, not guessing what all of them *knew*, that in
a minute he was going to KISS her!

And, when he finally did it, only right now he was kissing
some actress she had never heard of but who had the female
lead anyway, Mary Catherine wanted to drum her fists and
beat her feet and wiggle her behind. She didn't, because she
felt funny doing it on her own, but she couldn't help thinking
Boy! Will *we* have a lot to talk over tomorrow after singing
nine o'clock Mass!

Then it dropped down on her, all over again. How come,
they would say, you know all about the movie if you didn't
sit with us, how come?

Poor Farley, she knew just how he felt. It was like a punish-
ment to be all on your own, with no friends, with no one to
really care about you. He looked different and strange with his
sideburns, just the way she looked different and strange. Only,
because he was a famous star, he had fans because of the different way he looked. Maybe, if her dad got well and got
back working for the union again, he would be sent out to
Hollywood to look after the actors' union, and they had one,
too. Maybe because it was summer vacation or something,
she would go with her dad to Southern California, which Bob
Hope always made jokes about on the radio. And, because her
dad was working and had lots of extra money, she would have
a swanky haircut and clothes and some make-up and she'd go
to this party with her dad and Farley'd be there and she'd say,

without asking for his autograph or doing something dumb like that: "I've been an admirer of yours for a long time . . ."
No.

What would *get* him would be if she said, very seriously: "I've admired your *acting* for a long time. You really know how to show pain," and other things like that. Or, maybe, even before she got to this party, a talent scout would see her and get her cast, as a New Unknown, opposite Farley in his next picture, and everything would be perfectly ordinary until the first time the two of them had a love scene together and he would kiss her and she knew what she would do and just what would happen.

In the rehearsal, he would kiss her just the way he always kissed a girl, unless it was Joan Evans that old snot and it must be hard always playing a snot, and, when he did, she would gasp and draw back and run right off the set.

Farley would run after her and catch up to her and catch her arm and he would say, "What is it? Did I do something wrong?"

No. He would say: "Did I do something to *offend* you?" And she would shake her head, as if she had a high fever, and she would say, very weakly, "No . . . no . . ." And he would KNOW.

Just as soon as THE END came on the screen, she ducked out a side door of the Freshkill and took back streets all the way home. Her dreams were so real she didn't want to have to face the kids who had left her behind.

But, someday, they would all realize that embroidered basketball jackets and pretty homes and allowances weren't everything. Maybe she'd just let them read about her wedding to Farley in the newspaper columns and the movie magazines. Of course, she'd have made herself famous by that time so that their wedding would be the Wedding of the Year. Nobody paid attention when a somebody married a nobody. Well, maybe she would be kind and let them come to the wedding in the St. Patrick's Cathedral of Hollywood because she would have converted Farley because nobody who looked the way he looked could be a Catholic to begin with. Anyway, it would be her secret until then.

⚘

When she got back to the flat, her mam and her dad were talking about money, which was what they always did when she went off to the movies.

Her father gave her the funnies from the Freshkill *Daily* and told her to beat it into the living room. She did, and read the funnies first, in case he asked her if she had seen this joke or that, but she could hear that their talk was more serious than usual. Serious enough to keep her from looking up the Hollywood gossip column which was really her favorite part of the *Daily*.

"You saw — the letterhead — and who it was who — signed the letter."

ach I never did trust him with his red hair his red-haired wife too neither of them Irish he says nothin' in that letter 'cept hello good-bye

"All right, all right! So I was the one — wrote him first — told him about — the sad state of — affairs here. Told him how — I was the one suggested — the subregional office be — moved from down here — up to Al-bany — where the

legislature — sits, That wasn't — *bragging;* he understands
— the *import* of such — things! More than you! The only
reason you're — down on this thing — is because of old lady
— Eustice!"

don't care I just don't care what you think old lady Eu-stice
now she's had that stroke is sure to retire soon and whether
you like it or not by this time next year Rory I'm the one
who'll be town clerk on full salary I know this town inside
out an' backwards further-more

"You read — between the lines — I tell you! He's offering
me a — job when I re-cover. All right — an inside job —
not one — as I would like — out among the workers — but
a real — de-manding job — nonethe — less."

the only thing that's de-mandin' is you ought to be in your
bed right now and put out that ciga-rette you've al-ready had
one this after-noon what if Father Raffer-ty or Jim Kenned-y
with his black bag should de-cide to drop in

Mary Catherine pulled her eyes from Louella Parsons
which was only, entirely about Virginia Mayo today, and
paid attention. They were talking about a job, a job for her
dad!

"Read between the — lines! A job — either down in head-
quarters — in Washington, D.C. — or maybe even — in
Deetroit. I wouldn't mind going — back there because —
back there — I'd be right — in touch!"

whether you like it or not I re-peat by this time next year
I'll be town clerk on full sal-ary which is what we must count
on Rory dear to keep us go-in' what-ever your wishes and
dreams may be

"This — job — is — a — *fact!*"

So! So! So! Mary Catherine thought, as she heard her mam helping her dad back to bed, I knew it! I just knew God would hear me sooner or later.

She could hardly believe it. She had come home from the movies ready to die and, in half a minute, her whole world and her dad's whole world had changed around altogether.

"Thank you, God," she said, bowing her head to Him. "It was worth the wait."

⚘

She grabbed Annette's hand so that the two of them were the first ones down the spiral staircase from the choir loft after Sunday Mass.

"I have a real big secret to tell you and you have to promise you won't tell a single living soul."

"I *promi*se," Annette said, her feet barely touching the pavement of Sycamore Street as the two of them raced for the back booth of Pappas' on Main Street. Mary Catherine had her own dime to pay for her own cherry Coke.

"*Tell me!*" Annette threatened to grind to a halt and Philly was close on their heels in spite of the fact that her legs were so short.

"Well, it's something I'm not even supposed to be talking about!"

"EeEEee!" Annette said. "I promise on a stack of Bibles, *two* stacks of Bibles."

"Well . . . my father has been offered a big job by the CIO, that's his union, and we're going to move to either Washington, D.C., or to Detroit."

Annette stopped dead still and let her mouth drop into a big O.

"Oh, that's just wonderful," she said, "But that means I'll lose my very, very best best friend."

Mary Catherine was so delighted at how Annette was taking it that she almost forgot to be sorry she'd be losing her best friend, too.

"What is it? What is it?" Philly demanded, catching up.

"That's for me to know and for you to find out," Annette said, snapping her mouth shut.

"Oh, yeah? Hey, Mary Catherine," Philly said, trying to be as casual as anything but she couldn't manage it, "how come you didn't go to the movies with us yesterday? I rang your bell good and loud."

"You did? *I* didn't hear a thing. You got a weak finger or something?"

"Come on, Maryooch!" Annette said, giving her a friendly shove. "Let's *go!*"

As they burst into Pappas', red-faced Philly miles behind them, Annette said, "My treat!"

"Oh, no you don't. I can afford to go Dutch treat for a change!"

"You're rich already!"

Gasping for breath, the two of them hurled themselves into the back booth at Pappas', the best booth of all.

❧

By the time she got to school on Monday, everybody knew about it. They clustered around her, on the playground, asking questions.

"You aren't even supposed to know," she said, smiling at Annette and feeling only a little nervous.

❧

On the way home from school, after she had left off Annette, Billy McCarthy caught up with her. At first she had pretended she hadn't seen him following her.

"Mary Catherine," he called, just as she was about to go upstairs to the flat.

"What."

"You have to go up right away?"

"No." But she acted as if she didn't care one way or the other. He was kind of tall but still not as tall as she was.

"I really have to go to the library," she said. "I was just going to put my school books in the hall here."

"That's swell," he said.

"Oh?"

"I wanted, I mean, I was thinking about going to the library myself."

"Oh."

"I wanted to take out this book on sign language. So I could talk to the guys in class without Maggie-Baggie knowing. She has eyes in the back of her habit! Only I need somebody to look it up in the card catalogue for me. Miss Verplanck is such a crab."

"Yeah, she is. She even hollers at me sometimes."

"She does? But you go to the library all the time."

"Well, she does." She never had, but it sounded good to say so.

"Anyway," he said.

"I can look it up for you, if you want."

"Oh, that would be swell!"

"Okay, just let me stick my books in the hall." She thanked God a whole lot that she had her library card in her pencil case. She hadn't really planned to go to the library today. Her books weren't due until Friday. Even though she had read them all, she wasn't going to go upstairs to get them. Her dad might have an errand for her.

She felt very funny, but very nice, walking along Main Street with Billy to the library.

"Are you really going to move away?" he said.

"Yes," she said, "but I don't know when. It depends on how my father feels."

"Yeah, I know. He's been very sick."

"Yes."

They didn't talk for a long time.

Finally he said, "A lot of people will be sorry when you move away."

She couldn't think of anything to say so she kept quiet.

"I mean they'd miss you."

She almost asked him about Carol Devine but she thought it would be better if she didn't.

"I mean, I'd miss you, too."

"You *would?*" she said before she could stop herself.

"Yeah," he said and he moved a little way away from her and began to walk along on the curbstone. In a way, she was glad, because when he was right next to her, he had kept swinging his hand right next to her hand, almost as if he wanted to hold hands. She'd just die, right there on Main Street, if he ever did that. Because even though she and the kids had talked for hours and hours about how they would act with their boy friends when they got one, she couldn't remember a word of it because it was just like in the love comics — she felt as if big waves of electricity were shooting out of him at her. She also felt as if she were going to smother. So she didn't do anything but watch very hard, like a dummy, as he balanced on the curb.

"You *have* to move away?" he said, looking at his feet.

"Hey! McCarthy!" somebody yelled from across the street.

"Hey!" Billy yelled back, falling off the curb. It was Ralphie Sisco over there in front of the Chevy place, and he must have seen her, too.

"Hey! You gonna play ball? The guys got a game as soon as I finish my paper route." He pronounced it "rout," like in a war.

"Nah. I have to go to the library."

"Oh, yeah. I can see *that*."

"Seeya!" Billy yelled. His face was all pink.

"Don't do anything I wouldn't do!"

"Why don't you take a long walk off of a short dock!" Ralphie laughed, but it wasn't a mean laugh.

"That guy!" Billy said to her.

"Oh, he's okay."

"You think so?"

"Well . . ." Oh, had she spoiled it?

"Yeah," Billy said. "He's okay." He climbed back onto the curb.

She said thank you to God that Billy wasn't mad. One of his friends had seen him with her and he wasn't mad. Or ashamed. Here she was, wearing this dress of *Deirdre's,* the rayon knit one with red valentines all over its black and white checks that had the uneven hem, and he didn't care who saw him with her. He didn't mind walking on Main Street with her when she had on a dress with a droopy hem! She almost wished her dad wouldn't take the job he wanted so much.

"You didn't answer me."

"What?"

"You have to move away?"

"Yeah," she said. And then, without even planning it, she smiled at him. And he got all pink again and smiled at her and fell off the curb again. She had never felt so good in her whole life! If only she didn't have to move away.

But if she stayed living in Freshkill, it would mean her dad couldn't work and then Billy might get sick of the sight of her in Deirdre's hand-me-downs. After a while, he would get ashamed of her and then he would look for another girl. One smaller than he was.

But right now.

Well, it was all right, right now. She would find his sign language book for him and he would think she was wonderful. Just because she could work something easy like a card catalogue. She decided that tonight she would borrow some of her mother's little metal curlers and see what she could do to look pretty.

It was true, after all. A boy could like her.

5. The Last Days of Seventh Grade

"I DON'T THINK she's ever going to move away. I think she just made it up."

She was around the corner from Philly, only Philly didn't know it. The terrible thing was, maybe Philly was right. Her mother and father hadn't talked about the CIO job since that first time. And it seemed to her that not only wasn't her father getting better, he was getting worse.

It didn't make any difference who Philly was talking to, saying what might accidentally be true and not just one of those lies she sometimes swore were the exact truth.

But it was Annette she was talking to, because Mary Catherine could see the edge of her yellow dotted swiss dress that had once been Gina's but still looked okay.

☙

Mary Catherine sat still on a toilet in the girls' bathroom, listening to Philly, out there by the sink, talking. Even though it was Saturday morning, a lot of the seventh and eighth grade girls were at school, helping the sisters get ready for the closing of school. There were a lot of girls out there with Philly. She could see their feet. Annette's new sneakers with the dark blue tops.

"*My* mother talked to *her* mother, when she was in the clerk's office yesterday afternoon, to renew the license on my father's restaurant."

Romanelli's wasn't a *restaurant*. It was a tavern. A saloon. And they only sold pizzas and meatball sandwiches on the side. Mostly, they sold *drinks*.

"And my mother axed her mother and her mother said it was all up in the air and how did she know about it anyway? My mother said she was real nasty about it, too."

"Oh, she's a real crab," one of the girls said, and then she said something Mary Catherine couldn't hear which made them all laugh.

"Anyway, I told Ralphie and he's going to tell Billy. I mean, she told us all just a bunch of lies and stole him right away from Carol. Boys are so dumb!"

They all laughed.

"Yeah," somebody, Bobbie, said. "I'll bet he never even noticed the stupid clothes she wears. She really thinks she's hot stuff in those stupid clothes."

"Well, Ralphie's going to tell Billy . . ."

Mary Catherine stopped listening. She drew her feet up onto the front of the toilet seat so that if they looked they wouldn't be able to see her oxfords. She was the only one who still wore oxfords to school. She wrapped her arms around her knees and cried into her skirt.

Her bottom fell asleep before they finally left.

ॐ

When she went home at lunchtime, really only 11:30, Father Rafferty was there. The two of them, Father Rafferty and her mam — her dad was asleep — gave her a talking-to, not angry, but very serious. Eavesdroppers never got the whole story was what they told her. She couldn't think of anything to say to them or even how her face should look to show them she hadn't meant any harm at all. So she pressed her lips together very hard and her eyes blinked a lot and her mother said to Father Rafferty in a tearful voice oh there's ar-rogance in that ex-pression there on her face and Father Rafferty said, "Well, be easy on her, she's just a child," but he told her that maybe she had better come to confession this afternoon, even if she had only been there just yesterday, and have a chat with her confessor about truthfulness and responsibility.

After Father Rafferty had gone, her mother stopped almost-crying and yelled at her but in a low voice so she wouldn't wake up her dad. And she ended up saying she would just have to give up the movies for today so as she could get to con-fession right at four o'clock when they started up be-cause Father Rafferty *said* and in the mean-time I've got plenty for you to do

Mary Catherine knew that if she started crying now, she would never stop. So she pressed the tears and the yelling very hard into her brain. She could cry tonight when she was in her bed. Nobody would see her then.

At 12:30, the doorbell went DUMP, DUMPy DUMP DUMP, DUMP DUMP!

Mary Catherine sat still as a stone, looking at the stuff floating in her bowl of Scotch broth while her mother, faster than Superman, dashed down the front stairs and yelled at the kids for pounding on the doorbell.

After lunch, she took the laundry to the laundromat and

read the posters over and over again about how to use the machines and what to do and what not to do and listened to the usual lady who told her she was a pushy kid and that this was *her* machine, she had been waiting for it, when really the lady had just come into the laundromat, and she tried not to think about the movies which were today, the main feature, James Stewart who was very tall and seemed like he would give you a chance, being a baseball player. Her mam would make up a lie to tell her dad why she hadn't gone to the movies, Mary Catherine thought, very quietly.

At four o'clock, she went to confession and, even though she said a prayer about it and crossed her fingers for luck, she got Father Rafferty. He gave her, as penance, the Joyful, Sorrowful, and Glorious Mysteries of the rosary, which added up to three rosaries and about a million prayers. All she could think of was that she was glad it wasn't a school day so that everybody could see, but for real this time, that she had a big penance, that she was an eavesdropper.

When she got to bed, she was too tired to cry. But she couldn't get to sleep for a long, long time.

6. Summer 1948

IN THE SUMMER, with school out, with no kids she had to face, it wasn't too bad. She had plenty of time for reading, which was better than playing, because with reading you could get involved in the lives and worlds of all sorts of really exciting people from all over history as well as today. And, once a week, there was the movies, the best time of all, except it had presented a problem until she solved it.

There were three shows a week at the Freshkill: Thursday-Friday-Saturday, Sunday-Monday-Tuesday, and then Wednesday when they showed old movies for just one day. You had to get together with the kids on Memorial Field or at somebody's house in the summer to find out what afternoon or even, now that they were older, what night everybody was going to the movies together. The kids never went on Wednesdays. Who wanted to pay good money to see old movies when you could see old movies on television if somebody asked you over who had one? Mary Catherine went on Wednesday afternoons, no matter what was playing. She told her mam and dad she was making a study of old American movies and since she spent so much time in the Freshkill Library, or reading library books, they believed her.

The only problem was that a lot of the Wednesday movies

were horror ones. Ghosts or monsters. Mary Catherine knew the minute she saw the name of Bela Lugosi or Boris Karloff or Lon Chaney, Jr., in the credits that they were going to spend 99 per cent of the movie changing from themselves into somebody or some*thing* else.

Then, when she had finally gotten good at ducking in time to miss all the teeth and claws, along came Ray Milland and Gail Russell, who were *regular* actors, in a movie called *The Uninvited* and she had just sat there like a moron, not quick enough to hide her eyes when doors began to open with nobody there and the pages of a book turned and a flower suddenly wilted, and she had had nightmares for a long time about that movie and its ghost. Monsters were just made up by Hollywood, but ghosts might really be the tormented souls of people in Hell that the Devil set loose on the world because he was so mean.

So, one day, when the movie was called *A Damsel in Distress*, Mary Catherine just slid down right away in her seat as soon as it started, because of the *Distress* in the title, and she didn't believe for one minute in the cheerful music, the really cheerful music that was played while the credits were being shown. After all, Joan Fontaine was in it, and she had been in *Rebecca*, which had been about an English ghost just like *The Uninvited* and *The Canterville Ghost*. Any minute, all these ritzy people would suddenly freeze in horror as the music changed to the mournful organ stuff Sister Jeanne played for funerals.

It was only after a long time that she realized the movie was a musical.

When she did, she smiled and sighed and got comfortable.

She even put her feet up against the seat in front of her, which you could never do on a Saturday or a Sunday afternoon because the ushers were everywhere with flashlights because the theater was filled with kids. On Wednesdays there was hardly anybody but her and a few old people in the movies. Unless it was a rainy day.

The more she watched the movie, the more she wanted to be like the skinny man who was playing and dancing the matinee idol. He was elegant. That was just the right word for him. Nobody she knew for real was elegant, except maybe long ago her dad in the days when she used to walk through the streets of Freshkill with him. Those days, in addition to keeping his finger on the pulse of the people, he had had a good time showing her the beautiful and old things about Freshkill. Like how a house or a bridge or a wall had been built long ago and was still useful and good to look at. No matter how worried he might be about all the different locals, he would still take the time to show her things right around her that she wouldn't have noticed on her own. That was elegant. To be able to still see beautiful things when everything else was going wrong.

As the movie went on, she realized it was the music that was helping the dancing man (whom she had seen in a Technicolor movie but she couldn't remember his name) to be so elegant. There were songs about a foggy day in London Town and another one about nice work if you can get it (which was about Love) and then another really funny one about a stiff upper lip. The songs would have been *great* if you only heard them over the radio.

When the double feature was over — the second movie was

some stupid musical set in Hawaii in a funny color and everybody in it looked 110 and acted 120 — Mary Catherine raced out of the movies to look at the *Damsel in Distress* posters out in front. Of course it was, the skinny man was Fred Astaire whose today movies usually played Sunday-Monday-Tuesday so she never got to see them. The people who made up his music were George and Ira Gershwin, which was probably a husband-and-wife songwriting team, the best one in the world!

On the spot she fell in love with Fred Astaire and George and Ira Gershwin because, it was true, they had made her feel really happy and excited for the first time in a long time.

☙

Picking a good time and without making too much of it, she asked her dad about George Gershwin who was the Gershwin who had made up the music for the movie, the part of it she liked the very best.

"He was a Jew composer — died when he was very young. It surprised everybody. A year or so — after you were born. You can look him up — in the library — if you haven't got — something — better to do."

So she did. And the important thing she learned about George Gershwin was that he had started out from being a Jew in Brooklyn which, the book seemed to say, was about the same thing as starting out poor in Freshkill, but he was a genius and he had Made a Name for Himself, even though he died too soon. (*Thirty-eight* seemed old to her but not to the book.)

The funny thing about George Gershwin was that he was getting to be the most famous just at the same time her dad was getting shot at by Henry Ford and she was getting born. Their lives were all connected up, it was like a miracle! Or maybe a sign from God about something.

❧

One Wednesday afternoon, even though it was such a nice day she almost felt like taking a chance and going over to the playground, she was at the Freshkill fifteen minutes before the ticket booth opened. She wanted to get a good look at the posters out in front and at the shiny photographs that showed scenes of today's movies. Both pictures were Fred Astaire–Ginger Rogers musicals but the exciting thing was that one of them was *Shall We Dance*, a Gershwin movie! She was looking so hard at the photographs, staying a long time at each one, that she didn't even see Mr. Feinberg, who ran the Freshkill, come out of the lobby onto the sidewalk.

"Well, kid, it looks like it's just you and me today," he said to her, scaring her out of her wits. Mr. Feinberg was not an old man but he was almost entirely gray. Gray hair, gray eyebrows, gray eyes, gray suit, gray tie. Even his skin looked gray, which was because he had a heart condition and one Saturday afternoon a couple of years ago, right in the middle of the second feature, the rescue squad had to come right into the movies to rescue him because he was having a heart attack in front of the candy stand.

She smiled at him, a scared smile, because she was thinking that if maybe she was the only one going to the movies this afternoon, maybe he would decide not to run the two musicals, after all.

"Just tell me something. It's a nice day. The sun is shining.

What're you doing going to the movies? Nobody else is "
He looked very gloomy as he waved his hand at Main Street,
which was practically empty of cars and people.

"Fred Astaire," she said, trying to think up a whole sentence.
"And George Gershwin."

"What do you know about George Gershwin? He musta
died before you were even born."

"Well, he died when I was already born, but he wrote a lot
of good music anyway."

Mr. Feinberg shook his head. "That was some shock when
he died. Most people didn't even know he was sick and then,
one day on the radio, Walter Winchell, dead!"

"Yes," Mary Catherine said.

"You know something? I heard him play piano once. A
new theater was opening up in New York City, right around
the corner from the one where I was in the box office, so I
went. I heard he was going to be there, at the opening cere-
monies. So I went."

He stopped talking to her for a minute as he helped an old
lady up to the ticket booth.

"Good afternoon," he said to her, the old lady. "It's nice to
see you."

The lady smiled. She had something wrong with her that
made her head shake.

"Ethel," Mr. Feinberg hollered through the glass of the
ticket booth. "Open up and give Mrs. Sabinsky her ticket.
She wants to go in and sit down and get settled, right?"

Mrs. Sabinsky nod-nod-nodded. When she got her ticket,
she walked into the theater in a slow and stately manner, almost
like a queen.

"I'll bet these two pictures bring back memories for her," Mr. Feinberg said, scaring her again because she had been watching the old lady.

"Where was I? Oh, I remember. So. I was working b.o. in this place but I asked for time off. It turned out not to be necessary because everybody but Shubert himself took off on the chance of seeing George Gershwin play piano in person. They had this opening day program, see, with some very big names on the bill, but nobody paid attention. They were all waiting for Gershwin. He was a very dapper fellow to see, not exactly handsome, but dapper and full of life so that would of been enough, see? But, the important thing was, how he could really play piano."

Mr. Feinberg spoke these last words very slowly. Mary Catherine watched his face, waiting.

"He was supposed to play one number, right? There were a lot of other people on the bill, right? So he played it. 'I Got Rhythm.' You know that one?"

"I'm not sure," she said. No, she couldn't exactly remember that song so that meant there might be other songs of his she hadn't heard. That was exciting to think about.

"Well, he played it like nobody has ever played it, before or since, and he brought down the house. You know what that means?"

She nodded.

"He loved to play piano. And no wonder. He was a natural at it. Couple of years later, in fact, after that when the theater was opening, my memory's going, what *was* the name of that place? Metropolis? No. Gotham? No. Manhattan? Maybe. Aah, forget it! A couple of years later, he actually made a

symphonic music piece out of how he played 'I Got Rhythm'
that day. You got a record player? I'm sure it's still on
records."

"No," she said. And she almost said, because she suddenly
felt it, "I haven't got *anything* except maybe rhythm."

"Too bad. Too bad." Mr. Feinberg was looking at the sidewalk, shaking his head. "What a swell guy to have to go and
die so young. What style he had, what style! Even his mother
was still alive, still a young woman. We were almost exactly
the same age, you know, George Gershwin and me. Born in
the same month, September, of the same year, eighteen ninety-
eight, in the same place, Brooklyn. Only he was a genius. It
makes you think."

Mr. Feinberg wasn't talking to her at all. He was just simply
talking about somebody he liked. Somebody he hadn't even
known as his own friend. Somebody he couldn't even pretend
would fall in love with him and marry him, the way she could
with Farley. Somebody who was a genius at playing the piano
and making up songs that made Mr. Feinberg and a lot of
other people happy to be able to hear him doing it.

"And his *Rhapsody in Blue*, what do you think of that one?"

But he didn't even wait for her to answer, which was good
because, even though the name of the music sounded a little
familiar, she couldn't remember if she had ever heard it on the
radio.

"My kid sister got a Victrola one Chanukah . . . you know
what Chanukah is, you Jewish by any chance?"

She shook her head no.

"What's your name?"

He was going to tell her mother and father something, that

was why he wanted to know her name. She hadn't done anything wrong but now it would all be ruined and she wouldn't
even be able to go to the movies anymore. No kids and, now,
worse, much worse, no movies.

"Mary Catherine Mulligan," she said in a low voice.

"Mary Catherine . . . that what they call you — Mary
Catherine?"

"Yes."

"Mary Catherine, I'll make a deal with you. You and me
are the only regulars on Wednesdays, except for Mrs.
Sabinsky. And for the people from Blount House, that private funny farm out on the Mill Creek Road. Only calm ones
these days, though. I insisted. After that guy climbed up on
the stage, right in the middle of the picture, and kept yelling
how *he* was Tarzan. But we're the only ones who really watch
these Wednesday movies. What the hey? I'm going to look
in my book and see if I can get that movie they made about
George Gershwin's life. Before you have to go back to school.
Of course, they made up everything in it. I mean, the whole
thing about his life is a lie because, you know Hollywood, they
wanted to get some girls in it for romantic interest, but George
Gershwin never got married. Always too busy, even though
he could of had any wom — And on top of it, they got an
Italian actor to play him, which is really some joke. But in
that movie, *Rhapsody in Blue* — or have you seen it?"

She shook her head no. She couldn't believe it, that he
wanted to keep talking to her or what he was saying to her,
so it was better if she didn't say anything. Only looked very,
very interested.

"Okay. Okay. I'll book it! And you promise you'll come
and see it."

"Oh, I promise!"

"In it, they play a lot of his music. If you really like his music, it'll be some treat for you."

She stood very still, because she thought that the joy or whatever it was she was feeling inside of her was just going to kill her on the spot.

"All right. Go on and get your ticket. It's time. But don't *you* sit in the loge, see? I only let Mrs. Sabinsky sit where-ever she wants to, even if she only pays regular. It's not her fault she's gotten old and sick and not so well-off anymore. You can still see it, she's a lady of style. In her own way classy like George Gershwin."

"I'll sit in the regular seats."

She stood there in her dungarees and sweat shirt and looked at Mr. Feinberg with a look she hoped told him how happy he had made her. She wished that maybe she looked like Ginger Rogers or like Mrs. Sabinsky when she was young so that she could get across, with *style*, to Mr. Feinberg her thanks to him. But all she had was her twenty cents, which she gave up, happily, to Ethel. Once she grew up and got out of Freshkill and somehow got famous and got style, she would come back to the Freshkill and shake Mr. Feinberg's hand. And maybe *that* would make him happy, too.

"You watch the ads. And I'll be looking for you, pal."

⚜

The other movie, *The Gay Divorcee*, was better than very good, but *Shall We Dance* was the best movie she had ever seen. Even counting Farley. When it was done, she danced all the way down the back streets to home to get supper ready before her mam got home from work. She wanted supper to be okay, no mistakes whatsoever, because she wanted to see *Shall We Dance* over again tonight and she couldn't do *that* unless her mam came along. How would she do it, get her mother to come?

She would talk about how Ginger Rogers looked and the dresses she wore. In the old days, when all of them went to the movies together, even in Detroit, her dad had called her mam "Ginger, Ginger, my redheaded Ginger." And it was true. Even though her mam was old now, she was still every bit as pretty as Ginger Rogers, even if she didn't know how to tap-dance.

Her mother said, when they had finished the franks and beans and Boston brown bread for supper, it looks like I've made a cook outa you after all I'll do the washin' up tonight that was such a tasty meal Fred Astaire and Ginger Rogers you're teasin' me you know they're my favorites who'd be showin' such old pictures

"Oh, ma! It's so great! It'll just *kill* you if you see them again."

kill kill what of-fensive terms you young kids use hard hard as nails still still I'd love to see that pair of 'em again yes I would Rory Rory what do you think about me and Mary Catherine goin' off to the movies tonight could you manage

"I have this book — of Eisen-hower's — to finish. A prac-tical man. I'll be able to do it — if you go off — give me a little — peace and quiet — you two."

how gracious of you you old grampus entertain yourself child whilst I wash up

Mary Catherine didn't wait to be told twice. She ran down the back steps and along the alley to the cement loading plat-

form behind Rose's Furniture Store. Once there, she slipped
out of her dungaree pocket the card of thumbtacks of her
mother's she had swiped and pressed the tacks into the soles
and heels of her oxfords. Then she stood up straight, waiting
for the downbeat. There would be no one to see her, spy on
her, tell her mam and dad, because it was 6:20. Everybody
in Rose's had been long gone since 6 P.M. and the cop on the
beat, Ralphie Sisco's father, wasn't due until 8. She knew,
because she had watched. Once Annette had said, "You'd
make some spy." Well, she was right.

Mary Catherine stood up, lean and tall and elegant, in the
exact center of Rose's loading platform. In her head she went
One! Two! Three! And then she just eased out into some of
the classy I-don't-care steps, almost like walking, that Fred
Astaire did when he was pretending Ginger Rogers couldn't
see him. She could, though, and, just as Fred did, Mary
Catherine nonchalantly let her feet do fancier and fancier
things while she kept her hands tucked in the pockets of her
jeans: the slow buh-boom, buh-boom, buh-uh-uh-boomidy-
boomidy steps that got faster and faster and suddenly exploded
into rapid, complicated turns and twists and dips and slides.
She couldn't do them just right, but her feet pounding on the
cement sounded like good dancing so she just let go, no matter who saw, until her hands and arms were flying high over
her head and she was Fred Astaire and Ginger Rogers and
George Gershwin and his brother Ira all in one — "Ole man
trouble, I don't mind him, you won't find him, hanging . . .
ROUND MY DOOR!" — and the world was one giant swirl
of color and then she was dizzy as anything and sat down hard
on the cement.

The kids would never understand any of this, she thought as she lay there, her chest heaving. If they ever saw this, they'd think I was nutty as *two* fruitcakes! Well, that was just *their* tough luck.

She jumped up and skipped back to the flat because it was time to get her mam and her mam would just *adore Shall We Dance!* It was too bad she was getting stuck being town clerk because it was people like Rosalind Russell, pretty but pretty sarcastic, too, who got to be public officials in movies. But her mam was as beautiful as Maureen O'Hara and if she had been in a movie you would have known right from the beginning that Fred Astaire would have given her his heart and soul and tap-shoes to have her for his own.

When the two of them went through the lobby of the Fresh-kill at 7:10, Mr. Feinberg, who was taking tickets, made a wide smile and a small bow.

fresh Jew, her mother said after they were inside, I wouldn't look twice at him, but her unpleasant words couldn't spoil the evening for Mary Catherine, especially since she knew her friend Mr. Feinberg hadn't heard.

☙

If it had been her own life filling up the movie screen, Mary Catherine could not have watched *Rhapsody in Blue* with more care. It was true what Mr. Feinberg had said, most of the movie was just plain made up. She knew that from all she had read about Gershwin. But one thing in the movie, maybe the most important thing of all, was not made up at all. And that was the nervous, eager, headfirst sort of way that George Gershwin had lived and worked, as if you could separate his life from his work. She had to keep reminding herself that he hadn't lived that way because he knew he was going to die early, he had lived that way because that was the way he had picked. *He had picked.*

If she was going to make something out of her life and she *was*, she was going to have to pick. It was time to stop pretending she was going to be another Ginger Rogers, or one of Farley's leading ladies. Those probably weren't the kinds of chances that might come her way. Right there before her, George Gershwin was being pulled two ways — between classical music and jazz and, miraculously, he wasn't choosing one or the other, he was choosing his own, own way.

She sat, her eyes shut, through the other movie, trying to decide what was the classical music in her life and what was the jazz. No answer came to her.

"Gee, kid," Mr. Feinberg said to her in the lobby, "I'm sorry the second feature was such a dog. It sounded good on paper. You look like you got a headache. Dintja like *Rhapsody in Blue* at all?"

"It was very educational, Mr. Feinberg, and thank you very much for getting it."

"I suppose you could call it educational. What I liked was the music."

"Oh, me, too!"

"That's better. That's better. A smiling patron is a satisfied patron."

☙

How it came that Mary Catherine got her own little private place where she could read and study and imagine and just plain hole up was because she needed to know how to use *The Readers' Guide to Periodical Literature,* and that was because she had read everything in hardcovers the library had about George Gershwin, her ideal.

Miss Verplanck looked at the thick green-covered book Mary Catherine had put down on the check-out desk in front of her.

"*The Readers' Guide* . . . What on earth do you want this for? And nineteen thirty-five! I didn't even know this one was still on the floor!"

"I have this project. I want to read up on George Gershwin." What she *wanted* to do was see if she could find any more photographs of him. He was a bald-headed man with a biggish nose and a biggish smile who smoked long cigars, but he must have done *some*thing else besides sit at a piano.

"Read about, not read up on," the librarian said, pulling her mouth into a straight line.

"Read about," Mary Catherine said.

"What is it? A school project? No, school hasn't even started yet. Or did you have a paper to do over the summer that you left until the last minute? No, that couldn't be. They don't give papers in grammar school. Or do they? In *Catholic* schools?"

Miss Verplanck was always doing that, having conversations with herself. That was probably because she was an old maid and her mam said it was death to be an old maid no matter how hard bein married is God knows

"It's my own project. I've . . . admired his *music* for a long time."

"You haven't even been around a long time. He probably died before you were born."

Why did everybody keep bringing that up? Maybe God really was trying to give her a sign.

"When I grow up, I'm going to write a book about him." Her lie caught even her by surprise. But in the same moment she knew maybe it *wasn't* a lie.

"You are?" It was the first time she had ever seen Miss Verplanck laugh a kindly laugh. Then she stopped laughing. "You got this out of the adult side," she said, putting one of her twisted-up hands down on top of the big green book. She was not too old, her hair wasn't even gray, but she had very bad arthritis in her legs and hands. Mary Catherine often shelved books up in the gallery to save Miss Verplanck's legs on the days her part-time assistant wasn't there. She had just started doing it one day, and the librarian had never said a word about it, one way or the other.

"Yes, ma'am, I did."

"You have no business over there. You're supposed to stay on the juvenile side. That's in the trustees' rules, you know, and they're the ones who raise the money to keep this library open. This isn't a public library, you know that. It's on the sign . . ."

"Yes, ma'am. Open to the public but not a public library."

"Even if I should show you how to use this *Guide*, it wouldn't do you a bit of good. Back periodicals are stored in the basement, which is strictly out-of-bounds for juvenile card holders."

And she wouldn't be eligible for an adult card until she graduated eighth grade. Practically a whole year away from now!

"Miss Verplanck — " Mary Catherine's heart was pounding from the plan that had just sprung into her mind — "if I were

something like your volunteer unpaid assistant helper, something like that where I did jobs for you, then could I maybe
go downstairs and . . ."

"Hm. Hm. Hm," the librarian said, pursing her lips in a
thoughtful way. "I'll have to think it over. No," she said as
Mary Catherine started to pick up the *Readers' Guide*, "just
leave this volume here on the desk. I'll give you my decision
in a few minutes."

Mary Catherine went over and sat down at one of the tables
on the kids' side of the library and opened up the copy of
Today's Health lying there. Upstairs in the gallery, the old
grandmother's clock was tick-ticking away and she could
hear the pigeons cooing outside on the windowsills upstairs.

Victorian, her dad had called this building, but even though
it was made out of good rosy-red Hudson Valley brick, it
reminded her of one of the Swiss mountain houses in *Heidi*.
Probably because there was this wide wooden porch outside
over the front doors. Outside, the library looked like a big
solid two-story house. But inside . . .

Inside, in the main part, it was a single room that was two
stories tall with the gallery with its pretty iron fence running
all the way around the room just where the second story
would have started. The library was as tall and as arched inside as Holy Redeemer Church and, she hoped God would not
get mad, but she liked the inside of the library better. The
wood in here was dark and glowed softly, not like the yellow-
ish shiny wood in church. And the busts of the authors, on
top of the gallery bookcases, were plain white, instead of
painted a million different colors. And the big window,
which took up the whole south wall above the gallery book-

cases and was really three big windows side by side making up one huge arched window, was made out of etched glass, not full of religious colors, and when the sun was just right, you could see the shadows of the trees dancing on it. Even the check-out desk would have fitted into a church, as a pulpit, because it was made out of wide panels of dark wood and sat up on little legs. Not like the tinny one Father Rafferty stood in on Sundays when he made the announcements and gave the sermon and yelled about money.

"Come on, Mary Catherine," Miss Verplanck said in a regular voice since there was nobody else in the library, which was often the case. "I'll show you how to use the *Readers' Guide*, but if you had just used your head and followed the directions printed in the front, you wouldn't have wasted my time and yours."

⚜

"You might give these a dusting from time to time," Miss Verplanck told her as the two of them stood in the basement room and looked at the shelves and shelves of bound magazines. "There's a feather duster on that hook there. And if I need you upstairs, I'll just thump on the floor with my cane.

"And don't forget to turn off the light when you leave."

"Oh, no ma'am. Thank you, thank you so . . ."

But Miss Verplanck was already limping out of sight up the stairs.

Mary Catherine looked around her at the cave full of books and at the little worktable with its own chair and lamp. She gave herself a good hard pinch to make sure she wasn't dreaming it all up. But everything stayed just as it was.

7. Eighth Grade

EIGHTH GRADE WAS HARD, even though the kids elected her editor of *Holy Redeemer Highlights,* the mimeographed school paper that came out six times a year. Nobody was mean to her, but she felt shy talking to them, even Annette, because she was sure they would think anything she said was a lie, after the CIO business. They didn't seem to mind her going to the movies with them, on Friday nights now because they were big, but she was so ashamed of how her clothes looked, you had to look really nice to go to the movies on Friday nights, that she just stopped going with them after a while and went, instead, on Saturday or Sunday afternoons with all the dumb little kids.

The reason her clothes were worse than usual was Deirdre's clothes, which even though she hated them were at least clothes, had stopped coming. Deirdre had run off and gotten married, not even by a priest, to a man who painted signs for a living. So she needed all those clothes she used to give away when she was tired of them because a sign painter didn't make much money, even though he had a scholarship to the Rhode Island School of Design.

The whole thing about Deirdre was so upsetting that Auntie Kathleen had not even been able to be the one to write the

letter telling about it. It was Uncle Blaise who wrote the
letter and, even though he and Auntie Kathleen had six other
children, you would have never guessed it from his letter. It
was as if his only child had died. And the packages of clothes,
they stopped coming.

Just to be mean, her mother sent them a spiritual bouquet,
which was only usually sent to the families of somebody who
had really died. But Auntie Kathleen sent a thank you note
back right away.

serves her right serves her right, her mam said and laughed
in a way that was not nice at all. That was mean as mean.
Especially when you considered that her mam would never
have met her dad if it hadn't been for Auntie Kathleen and
Uncle Blaise. She knew the story because her mother liked
to tell it, even though she changed it around sometimes, depending on how she was feeling about Auntie Kathleen, or
how life in general was goin' in Freshkill this town

pretty as pretty that village it was and pleasant and 'umble
and decent but also poor as poor and to-tally lackin' in op-
portunities for a lass of talents and courage so off I go to Boston in America far away from all friends dropped down a-
mong strangers to try and earn somethin' to keep my fam-ly
from starvin' al-together even though I might well have
married the son of the squire who was just crazy about me
like a new-born calf he was over me or married his own father
who was a res-pectable widower except he did like his drop
and there was some talk about him and this gyp-sy woman but
I was such a child only sixteen mind you a no-table beauty
mind you in a county of beauties that I thought the streets of
Boston would be paved in gold and that even bein' a house-

maid there which was a po-sition far below my dig-nity would earn me enough to keep my fam-ly from the dole

That part she hardly ever changed, except to put in the exact names of all the people who wanted her to marry them and how they had all come to see her off and how many of them and which of them, exact names again, had wept and begged and im-plored her to stay at home.

well it was a simple fact that I had still have a natur-al ability in ad-dition to my brain power at house-keepin' and house-maidin' but through no fault of my own the masters one after another of them kept tryin' to get up against me thank God just thank God child with your looks you'll never have that prob-lem and the mis-tresses Irish names and all would get jealous and mean for no reason at all except any-one will tell you they were a stringy-lookin' lot one and all they would up and fire me and I was at my wit's end bein' so put up-on not knowin' where to turn next and

Here was where the story sometimes changed so com-pletely you could hardly recognize it as the one she had told you so many times before:

if it hadn't been for your decent Irish Christian Uncle Blaise kind man he was who made no secret of the fact he was mar-ried and to your dad's big and only sis-ter your dad's only livin' relative well Blaise saw the raw deal I was gettin' in the fam-ly he was show-ferrin' for so when I got fired through no fault of my own and he found me weepin' in des-pair over what was goin' to happen to me and my dear fam-ly on the other side he said come home with me my wife'll know what to do and they took me in even though the house in South Boston which had been bought with what was left of your grand-

dad's es tate your Auntie Kathleen bein' the elder and therefore the in-heritor and this house was crammed to the tippy-
top with babbies and roomers even so they looked after me
and they found me a job in a mill where the wages was good

Because, sometimes, when her dad was asleep, her mam
would say:

Blaise in his smart show-ferr's uni-form was always sniffin'
after me and you know but I never gave him one tiny tiny
bit modi-cum of en-couragement and when I was out of the
blue given notice even though that damn house yes damn
house had never been clean until I was hired and in fact overworked because they were such an untidy dirty filthy piggy
lot well Blaise as you ex-pect was right there and said to me
with a wink come home to South Boston with me there's help
there my old lady will know what to do with you and she
did too she had me boilin' nappies dia-pers within five minutes
of my arrival and even after I in out-right des-peration went
out and found myself a job in a mill a common mill which was
far beneath my dig-nity just to get away from that house full
of in-fant stink they still expected me to help out and to give
in some of my wages as well and the whole time Blaise tryin'
to catch me alone

Then came the part where the story was usually the same:

your dad dear man came from where he had gone off to
work in Deetroit to spend Saint Paddy's in South Boston
amongst the Irish and we hit it off straightaway and I wore
Kathleen's weddin' frock and veil there was just time to
publish bans which had been the frock and veil your grandmam and your dad's grandmam as well had worn they had to
take it in for me and your dad took me away from all that

babby smell in South Boston off to Deetroit and I felt like the queen of the world because Rory that dad dear dad of yours in those days even though he had already gone gray from the shock of your grand-dad's sudden tragi-cal death in the first re-corded auto accident in Paw-tucket and your grandmam's squanderin' in a year less than a year all that money well he was goin' gray but tall as tall and fresh-faced and gentle as gentle and without me even askin' he always sent a bit of his wages to Ireland to my people and then you came along and I had to give up my job in the head-lamp mill

Even though, if it *hadn't* been for her aunt and uncle her mam would probably never have met her dad, that never bothered her mother. It depended, when her mam was telling the story, on how the office had been that day or if somebody had been nice or nasty to her in the A&P, whether her mam talked of Auntie Kathleen and Uncle Blaise as her saviors or as a pair of fools and they de-serve her runnin' off like that no priest or anythin' with that fake ar-teest when it was a doctor or a law-yer or a dentist they were plannin' to snare for her

When it was clear even to her mam and dad that she just had to have something new in the way of clothes, her mother gave her $7.50 it's all I can spare child and after a long search she bought in Woolworth's one skirt, brown, one sweater, she picked kelly green, and with the fifty-four cents left, she bought a forty-nine-cent scarf, green and brown. Her winter coat, Deirdre's, yellow fleece with nailheads and a suede insert, was way too short because, all of a sudden, the skirts had gotten very very long. What she did when she had to put on that coat with her oxfords and her other clothes, old or new, was to walk kind of slumped to hide how short everything, except her, was — but with her head held up high, so she didn't have to look into anybody's face. Especially Billy McCarthy's.

She spent a lot of time in the library, upstairs but mostly down, dusting and reading not only the articles about George Gershwin but also all the other articles in those old magazines. There were lots and lots about Detroit when her dad had been there and she began to get excited. When she did the confidential mail for him these days, she also took brown envelopes and put them in a safety box in the cellar of the bank.

"Those are notes — " he had frowned at her — "of my organizing — days. Here — and out there. Valuable — so be goddamned sure — you lock them up — right. Make a useful book — one of these days."

She tried to tell him what she had been reading, but he told her to shut up and leave him alone. When she offered to bring home from the library some of the bound magazines with union articles in them he said, "Whatta yer tryin' to do to me!" He had been very sick again in the winter, had spent two weeks in Freshkill Hospital worrying so much about how much it cost that Dr. Kennedy had finally had him checked out, and now he was always in a bad humor, mostly yelling about how the money was going out faster than it was coming in. He had stopped reading anything but the *Daily News* and the *Journal-American*, even though he still insisted that she buy the *New York Times* and the *Herald Tribune*, and he spent every free minute watching the spare TV set that Rafferty had lent him.

In the spring, Mary Catherine took the entrance exam for Mount Saint Michael's Academy over the river in Westburgh.

They gave a four-year scholarship each year to the best girl from one of the two Catholic schools in Freshkill, the other school being Saint Anne's way up in the part of town called Beacon Hills (from the beacon lights lit on top of Mount Freshkill during the Revolutionary War) at the foot of the mountain. She tried not to think that there might be a girl smarter than her up at Saint Anne's because she really wanted that scholarship more than anything. One reason was because they wore uniforms at Mount Saint Michael's and everybody *had* to wear oxfords. Which was good because her mam would never let her have anything but oxfords and, too, her brown skirt and her green sweater and even her brown and green scarf were wearing out and she would have to go in rags to Freshkill High.

The other reason, the important reason, was that Mount Saint Michael's had the reputation of being a really tough school that turned out topnotch students who often got scholarships to colleges. Mount Saint Michael's and college were the places she *had* to go if she, like George Gershwin, was going to Make a Name for Herself!

8. Graduation

"AND THE ONE-YEAR SCHOLARSHIP to Saint Brendan's High School for Boys, Westburgh, New York, paid for by the joint Holy Name Societies of Freshkill and . . ." Father Rafferty drew out his words, "what do you think? *Our* school has won it! And not Saint Anne's! Think of it, Holy Redeemer, with God's help has won both the four-year scholarship and the one-year scholarship to Saint Brendan's, am I keeping you in suspense? Congratulations, Kenneth Damone, you've brought home the bacon for us!"

Kenny, all red and embarrassed, got up and right away caught his foot in his chair and almost fell down in front of all the people in the church. But, even if he had fallen flat on his face, nobody would have said anything, Mary Catherine was sure, because you could just see how excited he was. And why is it that the Mount Saint Michael's scholarships are the very last things on the program unless it's because Saint Anne's got *both* of them? She tried to put the whole thing out of her mind.

She could see how proud Father Rafferty was. Even the bald spot in the middle of his white hair was bright pink and he was making little jerky movements with his head as if he were planning, in his mind, while he was waiting for Kenny, just how he would tell all the priests he knew what a good school Holy Redeemer was.

And, of course, Kenny tripped on his chair, again, sitting down, but nobody noticed because Father was now giving out the Perfect Attendance Awards, starting with the first grade.

The eighth grade, the graduating class, was sitting in three rows of folding chairs right inside the altar rail, which was an honor, looking out at all of the people filling up the church. The graduating boys were dressed up in suits and white shirts and ties and they had the long green and white class ribbons hanging down from their lapels. And every girl was dressed in a white dress and nylons and white shoes and white gloves and they all had the same hat from Freshkill Dry Goods and some of them were wearing corsages of flowers in addition to their class ribbons. And they were all sweating like anything in the hot June evening.

Down in the front two rows, Mary Catherine saw, was sitting the entire D'Artaglia family, which included millions of aunts and uncles and cousins. They were going to entertain the whole class and its families at a big party after and Annette had specially asked her to come. Tears came into Mary Catherine's eyes at the thought of how nice Annette had been, asking her: "Please come, and bring your mother and father, too, if he can come. We'll have a swell time, Mary Catherine. Maryooch."

Far down the aisle, but in an aisle seat, she could see the red and black dot of her mam's head with its bright hair and dark straw hat.

ach what can you be thinkin' of, she had said. it'll be noisy and common at a party full of all those Eye talians for the love of God gettin' drunk on that wine stuff

The heat left over from the day plus all the lights on plus all the people plus the smell of the candles on the altar was making Mary Catherine feel drowsy and a little sick to her stomach. She tried to pray about the scholarship but she knew it was no use because all of that must have been decided long ago, right after the entrance exam. To keep from thinking how upset her stomach was feeling, she started to talk to George Gershwin in her mind. She had learned so much about him, he seemed as real to her as any of the kids here.

Do they let you play the piano up there in Heaven or are you stuck with a harp? Do you get to put on your opera or do the colored people have to stay in another part of Heaven? Please find out, George, dear George, if I got the scholarship, because if I didn't . . .

She just shut her mind off altogether because none of what she was thinking made any sense and it was bad enough to behave like a jerk in God's own house without having George think she was a dummy, too.

"Well, Mary Catherine, aren't you going to stand up?" She had lost track of what was going on and Father Rafferty was turned around and talking to her in the back row, asking her to stand up and all she wanted to do was say NO! Everybody will see how short my dress is even if it is brand new and I know *you're* the one gave my folks the money for it and my shoes and hat and gloves, I'm sorry I still don't look right.

"Yes, Father," she said instead, and stood up and climbed over everybody's feet and went over to him. Probably, he was going to tell all of them out there what a good girl she was and what a fine man her dad was and how her mam was town clerk. That was exactly what he did whenever he was taking visitors around school and stopped in her class. It made her feel not like herself but like one of the 100 Neediest Cases they printed in the paper every Christmastime, and she hated, hated it.

"Let me tell you something," Father Rafferty said to the people, at the same time putting his arm around her right up there practically on the altar. "I've known for some weeks that Mary Catherine had won this scholarship and I kept it to myself even though her father was, until his serious illness, one of the most valiant, if not *the* most valiant worker this parish has ever had, and even though her mother helps keep this town running as town clerk, a position involving enormous responsibilities."

Mary Catherine looked at the floor. Marble squares, white, gold, green. God's churches must cost almost as much as God's schools. She had won a scholarship, but it had to be the four-year one or else she hadn't won anything at all.

"The reason I kept this secret was because, just as her parents before her, this little girl has brought a singular honor on her parish. Mother Mary Adolphus, who is the headmistress of Mount Saint Michael's, wrote me especially to say that Mary Catherine had attained the highest score ever achieved by a student taking the Academy entrance exam in the sixty-seven years of its existence."

The people in the church started to applaud.

"Stop that! Just remember where you are!"

She didn't care. She had won it, the big scholarship. She was going to go to a hard school where they all wore exactly

the same clothes and shoes, no matter how rich or poor. She
wouldn't have to wear funny clothes in front of public high
boys and girls she didn't even know, who might not be kind.

⚘

Father Rafferty said, "I don't blame you for not wanting to
attend, Maureen, it hurts me I'll have to put in an appearance.
All those children the D'Artaglias have put through Holy
Redeemer, they pledged only five hundred for the school
addition fund and I'll probably never see a penny of it, but
they always seem to have money for parties." And he drove
them home in his Buick so they could tell her dad the good
news.

"That's all very well — you've done a good job — Mary
Catherine — more'n I expected — though I sus-pected you
had it — in you," her dad said as he lay back in his bed where
he had been when the three of them came in.

"The fact of the matter — is," he said from his pillows,
"well," he said, "you know what it is."

She stood there in the dim bedroom, trying to understand
what he was saying.

"What is it, Rory?" Father Rafferty asked.

"Well — the com-mutin' — for in-stance. Then — there's
those uni-forms."

She couldn't believe her ears. He was imitating the way her
mam talked.

"And then books — and then — all the other — extras.
There's no money for it. Christ," he said, and she could see it,
the silver of tears spilling down his cheeks. She had never
thought about all the extras, it didn't matter she had gotten

the highest score, she couldn't go after all. All she had done, when you counted it up, was make her dad so unhappy that he just gave in and cried in front of people.

"Don't worry about that, man," Father said in a soft voice. "There's ways. Means. You know that. Funds can be found for all of that. She's brought honor on the parish and the town. I gave the story to the *Daily* myself."

For a minute, listening to Rafferty's unfamiliar kindly tone (every kid in Holy Redeemer hated him as soon as they knew how because his favorite game was being snotty and sarcastic with kids, even first graders), Mary Catherine had felt drawn to him because he wanted her to have what she had gotten on her own. But, probably, all he was worried about was keeping the story in the Freshkill *Daily* true. Why wasn't it Father Cassidy who was the head priest? He knew all about kids and sometimes he would come on the playground during recess and join in a game of punchball and horse around with them and all the kids loved him because they knew he really was interested in them.

Her father made a snuffling noise.

"Rory," the priest said, putting his hand on her dad's back because he had turned away from them to hide his face, "I'm telling you that, without question, you don't have to worry about this child's expenses over and above her tuition scholarship."

But her dad didn't answer. Mary Catherine felt torn in half.

"You understand what I'm telling him, Maureen. Speak to him."

Father Rafferty took her out into the living room with him

and sat her down on the old sofa and, for the first time in her
life, had a conversation with her. She didn't trust him but she
wanted to listen anyway.

"Listen, Mary Catherine. Don't you worry. I'm going to
fix it so's you can take that scholarship. Understand?"

"No, Father."

"Well, the Academy has seen fit to give you free what they
charge other girls for, and that's a big gift. Do you understand that? Four hundred a year, for each of four years."

Sixteen hundred dollars. She couldn't even imagine what
that must look like, piled up in one pile.

"So you *have* to go. It would be shocking if you didn't go,
just because of money, and a blow to the parish. The cardinal
watches such things."

The cardinal. The cardinal. Even more important than a
not-true story in the *Daily*.

The cardinal lived next to Saint Patrick's Cathedral in New
York City, which was near the Radio City Music Hall. She
had been there once. When her dad was at a union meeting
and he had taken her and her mam. And he had taken her on
her own with him to the top of the Empire State Building,
which was the tallest building in the world, and he had said to
her, "There it is, Mary Catherine. Don't forget the way it
looks. The world at your feet."

She could never tell Father Rafferty about that. He would
never understand, even though he was her dad's close friend.
And maybe her dad, the way he had changed, wouldn't understand anymore, either. She tried to hear if her dad was
still crying.

"There are funds," Father Rafferty was saying in his unfamiliar sweet voice, "and you must take them and use them and not let pride enter into it. Charity has nothing to do with it."

What he was saying, she realized from far away, was that she *was* one of those needy Christmas cases in the paper. And that charity, which meant poor people, not only *did* enter into it, charity was the whole thing.

"You go in there," Father Rafferty was saying to her numb ears, "and you tell your dad that he has nothing to worry about when it comes to you. That getting this high honor from the Academy means that, most likely, when you're a senior, you'll probably win a scholarship to some very good Catholic college or, even, and it's possible perhaps, to a college in, say, Rome within the shadow of Our Holy Father, so you might even wind up a jewel in the crown of the Vatican. It's just too bad you're not a boy."

She had had the same thought herself, once or twice.

"Go in and talk to him. Tell him you have my word on any and all extras. Do you know why he's worried? He had a lot of promises made to him when he was growing up and he was planning on being an architect and it all came to naught which is why . . ."

She was on her feet, headed for the bedroom. Her mother backed away from the bed, out of the room, out to where the priest was.

"Dad."

"Whaaaat," he said, his jaw dropping down, shiny with tears.

"If it's okay with you, I can go to the Academy because the parish has money specially set aside for the extras I cost.

Father says it would be a sin and a shame if I didn't use the scholarship."

She hated all of this, talking to him, her own father, in a pleading voice. She had won her scholarship fair and square and in regular competition and they shouldn't give them at all unless they included the extras or else how could kids who *needed* scholarships afford to take them? And there was no school in the world, however good, that had the right to make her father break down and . . .

"All right, okay," her dad said, sighing and rubbing his face with the back of his hand. "It hurts me," he said, "to have to ac-cept charity — after years of hard work — but I'll do it — for you — kid. Tell him — it's okay with me." And he looked so sad and miserable that she couldn't help it, she cried out, "Don't, please don't . . . I'll go to Freshkill High and this summer I'll get my working papers and I just know it, I can get a job at Woolworth's because I look older than I am. I didn't mean to make you cry." She was crying herself. "There isn't any school in the world that's worth making *you* . . ."

Her dad snapped over in his bed and fixed his eyes on her. "Just tell Rafferty — I said okay — got it? Never mind *your* — tearful — little — speeches."

She backed up, away from his look and his sharp words, bumping into the door frame. In his worst times, when he had been sick and out of his head and shouting awful things at everybody, she had never felt so far from him.

He was whispering angry words. "Let the Church spend — it's got plenty — get me? It's got dough. Velvet robes. Rec-tories like mansions. I did my share. I had my — heartbreaks. Worked off my ass — for all of 'em. They can pay — now. They can pay. They owe me. So — just — get out there — tell him — it's okay — with me!"

"O . . . kay, okay." Her voice seemed to be coming out of her ears. George, George, she was thinking, don't pay any attention to any of this. What she meant to say was *God*, not George, but *God*.

When she told Father Rafferty, he clapped his hands with delight and then told her what date in July she had to go over to Mount Saint Michael's to be measured for her uniforms.

Her mother cut out the piece in the *Daily* the next afternoon and pinned it up in her office. Because of his TV programs he liked to see, her dad never did have time to read what nice things the reporter had said about her.

III

The Academy

1. Friday of the First Week

MARY CATHERINE FELT like one tiny blob of color in the biggest painting in the world as she walked across the mammoth, steeply sloping front lawn of the Academy. She was hunting for a place to sit while she ate her lunch, but she kept stopping in spite of herself (they had only half an hour for lunch) to gape down at the miles and miles of countryside and river laid out practically at her feet. It might just be a matter of perspective, the topic in Drawing this morning, but she felt as if she were seeing the whole world at once and it made her sort of dizzy. She found a stone bench under a ginkgo tree and sat down.

The Academy was an amazing place and she still was not used to all its wonders, even after almost a week here. There was so much of *everything:* buildings, grounds, views, nuns, kids (the boarders came from all over North and South America), classes, subjects . . . *well,* there was *one* thing she had already gotten used to—homework! Every nun seemed to think she was the only teacher giving homework — Algebra, Bio, Catholic Philosophical something (which was the fancy name they gave Religion here; their teacher's teacher had written the textbook), English I (grammar, her favorite), Latin, and Social Studies. Only the Drawing nun hadn't given any homework, and her mam and her dad were mad because she had signed up for Drawing instead of Cooking like the rest of the Freshkill kids. Well, she *wasn't!* Here she was, sitting around in a whole lot of perspective and *knowing* it.

She opened up her lunch bag and took out the sandwich. Peanut butter and jelly, again. Now why was that a surprise? She was the one who made her lunch to carry to the Academy because there was no cafeteria and, so far, peanut butter and jelly had been the only thing that crossed her mind at seven in the morning during her struggle to eat, get dressed, get her uniform tie tied straight, and make it out onto the corner to get the bus at eight with Annette and some of the others. She forgot her sandwich and looked down from the Academy's heights, even the nuns called it *the* Academy, at the Hudson, blue and spark —

A green uniform thumped down onto the bench beside her.

"You picked the best place to escape to," the uniform said, and Mary Catherine looked up, meekly, in case her companion was higher than a freshman.

"Oh, hello!" she said, immediately losing all fear. It was the girl in Freshman B with her who was called Jimmy. Jimmy's real name was Gemma McNaughton but the nickname fit her because she had the plain face and the flat figure of a boy. Even her smile was a thin but nice smile, like a boy's.

"I hope one of Them isn't out on patrol," Jimmy said, opening up her lunch bag, "because we'll catch it if they are. 'The front lahwn, young ladies, is for looking, not for using.' Oh, thanks be to God," she exclaimed happily, unwrapping a chicken leg. "*Yes*terday, my mother made me a spag*het*ti sandwich because her motto *this* week is Waste Not Want Not. She's a real nut. You'll have to meet her sometime."

Mary Catherine felt joyfully overwhelmed. All week long she had been admiring Jimmy and her funny, sarcastic friend Mim Shepard and right now Jimmy was making friends with *her*. She also felt nervous at the prospect of being caught by a nun in a place where she wasn't supposed to be.

"I thought when they said we didn't have to eat in the day-hops' cloakroom today, that meant we could eat anywhere on the grounds."

"No, you're supposed to stick to the south terraces where you can be Overseen."

"Then why are *you* here, eating away, so calmly?"

"Same reason as you. I like the view. Might as well be hanged for a sheep as a goat."

Mary Catherine agreed, and the two of them ate in silent contentment, enjoying the shade and the scenery. The Academy stood on the highest hill in Westburgh, a city noted for its many high hills. That meant you could see straight ahead without interruption to the distant line of old, worn-down mountains across the Hudson that went along the horizon and then turned toward the river until they ended up at Mount Freshkill, where some of the trees near the abandoned casino up on top had already begun to turn yellow or red. Mary Catherine's eye followed a scar, which was the track of the funicular railway, down the side of Mount Freshkill to Freshkill itself, spread like a lovely green and gold skirt to the riverbank. Here and there, she could see church steeples and taller buildings sticking up through the trees. There wasn't one of them she couldn't name and place exactly on its street. In spite of all that had happened there, she still loved Freshkill the way she had when she was little and walking with her dad.

"Look!" Jimmy said, pointing. "There's a lot of people

going somewhere, *fast!*" A long silver train was streaking
north on the New York Central tracks on the Freshkill side.
It disappeared for a moment behind the long low shapes of
the Freshkill station and the ferry-house. Then, the sun bouncing off its windows, it reappeared, overtook and passed the
mile-long patchwork freight train crawling along on an inside
track, and was gone from their sight.

"When I make my fortune," Mary Catherine said, "I am
going to do absolutely nothing but ride on trains like that."

"It's so much fun, isn't it?" Jimmy said. "We came from
California on a train like that and I don't think I slept a wink
the whole time!"

"When I was little, we came from Detroit on the bus and I
didn't sleep, either. I just threw up and threw up and threw
up."

They both laughed. "How come you came from Detroit
to here?"

"My father works . . . worked for the CIO getting industrial unions set up. He's . . . he's a semi-invalid now — "
she was surprised at how easily the unfamiliar term slid out
of her — "so he's had to retire."

"Oh, I'm sorry. My father is initials, too."

"What?"

"WHO. The World Health Organization. He's a doctor
who goes around trying to stop epidemics before they start."

"An epi-demi-ologist?"

"My God," Jimmy said, drawing back and looking at her,
"I told Mim you were smart but where did you pick that one
up?"

"Did I say it wrong? It was in a book by René Dubos."

"Mim said," Jimmy said, continuing on, "that you looked all right but that anybody with a name like Mary Catherine was probably a goody-goody. Oh, don't look so upset. Mim looks at the whole world through jaundice-colored glasses. She hardly believes in anything."

"Then how can she be a Catholic?"

"She practically isn't, but that's another story. Her father is a Protestant," Jimmy explained. "He's an Army officer and teaches at West Point."

"Oh." Mary Kate felt she had been plunged into worlds beyond her imagination.

"Anyway, I don't think Mary Catherine fits you, either. It sounds like some kind of Confirmation name or nun's name or something. So I'm going to call you Mary . . . Kate! Okay?"

Mary Catherine tried it out: "Mary Kate Mulligan. Okay. It sounds okay to me. Shall we have the baptismal ceremony now or later?"

"We'd better eat or there'll be an execution ceremony!"

They lapsed into a comfortable silence again while they ate. Mary Catherine, her mind filled up with the last ten minutes, looked down at the river, busy with traffic. Going north and south were oil tankers, and tugs pulling barges filled with gravel and with bricks; going east and west, the big old dark red ferries she crossed on, morning and afternoon.

"Oh, look at that, Jimmy! You know what that gray boat is?"

"Some kind of Navy thing? It has those big numbers, like in war movies."

"It's the Coast Guard ice-cutter that keeps a channel open in the winter. All the way up to Albany from New York City. My dad showed it to me once. They must be doing their shakedown cruise."

"You know which boats I like the best?" Jimmy asked.

"Which?"

"Those ferries. They look like nice old grandmothers out for a stroll."

"Oh, they're old, but they're not like grandmothers at all. You should hear it when the engines reverse when we're coming into the ferry slip. They sound like growling giants with insides full of clanking chains."

"Boy, will Mim be glad she was wrong about you!"

Going back up to the main building, which was called Main and which looked like Parliament in London except one half of it was the Academy and the other half was the convent where nuns for the Order were trained, they cut across the lawn in back of one of the five spacious houses which were, here and there, scattered over the acres and acres of campus. Those houses, lumped together, were called The Villas, which was an expensive elementary school where you had to pay to go and where you got, even if you were a boy, sketching and ballet as regular classes.

Jimmy and Mim had gone to The Villas but they didn't seem a bit snobby. Which was more than you could say for some of the Freshkill kids, even Annette, who thought, just because they wore the Academy uniform (green serge jumper monogrammed MSM in gold, tan long-sleeved shirt, green boy's tie, runless nylons, green socks, brown oxfords:

A decent chine, young ladies, and *no* rubber heels, they mark the parquet) on the streets of Freshkill, that they were practically royalty, and so were snotty as anything to the bus drivers and ferry-token men. Well, she was at last friends with somebody who had a decent vocabulary and who knew the world didn't begin and end in Freshkill and Westburgh.

Cutting across the lawn, Jimmy was talking about Odahilda Suarez (pronounced Sue-are-aze and she was from Havana, which was pronounced Ha-ba-na) because she felt responsible for Odahilda.

"My dad's down in Cuba, advising, right now, and he met her father and they got to talking about their daughters and, before you could say Jackie Robinson, my mother and my brother and I were picking her up at Idlewild and dumping her off here at the Academy so she could improve her English. Her father doesn't expect her to pass any courses or anything. Doesn't that kill you? He just wants her to be in a nice place among girls her own age who speak English and so what if it costs a million bucks!"

"Oh, I know all about Odahilda," Mary Catherine said excitedly. "She's in love with a boy called Cesar, excuse me, Say-sar, and I mail letters for her."

"For corn's sake! You could get kicked out doing something like that."

"You know why I do it?" Mary Kate confided, feeling frightened all the same. "The Freshkill kids didn't think too much of me until I mailed a letter for Odahilda. Then they thought I was just great." She was immediately and profoundly sorry she had said it, especially when she saw Jimmy frowning and shaking her head.

"Listen, Mary Ca — Mary Kate, I know they're your

friends but, don't get mad, they don't seem too bright to me."

Before she could say yes or no or I'm as big a jerk as they are, they had come upon Odahilda, who was reading a thick, air-mail letter.

"Hey, Odahilda," Jimmy called, "how are things at the castle?"

"Jew mean ma how-us?" Odahilda came over, folding up the letter. "Oh, Jeemy, jew joke. Eet's a big how-us, bot snot a cahstle."

"You miss it?"

"Jes. Bot my boy fren Saysar, heem I mees zee most!"

"That's a wicked smile if I ever saw one," Mary Kate said. "Are you engaged to marry him?" It seemed the right thing to say to a very rich, very beautiful girl who sported a huge emerald ring plus enough bosom to fit out three or four other girls. She looked twenty instead of fourteen. *All* the South American girls in Freshman B looked twenty instead of fourteen!

"Oh, no! Heem, I *luv*. My famly sayus who I *mar-ree*. Eet's nevair who jew *luv*."

"God," Mary Kate said, caught up in it all, for the second time in half an hour. "How awful!"

"No, no! Zat way jew are shoe to mar-ree a reech one. Jew *haf* to mar-ree a *reech* one."

Jimmy and Mary Kate exchanged glances over Odahilda's head. South America, take eet away!

"Listen," Jimmy said, clearly getting down to business. "How about the two of you spending the weekend at my house? My mother can fix it with Mother, Odahilda. Because when my father's away, my mother likes the place

filled up with friendly types. And don't let the fact that I
have a twin brother who looks just like me, except he's *handsome,* influence you in any way. *Or* the fact that he'll probably have some of *his* friends staying over, too."

"Oh, deer Jeemy, here I am!"

"I can't!" Mary Kate said instantly, then groped for a
reason. "He's . . . it's my dad's birthday and he gets a big
kick out of things like family parties." A lie.

"Oh. Well, I wish you could come. Promise you'll come
soon?"

"I promise." But she did not know whether she meant it
or not. It was one thing to know Jimmy at school, quite another thing to go to her house. It might end up the way it
had with Annette and she didn't want that to happen. The
reason she had told Jimmy *why* she mailed the letters for
Odahilda (and why couldn't she have done it without sound-
ing like Miss Gooky Grub of 1949?) was because she could
feel it, she could trust Jimmy to understand. If only something didn't go wrong, she and Jimmy were going to be the
sort of friends who could have real talks with each other
about important things.

2. Academy Rubrics

Friday night of the second week of school was the chapel ceremony dedicating the freshman class to the Blessed Virgin Mary. The rest of the school attended in civilian clothes, but the freshmen were required to wear their long white procession gowns.

Mary Kate stood still in the middle of the living room while her mother fussed at the dress, smoothing the Peter Pan collar, lining up the little pearl buttons, pinching the puff sleeves, tying and retying the long sash.

it'll be freezin' in that stone chapel place put on your school cardi-gan mind or you'll catch your death

"I can't wear a green sweater over a white dress. It'll show!"

vanity vanity

"Anyway, it'll be warm in there. They know we're all in organdy and, besides, there'll be parents there, too. The nuns wouldn't freeze parents!"

Her mother wasn't going, even though the D'Artaglias had offered her a ride and, even though, as president of Freshman B, Mary Kate was going to lead one of the two lines of freshmen into chapel.

oh you understand child don't you I'm bushed after a long

day long week at the office what with my assis-tant sick and
away and the property taxes bein' re-assessed I'd nod off there
in the middle of it all embarrass you a Saturday night maybe
but not a Friday that's the simple fact of the matter

The simple fact of the matter was, Mary Kate thought bitterly, that her mother didn't want to ride in any car with any
Eye talians, no matter what.

☙

The big vestibule outside the chapel was entirely marble,
except for the ceiling, and it was as drafty as the North
Pole. The sixty of them, chilly and nervous, stood in silence,
shielding the flame of the candle each of them was holding.
The prospect of yet another ceremony had dried up all their
talk and jokes. That afternoon there had been a long assembly
in the auditorium underneath the chapel in which the four
years of new class officers plus class representatives had been
sworn into the Student Council Association. Father Randolph, the school chaplain, had given an endless talk on the
responsibilities facing them, and so had Mother Adolphus. The Academy, the freshmen were realizing, was Serious Business.

Mary Kate kept turning around to see if her line was
orderly and straight. It really took your mind off yourself to
be responsible for twenty-nine other kids, she thought in
wonder. They looked beautiful, though, in their white
gowns with the candles casting restless shadows on their faces
and short white veils.

Getting used to being part of the Academy, an accepted
part of the Academy, must be what it was like learning to

live in a foreign country where the language was the same, but the customs and terms were different. For instance, floor-length dresses for a procession instead of the regular-length dresses they had worn, but always in the daytime, for processions at Holy Redeemer. For instance, Father Randolph in his long white habit instead of Father Rafferty in his plain black suit or his plain black cassock. For instance, the 1890s outfits they wore for gym, which weren't a thing like the one-piece shorts-suits they wore at Freshkill High.

Mary Kate looked up with a start at the nun bustling toward them through the double doors of the chapel.

For instance, real mahogany doors instead of pine painted to look like oak.

But the nun hurried past them, her hands tucked in her sleeves, utterly unaware of the sixty of them with their flickering candles. Mary Kate was impressed. Maybe one day she, too, would take all of this for granted.

This nun, this second one whamming through the double doors, meant business.

"All right, young ladies," she whispered in a voice that reached the very end of the double line of girls.

Mary Kate had never seen the chapel at night before. All of the beautiful stained glass (not painted glass like Holy Redeemer) windows were blanked out by the night. There were a few lights on, high, high up in the very tip top of the soaring chapel ceilings (Tudor Gothic), but most of the light came from the banks of candles on the main altar and the two side altars. They could hear whispers and breathing, even over the organ music, as they walked down the aisle between the pews containing the parents and kids. Then the aisle

widened out as it passed between the two blocks of nuns' stalls
facing each other, just like in a monastery, and then, suddenly,
they were in the huge marble-floored area outside the main
altar rail. Mary Kate and Bernice Gronbach, the Freshman
A president, stood still right in the center of the big place
and waited while the kids arranged themselves in order around
them. When the kids were in place, Neecy and Mary Kate
took three long steps forward and genuflected in front of the
Blessed Sacrament. The kids behind them genuflected, too,
their skirts whispering against the marble. Then Neecy and
Mary Kate made a right-angle turn and walked, solemnly,
to the side altar of the Blessed Virgin. The freshmen also did
a right face.

Neecy began:

"Dear Mother Mary, we, the class of nineteen fifty-three,
humbly offer ourselves to your attention. We pray to you for
spiritual guidance and comfort during our coming years at
Mount Saint Michael. In the past, you have always been here
to listen to our individual fears, hopes, and joys. Your rosary
has given us consolation and through it we have been brought
closer to you and to Jesus, your Divine Son. Now, as a class,
we beseech you to continue as our source of solace" (She did
it! She did it! Mary Kate thought. All through rehearsals,
Neecy had kept saying it "our slource of saltz," which had a
kind of nice sound but clearly didn't suit the occasion) "however unworthy of your precious love we may be."

It was Mary Kate's turn:

"We know that our offerings and petitions, coming through
your hands, will be more acceptable to Our Lord. You have
been our ideal Lady in all that we have done; may you con-

tinue to remain our ideal, not only throughout our four years at the Academy, but also through the rest of our lives. Keep us close to you and protect us in all our undertakings. Help us to bring honor, by our work and lives, to the Academy and to our dear parents who have sacrificed so much for us. We pray that your rosary will be the means of binding our class together in all its efforts and aspirations and that we may never disappoint you, so that one day, with you, we may enjoy the bliss of eternal happiness."

"To you," Mary Kate and Neecy and the rest of the freshmen said in unison, "we therefore lovingly dedicate our class."

There was a moment's pause as the visiting monsignor, who taught at some big Catholic college, came off the main altar to where they were. They sank to their knees as he raised his hand in blessing.

Mary Kate was moved to tears by the beauty and seriousness of the ceremony.

"Dear Mother Mary," she prayed, "please help me to be worthy of your love. I'm sorry the dedication prayer wasn't better but the nuns kept changing the stuff Neecy and I wrote, they said it had to be fancier . . ." Her cheeks flushed. "I didn't mean that to sound like a sin of pride, dearest Lady, all I meant was . . . you deserve a really *great* dedication prayer!" She shut up then. The Blessed Virgin was full of kindness; she would understand.

When the blessing was done and the freshmen had settled in the pews set aside for them and had extinguished their candles, the monsignor gave a little talk on the Responsibilities facing you new "Mounties." Mary Kate concentrated on trying to keep warm. Her mam had been right; it was *freezing* in chapel.

She automatically resumed paying attention when she heard
the monsignor using the familiar winding-up tone that all
priests seemed to use.

"As Shakespeare, the Bard of Avon, so aptly put it: 'To
thine own self be true, and it must follow, as the night the day,
thou canst not then be false to any man.' Nor unto your
Blessed Savior Himself!"

My own self, my own self, Mary Kate thought, shocked
and alarmed, as she knelt for Benediction. "Dearest God, help
me, *please*. I don't know who my own self . . . my *real*
own self is. And I *need* to! This school is a serious place and
you gave it to me as a gift, made it possible, and I have to,
have to do well here, make the most of it here, because, otherwise . . ."

She had no more time to think because the lights around the
main altar turned on, revealing the creamy marble and gold
mosaic for the first time tonight. It was a beautiful altar, very
rich but very simple, and the crucifix over the tabernacle instead of being made out of gold like at Holy Redeemer was
made out of plain wood with a painted dead Jesus on it. In
the middle of all that gorgeous beauty and clouds of incense
hung Jesus in his pain and suffering, plain as day, so you
couldn't forget it. It would be very complicated getting used
to the Academy while she was trying to find out who she
really, really was. Very complicated and very hard and very
different and very educational.

❧

The freshmen came into the auditorium for other things
besides Assembly. Those who had been accepted, and that
wasn't everybody, came three study halls a week to practice

for the Choristers. Mary Kate had a lowish sort of voice and had to confess to Sister Felicitas, called Sis behind her back, that she couldn't read music.

"Very well," Sis said in her haughty voice, adjusting the sleeves of her angora sweater that snaked in under her veil and around her habit, "you'll do as a second soprano. We're short of them."

Mary Kate quickly learned, to her dismay, that second sopranos sang everything but the melody.

Then there were the special classes: Dramatics three times a month and Social Graces twice a month.

Miss Jantzen, who was the Dramatics lady and who looked just like a pointy-nosed Campbell's Soup kid, struck a note on the grand piano.

"On that note, Miss . . . ?" Miss Jantzen looked at her inquiringly.

"M-mulligan."

"Em, Miss Mulligan, on that tone, in a monotone?"

Mary Kate shook her head yes to indicate she understood monotone.

"In a monotone, please say 'Joan of Arc Saint of God.'" Miss Jantzen, who had acted on the Broadway stage and on the London stage, bit off and chewed each word. Mary Kate was terrified. Like the rest of the kids, she had spent the time waiting for her turn making fun of the teacher and her one-line opera.

But standing in front of Miss Jantzen was not funny at all. For the first time in her life, Mary Kate was facing a real actress and all she wanted to do was measure up. But how did you do that?

The drama coach struck the note on the piano again.

"Joan-of-Arc-Saint-of-God," Mary Kate said softly.

"No, no! Let me *hear* you." She repeated the note.

"JOAN OF ARC SAINT OF GOD."

"All right. Again, please."

By the time they had done an entire scale, plus some higher and lower notes, Mary Kate was exhausted by the strain of it all. She was glad to sit down again, but sorry, too.

At the end of the class, Miss Jantzen referred to her notes.

"The following young ladies will commit to memory for the next session the speeches I will assign. Marguerite Connery, Alice LaSalle, Gemma McNaughton, Mary Catherine Mulligan, Virginia Santa Cruz. You may collect your speeches now. The other young ladies are required to select a passage of either prose or poetry to be recited, from memory, at the next class. Please do not choose 'Fog' by Carl Sandburg."

"Yours is a short speech, Miss Mulligan, something of Hamlet's, short but more difficult than it may at first seem. Memorize it carefully, please."

"Yes, ma'am."

Even as she started up the aisle of the auditorium, in a rush to get to Latin, she read the typewritten words:

What a piece of work is a man! how noble in reason! how infinite in faculty! in form and moving how express and admirable! in action how like an angel! in apprehension how like a god! the beauty of the world! the paragon of animals! and yet, to me, what is this quintessence of dust?

It hardly made any sense at all, except to say, maybe, that

Miss Jantzen was a Protestant. She would really have her work cut out for her. It didn't seem fair, either, to get homework for dramatics, which wasn't even a regular class that you had to pass to get your diploma.

❧

The Social Graces lady was called Mrs. Fox Marsham, instead of Mrs. Edward Marsham, because she was divorced.

"Boy, I never thought I'd live to see the day *nuns* would put us in the power of a divorced old bag!"

The Freshkill kids were bitching on their way to the auditorium.

"Anyway," Annette said, "I think if our parents can afford to send us here, it means we're high class enough so we don't need any old . . . anybody teaching us table manners."

Mary Kate liked Annette but it was true, Annette wouldn't recognize an oyster fork if it knocked her down and ran right over her, even *after* they had had the table-setting lesson.

"Come *on*," she said to the kids. "Loyola said Mrs. Marsham's going to teach us receiving lines and stuff like that, too. *You* don't know how to do any of that, and the Academy is always producing receiving lines at the drop of a habit!"

They well-welled.

"Well, well, yourselves! Suppose you end up marrying the President or somebody, then won't you look like a dummy, shaking all the wrong hands and stuff!"

They laughed but still grumbled a little as they went in and settled down in those miserably uncomfortable auditorium seats. The only thing wrong with Social Graces was its timing — 2 P.M. on Friday, last period, a time when absolutely everybody was crabby and half-dead.

The lessons themselves were pretty interesting, at least she thought so. Although the first time she'd seen the teaching table set up with all the plates and glasses and acres of silverware and salt with a spoon and sugar with tongs and the other things that were used at a formal dinner, finger-bowls, too, she thought she'd never be able to get any of it straight.

But, as Mrs. Marsham was always saying, "Logic applies." That meant, if you just kept your head, you could work your way through all those forks and spoons and glasses because they had been put there in a certain way, not as a trap, but to help you through all ninety-six courses.

And Mrs. Marsham was interesting, too. Mary Kate wondered if she, like Miss Jantzen, had once been an actress. Her clothes and shoes and hat (she always wore a hat) seemed to have been made especially for her, and she had a way of slightly turning her head away while she was talking to you and then suddenly turning it back and giving you a dazzling smile. Even though she was pretty old, maybe fifty, she was still beautiful with her big violet eyes and her delicate nose and her heart-shaped face. She could have been Elizabeth Taylor's mother.

She wore her hair, which was a dark blue-y gray, in a French twist which made a nice little perch for her silly hats. She was tiny and probably didn't weigh a hundred pounds soaking wet. Best of all, she had what sounded like an English accent. It *wasn't* English, it was Refined American and maybe, therefore, attainable, especially if you had somebody like Miss Jantzen standing on your neck saying things like, "For heaven's sake, Mary Catherine, speak more clearly. You have it in you to do so."

From the first moment, scared or not, Mary Kate became Mrs. Marsham's devoted pupil. (She was even letting her hair grow so maybe *she* could wear a French twist.) It was entirely possible that a lady like Mrs. Marsham who, after all, did live on Park Avenue, might know Fred Astaire. After all, she wasn't going to live in Freshkill forever! One day, she was going to live and do whatever work she decided on in New York City and maybe even have an apartment overlooking the Hudson on West 72nd Street the way George Gershwin had had.

"Dear gels," Mrs. Marsham addressed them from the stage, "you're looking SIMply dreadful this afternoon. SLUMPed about. Like a roomful of CHARladies after a hard day's work. That's PEARfectly all right, of course, if you are interested in acquiring a JANitor for a husband, but, but, BUT . . . if you have HIGHer ambitions . . ."

The auditorium was filled with the sound of them shifting and straightening.

Boy, Mary Kate thought, just mention the word husband . . .

"There. How *nice* you look. And now . . . to the business at hand! Before long, dear gels, your lives will be filled with parties, dances, receptions, balls" (Bobbie Covetti sniggered; she thought she was *so* sexy because she knew more dirty words and double meanings than anybody) "weekends in the country, college weekends, perhaps, perHAPS, a weekend devoted to getting to know *his* family."

There was an explosion of whispers in the auditorium. Mary Kate was glad Mrs. Marsham couldn't hear what some of the dumber, *cruder* kids were saying.

"You, you see that *does* interest you, doesn't it? As well it should. Dear gels, my only task, the very *reason* for my being here, is to help you to enjoy to the utmost all these GLORious occurrences that soon will be filling up your lives. Because, you know, there are PITfalls!

"A reception or a formal dance, for example, surely means a receiving line. How awful for you if, in front of your young man, you make a BOTCH of going down the line of sponsors and chaperones at your Senior Dansant. Men simply don't care for FORmalities like reCEIving lines but, if on top of that, you embarrass him with your inEPtitude, oh, dear gels!"

The freshmen sobered up, stopped being snotty, snapped to attention.

"Let me see," Mrs. Marsham said generously. "The young ladies in *that* row — " she indicated them without pointing, they all noticed that refinement, jotted it down in their heads for future reference — "will please come up here with me to act as that — " she shivered daintily — "as that DREADful receiving line."

The row got up.

"And the rest of you — " the twenty-thousand-watt smile — "are the poor souls who must endure meeting the OLD folks."

Even the Freshkill grumblers rose to their initiation into Society with great good humor.

☙

If Mary Kate got killed off at the Academy, she knew it was not Latin or Algebra or an overload of homework that would do it, but gym as prescribed for Young Ladies.

The uniform told you a whole lot about the Order's attitude toward Sports (Modesty Above All) even before you fielded a team; it came in layers: short-sleeved white cotton blouse, voluminous navy wool serge bloomers (itchy), a navy blue wool serge tunic (gold MSM monogram on the yoke) with pleats falling from the yoke down to the middle of your (whisper) calf, thick white socks worn over your nylons (nerve-racking), white sneakers. The one thing you didn't want to do in an outfit like that which covered up more of you, practically, than the regular Academy uniform you wore in public, was to sweat. Even the blouse seemed itchy when you were sweaty.

The one thing the Academy's ladylike sports did was make you sw — perspire.

Take this afternoon, for instance. Indian summer, 109 degrees in the shade, and the sunshine weighing twenty tons a ray. Gym: middle of the three afternoon periods.

At approximately 1:13, twenty-nine freshmen and one sophomore transfer student burst out of the side door of Main, plummeted down the south terraces, sprinted across the baking playing field to the gym, and plunged into the dim, dank basement locker room. Trying not to see or be seen, they exchanged their uniforms for the "freedom" of their gym tunics, hurrying to hang up clothes, lock lockers, safeguard nylons against careless fingernails, and get upstairs by 1:20 so that Miss O'Keefe, the gym instructress, wouldn't holler at them again. For a Lady, she had a very loud voice and precious little sympathy.

A short prayer in the gym, then out onto the playing field into that heavy sun, Mount Freshkill a faint blue shadow in the background, for, Mary Kate dreaded it, field hockey. It didn't seem like a ladylike game to her, stuck playing right wing. It seemed a dangerous game involving long sticks, a very hard ball, and a tremendous amount of running up and down. And there were kids who were worse at it than she was, so you had to look out they didn't clobber you when they swung too high and wide with their sticks. There were already five chipped elbows in Freshman B alone! And Miss O'Keefe ran right along with the line, screaming (coaching, she called it) so you could never slow up at all and you got a terrific headache. Miss O'Keefe never seemed to lose her breath or swea — perspire, either. In the time-outs, they would lean on their sticks, gasping, their faces blotchy red, while she told what they had done wrong and the usual stuff about how field hockey was *the* sport in the Seven Sisters college, which was probably some awful Catholic place for training gym teachers.

When Miss O'Keefe finished with them, it was always five to instead of seven to two and they were due in their next class on the hour. Every once in a while, a kid would burst out crying as she tried to peel off her sweaty clothes and get back into her regular ones, which kept sticking. Nobody helped her, though, unless by some miracle they had gotten dressed extra fast, because they knew the 2 P.M. nun was already pacing around her half-empty classroom, waiting to yell.

"Don't think you can use gym as an excuse for continually arriving late for Social Studies," Sister Rosaria squealed at them as Mary Kate and the others appeared, breathless, exhausted. "Man does not live by athletics alone." The little nun stalked up and down the aisles, glaring at each of the latecomers in turn. "Social Studies stands very high on your transcripts!"

They hardly had the strength to say, "Yes, Sister," as usual.

And to think she had looked forward to gym at the Academy, just because of that big building and all the fields and courts and tracks.

3. The Halloween Dance

ACROSS THE FRESHKILL CYO GYM, dim and full of decorations for the Halloween dance, Mary Kate could see Ronnie Ricatelli, who was the boy all the girls idolized. The kids were sneaking looks and sneaking looks at him and his almost-as-interesting buddies.

He didn't even go to Saint Brendan's Boys' Catholic in Westburgh, which was where the kids said most of the really great guys went. He was a senior at Freshkill High, but last year, just a junior, he had been the star forward on and co-captain of the varsity basketball team, the first time in Freshkill history a junior had been that! Once, last winter, she had tagged along with the kids to a basketball game and Ronnie had been breathtaking. It was hard to believe you could be so talented and so handsome, too. The most interesting thing about him, though, was that he had just broken up with Angela Reilly, whose father commuted to New York City, which meant she had all kinds of clothes and even a little red convertible of her own. There wasn't a girl in this room tonight, Mary Kate bet herself, who wasn't aching to fill up that empty space in Ronnie's darling heart.

Wow! she thought, even I'm getting goofy about him. But maybe all it meant was that she was getting the hang of how

to behave around boys all over again after that trouble at
Holy Redeemer about her dad's "job" when the kids had
even turned their boy friends against her, had even turned
Billy McCarthy against her.

That was all fixed up now. She was part of the gang again
because the kids were proud of her big name at the Academy.
Even though being part of the gang wasn't as important to her
as it had once been, it was okay and even nice because it meant
you had somebody to go to dances with, like tonight. She
laughed to herself, full of happiness, and at the same moment
realized, with horror, that she was looking straight into Ronnie Ricatelli's face. Quick as a flash, she turned her head and
pretended to be chattering with the kids. He had really been
staring at her with those sad brown eyes of his and he was
probably thinking Who does she think she is, looking at Me?
Whoever she is and *that's* not much.

Just to be on the safe side, she worked herself right into the
center of her bunch of kids. Not only the Academy freshmen
from Holy Redeemer and Saint Anne's but also the Holy
Redeemer kids who had gone to Freshkill High. All of them,
even her, were dressed up in sweaters and skirts and nylons
and their Sunday heels. Dances weren't so bad after all. She
had thought you needed fancy clothes for dances like this but
the kids said you only had to dress up when there was a real
band, not when they just played records.

She wished the records would start; maybe they would
play a Gershwin song to make it perfect. A Gershwin song
and all of them together at her first real dance.

No, not all of them. Philly Romanelli was way down on
the girls' side of the gym, acting as if she didn't even know who

they were. And she was wearing a black peekaboo blouse and how had she ever gotten past the CYO mothers, much less her *own* mother, wearing *that?*

Right in the middle of the kids like this, she couldn't avoid hearing all their dumb gossip. She liked them, but sometimes they were as bad as her mam, always trying to make something out of nothing. About how Roddy Walsh might get kicked out of Saint Bren's even though he was a senior because when the cop stopped him for driving without lights he found a bottle of beer, unopened, but *still* a bottle of beer, in the car; and about how Joe Montgomery, who *had* been kicked out of Saint Bren's and nobody knew for sure *why*, had kept Rosalie Parmenter out until 2 A.M. and everybody knew what *that* meant, she had probably come home with her bra up around her ears; and about what a shame it was that a cute guy like Sonny Policelli had ended up just being a barber like his father, and now he was mixed up with Fran Polinski, who wasn't much once you looked past that sexy figure of hers. *Everything* they talked about these days after a while turned out to be Sexy.

Mary Kate knew who Sonny was. Once on Ladies' Day, which was the last Wednesday of each month at Policelli's Barber Shop, Sonny, just out of high school, had cut her hair and she trembled the whole time, why? and he had trembled the whole time, why? He had had to adjust her chin once with his hand to get her head at the right angle and, even though she had been busy trying not to faint, she had noticed that he yanked his hand away as if he had gotten an electric shock. It had all been very confusing. And another good reason for letting her hair grow.

A couple of months after the business with Sonny, she got the curse for the first time and her mother had told her to ask her father about it and her dad had told her to go and have a talk with Father Rafferty about it. Instead, she went to the library, took a book written especially for teen-agers off the shelf, and went down into the basement room to read it, since they'd die of shock if she ever brought it home. She had sat down there and learned all about Sex. The book, which didn't have an imprimatur (she hoped God wouldn't mind), had been full of instructive, unfrightening drawings that made her realize that the kids didn't always know what they were talking about, but it really hadn't explained all that trembling between two strangers, one of them practically *twenty*, in the barber shop.

And now they were talking about Vic Guiliano and how the only reason he was taking out some girl was The Only Reason.

Oh, this boy and girl stuff was driving her crazy! Why couldn't you just be friends with a boy, like you could be friends with a girl, without all that Sex stuff getting in the way? It would be very interesting if you could just talk to a boy without worrying Was he going to ask you to go steady? Just hear what he thought about a book you had both read or a movie you had both seen without wondering Does he think I'm cute?

She had already made friends with Jimmy's brother Alex, who was as nice-looking as Jimmy had said, but he mostly liked playing football with his friends better than he liked talking to her or any of the kids Jimmy had over. Still, he had told her she reminded him of a character in a Shakespeare play he had seen at his school (Westburgh Free Academy, where he went because he had told his parents he wasn't going to go to any *Catholic* high school), a girl called Rosalind who had to dress up like a boy but, Alex said, you could never forget that she was a girl. Mary Kate didn't exactly know how to take that, but at least she had had *some* kind of conversation with a boy and she hardly knew any b —

This time she saw, with dismay, that *he* was looking at *her.* She hadn't even thought of looking at him and there he was, looking at her.

I can't dance! she sent him in an urgent burst of mental telepathy. Mr. Promuto at the Academy, social dancing, fifty cents a lesson after school, he always makes me take the boy's part because I'm one of the tall ones and anyway it's the Peabody, you never heard of it, it's an Ice Age dance *no-body ever heard of!*

She slumped a whole lot so her head wouldn't stick out so far above the crowd of girls.

You dope! He's probably only trying to decide how to get even with you for daring to look at him before. He doesn't know it was an accident.

She hunched her shoulders a little more.

For some reason, boys were very often mean to girls, not only to ordinary girls like her but even to really pretty girls. Just last week, because it was a sunny day, Bobbie and Annette (who were knockouts) had been practicing dance steps on the front deck of the ferryboat and one of the Saint Bren's freshmen had hollered from his side of the boat to their side of the boat, "It's lucky you creeps have each other to dance with!" You would have thought he'd want to make a good impression on them since he wasn't too good-looking himself but oh, no. Imagine what a boy like Ronnie would say to a skinny wreck like her! She hadn't even wanted to go to this dance really. She could just say that she had to go to the john, which was near the door, and she could grab her coat and run . . .

All of a sudden the *buzz-buzz* of the kids' voices stopped and she felt a hand on her elbow. Her lips got stiff and cold because she knew, without looking, Who it was. He had such warm hands; it went with the rest of him; the just-right pompadour, the dark plaid sports jacket.

She turned around because she had to. Everybody else was quiet and staring like in the movies when the two archenemies meet and everybody knows a terrible fight is going to start in the next minute, a fistfight or a gunfight to the death.

She struggled to say something to stop whatever he was going to say, but it was no use. That damned heart of hers was pounding so hard it was filling up her chest and throat. She tried to pull herself together because, if she could, then maybe she could think of a fast answer to his rude remark that would make him end up looking like a jerk, even if it meant she might as well move out of town on the spot. But she just stood there like a moron, her eyes popping out of her head, waiting for him to say it.

"Wanna dance?" he said.

She blinked in amazement.

He smiled at her sleepily and raised his arms, right there in the middle of all the silent kids. Dumfounded, she moved toward him.

"Hey, honey, I'm the one who leads," he said, rearranging

her arms, smiling that fascinating, scary smile at her, moving her out of the crowd onto the empty, empty dance floor.

Oh God, oh God, she prayed, please let somebody else dance and hide us.

"This is a fox trot," he said. "One-two-three, one-two-three," he said, his warm breath coming through his smile to brush against her cheek.

I am ruining all of this, she thought as she desperately tried to keep count. Every girl in this place is dying to dance with him, every girl in this place can do the Lindy standing on her head, and here I am, ruining, ruining everything!

"Relax, relax," he said and leaned forward to put his cheek against hers.

Relax! Relax! she ordered herself. It didn't help that every time she passed one of the Academy kids, who had finally started dancing, too, they smiled and winked at her over the shoulder of the boy they were dancing with.

"Come on, honey, just let the music carry you along. The Four Aces, they're just the greatest."

They are the absolute worst, she was thinking, just as he nudged the middle of her back with his hand. All of a sudden she felt like butter on a warm day. On July fourth! Even the Aces started to sound good.

Oh-h-h, this was some more of that Sex stuff, she worried, at the same time knowing, for sure, she didn't care, she didn't care at all. He felt good and he smelled good, like spices, and she just didn't . . .

"Good, good. *That's* the way."

Right away, she had the sobering thought that Ronnie, especially since the bottom of his cheek fit the top of her cheek so nicely, was probably a Near Occasion of Sin, page forty-four, *The New Baltimore Catechism.*

She still didn't care.

When the record ended, Ronnie kept his arms around her, somehow turning her around, so that he was clapping his hands, applauding the record, with his hands out in front of her and with her back close to his front. She could feel the hard buttons of his jacket through the back of her cheesy imitation angora sweater and she couldn't begin to imagine how many pink hairs must be coming off on his jacket. What upset her even more was his breath on the back of her neck.

The music started up, those Aces *again*, and he had her turned around and dancing before she knew what was what. For half a second, he held her off at arm's length.

"You have natural grace," he said with that same, same smile.

Her mouth made a downward boomerang which, luckily, he didn't see because he had already folded her up in his arms. And to be folded up in those hard, strong arms was all she wanted.

He was talking into her ear.

"What?" she murmured.

"Sure name."

"Oh. Mary Kate Mulligan."

"Come I've never seen you before?"

"Oh, well, I go to the Academy."

He laughed a groan.

"It's a good school!" she protested.

"Full of nuns."

"Yes."

"What's a nice girl like you doing in a place like that?"

"I got a four-year scholarship," she said without thinking.

"Oh. You smart or something?"

"Ha ha." She wasn't good at giggling. She hoped he hadn't noticed. His old girl friend Angela was famous for being a dumb blonde. And she was sure she could feel him stiffening up. All she wanted was for him to keep gliding the two of them around the gym floor, their own warm little island.

"I might get a basketball scholarship to some college," he finally said.

"Oh, you're wonderful! I've seen you play."

"Yeah?" He was loosening up again.

"Yeah, and I understand what a hard game it is. Everybody is always trying to get me to play basketball. Because I'm so tall," she explained. "But that doesn't make any difference, even with girls' rules. I mean, just because you're tall . . . I mean, you have to have . . . talent."

She could feel him nodding against her cheek. Wonderful, wonderful! For him, she'd even learn to play that stupid game.

"Yeah," he said. "You said it. You gotta keep in practice all the time. Even out of season. I had this girl friend, see, and she didn't understand that. She got mad and said she wasn't going to spend one more minute sitting home alone while I was practicing."

"Well, maybe she doesn't appreciate how hard basketball is. Maybe that's why she feels the way she does." What Mary Kate was feeling, right at the moment, was terribly jealous. "It's a tough game."

"That's right," he said, now doing more talking than dancing. His eyes didn't look sleepy anymore, and he had stopped dancing cheek to cheek. "Not many girls would understand that."

"Well, most of them are short."

"I never thought of that."

She smiled at him, trying not to look helpful. He had not picked her out to dance with him because she looked helpful.

"You know, I never thought of that. Maybe if she came to practice a couple of times, she'd realize, she'd appreciate . . ."

In a way, Mary Kate was glad the music was ending. It meant all that singing like yowling would stop, too. If only they'd played a Gershwin song . . .

He steered her over to where some folding chairs were set up.

"Listen. I have to make a phone call, but I'll be right back, okay? Wait for me right here, okay?"

"Sure."

"I've got a feeling, Mary, that you're my good luck charm!"

The kids swooped down on her as soon as Ronnie was out of sight. She could hardly bear their titters and whispers and questions. He was going to call up that old Angela and she had put the very words in his mouth that might fix the two of them up again. A lot she mattered. He hadn't even gotten her name right.

"Listen," the kids were saying, "get him to dance with me." "Me, too!" "*Me, too!*" "Oh, Mary Kate, you know *I'd* just drop dead twice if he ever danced with *me!!*"

"He's not going to dance with anyone," she said flatly, tired of their dumb voices. "I told him how to get Angela back and he's trying it out now."

"Wadja do THAT for?"

"Because he really likes her and the fight they had was silly."

"What was it like dancing with him? Tell us! Tell us!" they started up again.

"It was very, very nice," she said, feeling the tears way at the back of her eyes. It had been better than anything she had ever imagined, even dreaming about Farley, only somehow it had all turned against her, she must have done something wrong, and it was all over.

Ronnie dashed up to her, causing the kids to scatter right and left.

"You were right!" he said, all excited. "I got her to promise to come to practice. I told her what you said, the stuff about how basketball might seem boring if you didn't know how complicated . . . we're, she said she'd go out with me for a pizza."

He didn't even look old and interesting anymore. He looked like some kid talking about his collection of bubblegum cards. But she could still feel his arms.

"Listen, how can I ever thank you? I mean, you put us right back on the same wavelength. There must be some guy here you have your eye on. Say the word, and I'll make sure he dances with you all night."

"Oh, don't do that! I mean, you know, it's more fun just seeing what happens." She didn't believe a word she was saying.

"You know, being smart and all, you should study to be a teacher. If there were teachers like you at Freshkill, the kids wouldn't hate school so much."

"Thanks."

"God, don't thank *me!*"

She could see he was longing to hop into his car and be gone. "Hurry up. You don't want to keep Angela waiting."

He didn't even say good-bye, just gave her an old-buddy wave. His compliments tasted like ashes in her mouth.

Even before the kids could surround her again, another boy came up and asked her to dance. His breath was terrible and he danced as if he were sawing wood. Even she could dance better than he could. She very firmly extracted herself from his arms when the song ended.

"I have to make a phone call," she said.

"I'll come with you."

"No," she said. "There's this friend of mine who's been dying to dance with you."

"Yeah?"

"Down there. See?" She pointed out Philly and dashed for the coatrack. What she wanted to do was to lock herself in the girls' john and have a good cry. Instead, she got her coat and went out into Main Street. The bitterly cold air made her breath catch in her throat. It also cleared her brain. She had just better go home; there was noplace else to go.

Even though she didn't like walking on Main Street by herself, she walked slowly, trying to figure out why she wasn't at least enjoying the honor of having helped Ronnie out. It wasn't that other boy's fault, Dave, he'd said his name was, that he was such a drip. After Ronnie, any boy who'd asked her for a dance would have seemed like a drip.

The simple fact of the matter was that if she had been smart enough to help Ronnie get his girl back, she should have been smart enough to get him interested in her, especially since she liked dancing with him so much. Maybe later, after some dates,

she would have thought *he* was a drip because, ten to one, all
he could talk about was basketball, but she should at least
have worked things so she could have found that out for herself.

It's just not your time yet, she told herself. Sooner or later
it will come to you how to act with boys so they don't think of
you as a creep or as their big sister or their mother or their
teacher.

Damn it! He didn't pick me out to dance the first dance of
the first big dance of the year because I reminded him of his favorite teacher!

Boop-boop!

The car horn she had been dreading. Some Freshkill boys
had nothing better to do on a Saturday night than to cruise
their cars up and down Main Street honking at anything female.

"Oh, beat it!" she yelled, tears splashing down her face.
"I'm old enough to be your mother!"

"Hey, Ma! Hey, Ma!" they catcalled, coming back a second time. She ran the last block and let herself into her building before they had a chance to come back a third time. She sat
down on the stairs, not ready to face Them up There.

What she would do would be never to go to a dance again.
At least not until she was grown-up and out, out, out of Freshkill. She had enough to do holding A's in her subjects and
learning all the extra stuff Miss Jantzen assigned her.

And, too, Miss Verplanck had given her this novel by this
writer named Thomas Wolfe. It weighed a ton but some of
it, well, it was impossible, but it seemed as if Thomas Wolfe
had somehow gotten inside her head and had copied down

exactly what she was thinking and feeling. She knew one part by heart:

> *The girl is the youngest child. She thinks she would like to go away somewhere and see the world. Sometimes she hears the whistle of a train that is going to Paris. She has never ridden on a train in her life. She would like to go to Paris. She would like to have some fine clothes, she would like to travel. Perhaps she would like to start life new in America, the Land of Opportunity. The girl has had a hard time. Her people do not understand her. If they saw her listening to the lark they would poke fun at her. She has never had the advantages of a good education, her people are so poor, but she would profit by her opportunity if she did, more than some people who have. You can tell by looking at her that she's intelligent.*

Before she had discovered Eugene Gant, she had assumed that thinking stuff like that about herself was the sin of self-pity. But Thomas Wolfe was a famous writer, not some kid. He had thought these thoughts and had decided they were important enough to write down. And *he* was dead, too, just like George Gershwin, unexpectedly dead while she was just a baby. You'd think God would have left one of them around to help people.

She would lay off dances; there was still a lot of Thomas Wolfe left that she had to read.

As she opened the door of the flat, she realized she had no excuse to give to her mam for being home so early from the dance.

thank God thank God you hear that he's wheezin' somethin' dreadful hear it

"Yes. He sounds awful." Oh, God! Now this on top of it all!

She was shocked at her unkindness, instantly ashamed. He was sick; more than once he had been close to dying. Oh, to hate her dad for being sick just because she wanted to crawl into bed and cry herself to sleep. She was a selfish girl, a nasty bitch, to put her stupid cares ahead of her own dad who might be dying. God would surely remember that the next time she came sniveling around, asking Him for something.

His breath came in a loud rattle.

"*Ma!* Aren't you going to call Doctor Kennedy?"

that very thought has been on me mind all this evenin' except can you still smell it he smoked a coupla cig-arettes and Jim'll put this attack down to that and yell at me when all the time it was some com-mentatin' fellow on the TV tonight praisin' that jackass Harry Truman pre-cipitated this attack of you're home early aren't you it can't be ten ah child you look near on to tears no fellow asked you to dance is that it no one took no-tice how pretty you look in your pink ah well it happens it happens but you've a long life ahead of you sooner or later some steady chap'll notice you and oh listen to that Mary Catherine he's makin' that gurglin' sound God help us all fetch me my coat there I'm runnin' over to Jim's I'd never make a scrap of sense over the phone stay with him child talk to him make soothin' sounds

Mary Kate went in and sat down by her dad's bed. Trying to get his breath like that, he was all twisted up in his sleep. These days he didn't look like that dad of hers who had stood up to the mill owners and their hired thugs. Awake or asleep, he looked sour and disdainful. He didn't care about all the stuff she was doing at the Academy, always just told her to be sure and go and tell Rafferty, that damned Mike Rafferty, about it. She didn't want to tell any priest. She wanted to tell her dad! Maybe good news would snap him out of being so . . . changed. If he were still the way he had once been, she was sure of it, she could have told him about what happened at the dance tonight and maybe even discuss Thomas Wolfe with him.

Impulsively, she reached out and took his hand. At her touch, he raised up and flopped over, like a fish out of water. She pressed her hands to her mouth to keep the scream from coming out. He must be dying! God would get her for sure for thinking about herself instead of her dad at a time like this! He must be dying to move in that unhuman way.

She didn't care what her mam would say. She grabbed up the phone off her dad's night table and ran, trailing the long cord behind her, into the kitchen.

When she got through to Father Rafferty she told him to come, right away! The three of them, the priest, her mam, and the doctor, arrived at the same time. When Father Rafferty had gotten finished with his business with the candles and the holy water and the cotton with the blessed oil, the men carried her dad down the stairs into the ambulance with all its lights. It was like a movie. The worst, scariest movie in the whole world.

"Please, God! Please, God!" she beseeched Him. "Strike me down, flunk me in all my subjects, make me forget my lines, but save him, oh, please save him. *I need him!*" She put her head down on her knees, there on the bench in the hospital corridor, and she cried, and then she fell asleep.

She woke up, still dressed, but put to bed in the made-up
sofa bed.

No more dances, was her first thought on waking.

She roused herself. On the kitchen table she found her
mother's note:

> *Dear MC, Yr. dad has passed his Crisis and is okay.
> They made us come home but I am taking a taxi back
> so as to be there in case he wakes up. Go to Mass like a
> good girl. There is some Stew in the Frig. Heat it up for
> a bite then come to the hosp. Fr. Rafferty will give you
> a ride.*

It was signed "Yr. mother (Maureen)."

Mary Kate felt as if she were a million years old.

4. Ev and Akky

IT WAS ENOUGH to make you want to quit the Academy altogether. Five mornings a week, 9 A.M. Mother Bernadette (Ev), English I and, right after *that*, 10 A.M. Sister Aquinas (Akky), Catholic Philosophy for Young Moderns (it was a new style of teaching Religion I she had learned from her teacher out at Principium University and they were using exactly the same textbook, she told them over and over, that real college kids used).

Mother Bernadette was called Mother, instead of Sister, because, until she had retired a long time ago, she had been entirely in charge of the convent side of Mount Saint Michael and the training of nuns for the Order. But then there had gotten to be this shortage of teaching nuns on the Academy side, so Mother Bernadette had volunteered to help out. The problem was that English I was grammar and Mother didn't know a pronoun from a hyphen.

You could never tell *that* just looking at her, though, she appeared so grave and wise when she wasn't talking. In fact, she looked just like a distinguished U.S. senator, the one her dad said was about the only one who could straighten out these new modern workers with all their fri-volous de-mands.

Even in April, though, it was still a shock to walk into

English I and see Everett McKinley Dirksen sitting there in his black and white habit. Mary Kate hoped the senator was better at his job than Ev — Mim was the one who had started calling her Ev — than Ev was at her job.

It was an accident that the four smartest kids in the freshman class, Jimmy, Mim, her, and Ginny Masterson, had all ended up in Freshman B, if you could call alphabetical order an accident. They sat together so that when Ev really went off the tracks and started teaching the class the stuff wrong, they could pop up, very fast, one after another in the same part of the room, and bully her into the right answer. They were never mean about it, not too often anyway, but when they questioned and answered, bang, bang, bang, bang, without giving Ev a second to interrupt, they gave her the chance to act as if she had known what the right answer was all along. None of them liked this job they had taken on, not even Mim, who was the original person who did not suffer fools gladly. Ginny always had the last word in one of these machine-gun episodes because her combination of blond curls and big blue eyes, sweeter than sweet, seemed to soothe Ev.

Last night's homework in the grammar workbook had been a long review of adjectives and adverbs.

"She's never going to make it this morning," Jimmy whispered as she slid into her seat.

"Yeah," Mim said, "she's always feeling bad-ly and I'm not feeling too friend-ous this morning. I hope the old dear is on *some*body's prayer list."

Mary Kate wasn't feeling too friend-ous this morning, either. She was fed up with Ev, who didn't give a damn that she didn't know the subject she was teaching and just tried to bluff her way through, and she was even more fed up with Akky, the sneaky parrot-faced Akky, who had found out about her dad's being a semi-invalid and was trying to use that to get at her. Akky was the only nun on the staff who taught kids for their entire four years at the Academy, so if she once got you in her power, she had you as a spy or a stooge for practically your entire life. It wasn't a nice way for a nun to behave. Father Rafferty might be a nasty, dumb person, but at least all he was was a secular priest who had been trained in some crummy diocesan seminary (free for poor boys) and, at least, he could be excused as a test God had set up for the Holy Redeemer parishioners, most of whom were hard up and not too well educated themselves.

But Ev and Akky, they were Order nuns, they had gotten expensive training, they were high-class Representatives of the Church, they had no right to be as crummy as they were. After all, the Church was what was going to save you.

Oh, she knew that a lot of Freshkill kids who had gotten really boy-crazy were breaking a lot of the Church's rules in parked cars so they could get boy friends, that's what they talked like on the ferryboat, anyway. But she didn't have her head all muddled up with that Sex stuff, not anymore, so she still knew the Church with all its rules was there for your own Eternal Good. Ev and Akky, though, when you kept getting them five mornings a week, back to back, could go a long way toward shaking your faith in the Church.

Mary Kate was glad that Mim had gotten out of the bed on the wrong side. The two of them out of sorts were enough to sabotage any rescue missions this morning in the mine-fields of adjectives and adverbs.

She was in such a bad humor that she didn't pay attention at all to the workbook correcting. She just sat on her hands and looked at the pictures of Jesus, the pope, and G. K. Chesterton pinned up on the bulletin board. Ev, however, finally got to her.

"Number sixteen. The correct answer is 'Go slow.' 'Go slow.' "

Repeating it like that, like some dumb bingo caller.

Mary Kate raised her hand.

"Mother?"

Ev looked nervous.

"Yes, Mary Catherine?"

"I believe that 'Go slow' is the form in common usage, I know you see it everywhere on road signs, but isn't 'Go slowly' the *proper* form?"

"Well, uh," Ev said, as usual.

"Yes," Jimmy said. "They have to shorten messages on road signs so you won't have an accident while you're trying to read them."

Mary Kate had to stop herself from giving Jimmy a delighted kick in the ankle.

"Oh, for heaven's sake!" Mim beetled her dark brows. " 'Go slowly' even *sounds* correct unless, of course, your ear has become *polluted* by the vernacular."

Ah, Mim! They had just learned about the vernacular in Latin last week.

"And adverbs mostly end in l-y, don't they, Mother?" Batbat of Ginny's baby blues.

"Of course," Ev said. "I was just testing you young ladies. You looked lothargic to me. 'Go slowly.' 'Go slowly.' "

"Just like in the song," Mim whispered. "Swing low-ly, sweet chariot."

Mary Kate felt a little cheered up. If only the old jerk would just write away for the answer book instead of only threatening to do it. And there was no use complaining to Mother Adolphus, who was fair as fair. Ev was a big shot and that was that.

The old nun's voice droned on. Even Akky would be a relief after this. Well, at least this time, she did have the answer right.

Mary Kate felt the devil rise in her, suddenly and over-poweringly.

"Mother?" she said.

Ev sighed. "Yes, Mary Catherine?"

"I thought that if an action verb was being used as a state-of-being verb, the modifier following modifies the subject rather than the verb and would, therefore, be an adverb rather than an adjective. The modifier, I mean. In this case, I mean. If you see what I mean." Even she couldn't make any sense out of what she'd said.

"Of course I see what you mean!"

"Well, Mary Catherine," Mim said without waiting to be called on, "that would be true if you didn't apply the test of substituting a form of the verb *to be*, even a *child* knows about the test of substituting a form of the verb *to be*, if you'll excuse me for saying so, for the state-of-being verb but, of course . . ."

"I think Miriam's right," Jimmy said.

"No, I agree with Mary Catherine," Ginny said. "It comes down to a matter of whether . . ."

"I think the class should take a vote on this," Ev interrupted, "since there seems to be some difference of opinion."

Mary Kate crossed her fingers. The kids in this section weren't dumb. They probably knew what was going on. Now if they just . . .

"All in favor of 'We built the raft strong enough to hold us,' raise their hands."

Mary Kate could feel the rest of the class watching the four of them.

She raised her hand, and so did Mim, who had "disagreed" with her.

"But, but," Ev said.

After some confusion, thirteen of the thirty kids raised their hands in agreement. That left exactly fifteen kids to vote for "We built the raft strongly enough . . ." which was just what that version got, without a moment's hesitation.

Ev dismissed them early because she said she had a convent assignment.

The only reason that Akky had let up on trying to trap her, Mary Kate knew, was because she had better game in Sharon O'Neill, a dayhop from Cornwall who also had a sick dad . . .

Had was just the right word. Sharon's dad had died last week. Funny old Sharon with her coal-black hair standing up in spikes. She was a poor kid, too, and right from the beginning of school she and Mary Kate had been friends.

"Now tell me, Sharon, just tell me if you don't want to talk about it — " Akky's eyes narrowed down to slits behind her silver-rimmed glasses and her face got redder than any parrot's Mary Kate had ever seen — "but I think it would be helpful for all of us to know just what you felt at the exact moment you knew your father was dead."

Sharon was standing stiff as a ramrod, tears leaking out of the corners of her dark eyes, her face dead white. The class sat silent, sick with embarrassment, not for Sharon, but for the damned nun who didn't seem to know when to shut up. Sharon was so quiet these days, so unlike her usual self with her same joke about how once her shipment of Dior dresses came in she was going to take over Saint Bren's single-handed.

Mary Kate's pulse was hammering in her ears. It could be *her* standing up there, mute with grief under that . . . yes! that *bitch's* bullying. Oh, she thought with hate, that bitch is always going on how she's one of the two nuns on the staff with a Ph.D. and how the professors out there at that snobby Principium University keep telling her she'll never be able to teach Scholasticism to a silly bunch of schoolgirls but we're showing them, aren't we, young ladies? We're showing them!

Yeah, you bitch! We're showing them how to crucify a poor kid who never did anybody any harm. You fat, stupid, sneaky, mean bitch!

Well, she wasn't much better. She'd never say any of that out loud, no matter how bad Akky got. None of them would. You could get kicked out.

"Now, Sharon, don't dramatize. It is your duty as a Christian to relate your experiences to us . . . ."

There was a noise at the back of the classroom. No, not at the back of the classroom. Outside the back of the classroom. Outside of the classroom altogether, in the uninteresting part of the Academy grounds. In the driveway that led up to the

loading platform outside the kitchens that served the Academy
and the convent. The kids, despite the terrible situation in the
classroom, began to look at each other questioningly. Only
Sharon and Akky were unaware of the noise: car doors slam-
ming, feet, lots of feet, on the cement.

"Sharon O'Neill! I don't like to threaten you, but a display
of such infantile . . ."

"Way!" "Ho!" "Hey, Sister Benedict! What treats have
you got for us *this* year!" "Wandering players are we — "
a voice yodeled above the rest — "and half-dead with . . ."

"The Buskers! The Buskers!" The news spread rapidly
through the class.

Mary Kate summoned up her thoughts, still watching
Sharon. The Buskers, the actors from that miserable damned
Principium U. — they were giving *Macbeth* at the Academy
tonight.

"Let me see just see what this disturbance is," Akky said,
waddling swiftly down an aisle toward the windows. The
class, like a wave, rose up behind her and broke for the windows.

The kids nearest Sharon, Mary Kate included, rushed to
Sharon, Akky's back turned, to comfort her. Mary Kate put
her arm around Sharon's waist, grabbed Sharon's hand with
hers.

"Come on, Sharon, it's okay." "Hey, wake up! The Buskers
are here!" they whispered at her, trying to find the right
words.

"Use this Kleenex, come on. It's clean! Would a Mulligan
give you a shot-up Kleenex? You sure you're not Orange?"

She steered Sharon to the window, feeling the terrifying

quakings and shiverings in Sharon's body and hand. She wanted to let go, all that shaking scared her as much as any of her dad's attacks, but she decided that if they killed her she would not leave her friend now.

"There they are." Cheerful, be cheerful. "Oh, Share! Look at that tall guy! He's even better-looking than Gregory Peck!" Gregory Peck was Sharon's ideal. It just killed her that he was married to this Swedish lady and had all those kids.

Sharon blinked and blinked and used the Kleenex.

"Oh," she said. "He doesn't look like Gregory Peck. He only looks like Farley Granger." She blew her nose again.

"Thanks a lot. I think you're nice, too."

They watched the actors and actresses pulling suitcases and boxes out of the car and the station wagon, watched them unload bigger things from the back of the little van.

"Gosh," Sharon said. "I thought they'd be dressed up. I always thought actors always went around dressed up."

"Yeah," Mary Kate said. Mackinaws, oilskins, babushkas, a whole lot of khaki stuff. Even dungarees! Where were the matched ostrich-skin luggage, the poodles, the long cigarette holders? And even though they were still yoo-hooing for Sister Benedict, not one of them was yelling Yoo hoo, Sister Benedict *dah*ling.

"I don't know, Share. Maybe they were afraid of getting dressed up because of the weather. April is tricky, you know."

"I wonder if *Gregory* goes around like that when he's working."

A small, interesting thought was dancing around in Mary Kate's head. She liked acting very much, so much that she had even played around with the idea of maybe becoming an

actress instead of the private secretary to a famous man who
might marry her. What had stopped her playing around with
that idea was that she wasn't really pretty. Not *ugly*, but not
pretty.

Well. Not *one* of those ladies down there, and one of them
must be the *starring* actress, was a raving beauty. Not ugly,
but not a raving beauty . . .

"They don't look any different from us," Sharon said, as
if to confirm Mary Kate's thought. "Only older."

"Just wait'll your Diors come in . . ."

There was a whoop from the actors as Sister Benedict
appeared on the loading platform. She was the little dried-up
hunchbacked nun who not only ran the convent and the
academy kitchens but also did duty in the Academy candy
store (12:15-12:30; 3:15-3:30).

"Oh, look at *that!* Just look at *that*," Mary Kate heard
Akky snarl. "She hasn't even got the sense to take off that
apron! Doesn't she know she's dealing with *university*
people!"

"Hey, Sister Benedict!" a pudgy player, a man in old Army
clothes he was, yelled. "I've been waiting all year long for a
good feed out of your kitchen!"

Sister Benedict's withered face broke open with a smile.
The kids who bought candy from her mostly didn't like her
because she never made any conversation with them. Never
gookily thanked them for their nickels and dimes. Only paid
attention to all those papers caught up on her clipboard.

One day Mary Kate had said to her, handing over her nickel,
"I think, if I go before my time, it will be entirely due to coco-
nut bars."

"There are worse ways to go," Sister Benedict had said. "Peanut clusters," she had added, looking over her clipboard, admitting her own vice.

"Oh, she's giving the whole establishment a bad name," Akky complained, looking around for agreement. Mary Kate put her height between Akky and Sharon.

No need. Akky's eyes had returned, like a flash, to the driveway.

The heavy sky suddenly gave way to rain, driving the actors away from the cars and toward the kitchen. The kids, in a mass, leaned up on tiptoes, hungry for every last glance of the Buskers.

Oh, they can't go. Not yet. Not yet, Mary Kate begged.

She threw caution to the winds and waved at the tall actor, even if he did look more like Gregory than Farley. She realized, at the same moment, she had a Kleenex fluttering in her hand.

The tall actor, rain glistening on his face, rivulets sliding down his black rubber rain cape, stopped dead and waved back.

"Don't forget to come and see us," he shouted to them. "We need paid admissions, but we need pretty faces in the audience, too!"

The kids, especially the short ones who could hardly see out of the windows, began jumping up and down and waving back.

"Young ladies . . ." Akky started to say, but it was easy to see that she was as distracted as any of them.

"Hey! Sister Benedict!" the fat actor shouted. "Get out of the rain! All your starch'll melt!"

In the most beautiful movement Mary Kate had seen in her entire life, the tall actor raced forward, swooped little Sister Benedict under his cape, and carried her off to the kitchen doors.

"Aw, Larry!" the fat actor yelled, hurrying to catch up. "You *always* get the girl!"

The kids all laughed and then began moving away from the windows.

The show is over, Mary Kate thought, and now we're going to get the lecture about how some young ladies and some nuns have no dignity and Dignity Is a Virtue.

Just then, a priest, you could tell he was a priest by his collar but the rest of him was certainly out of uniform, climbed out of the back of the jeep station wagon.

"Father Herrick! Father Herrick!" Akky bellowed, yanking up the window. The leader of the players. There had been an article about him in her dad's *Herald Tribune* which he never read anymore.

He looked up, a little dazed. He must have been sleeping, Mary Kate guessed.

"Ah. Sister Aquinas," he said, saluting with a wide wave of his arm. "How's my favorite student?"

The kids looked at each other in amazement that Akky could ever have been anybody's anything.

"Father, you're embarrassing me in front of my girls."

"Nonsense! You should have stayed in Speech and Drama. Left the philosophizing to the graybeards. I have to run now, the rain," he gestured. "Make it your business to stop by and see me sometime today."

Akky called good-bye and slowly closed the window.

"All right, girls. In your seats, please." Not a hint of a yell.

Mary Kate sat down, transfixed. Had Akky, too, thought about being an actress? Was she so mean . . . was it like her own dad? If you couldn't have the job you really wanted, you made life hell for everybody around you?

"Father Herrick is the director of the Buskers," Akky said. "He's very brilliant. Well-known. He could have been the most famous director on Broadway today if he had ignored God's call."

She was wandering back and forth in the front of the classroom as she talked, stopping once or twice to rearrange things on her desk.

"Not only brilliant but a thrilling . . . lecturer. You have quite a treat in store for you tonight."

Mim raised her hand. Mim, who could always be counted on to keep a teacher off the track. But Akky didn't seem to see her. What was she going to say? What incredible thing was she going to reveal about herself? Mary Kate edged forward in her seat.

"Now, where was I? Oh, yes," she said softly. "Sharon? Up on your feet, please."

The class gasped as Sharon got up.

"Now, no nonsense, please. I want you to tell the class . . ."

Sharon let out a terrible howl and, almost bowling Akky over, ran out of the classroom. Akky was right after her, but she *was* fat.

Akky stuck her head back through the door.

"I'm going to Mother Adolphus' office to put Sharon on report. There will be absolute silence while I am gone.

Mother might like to be filled in on the behavior of certain people in this class who think shouting and waving out of windows is acceptable Academy behavior."

The door shut and, for a full minute, there was silence.

Then an angry voice, not even in a whisper, burst out: "If she ever *had* gone on the stage, the only part *she* could get is Moby Dick!"

Mary Kate was astonished to discover the voice was her own.

5. The Flame

"WELL, WHAT DO you guys think? I mean, I know she was really only talking to the upperclassmen when she asked for ideas for news stories and features, and that she didn't mention anything about a *series*, but I think it's such a good idea that . . . don't you have *any*thing to say?"

Mary Kate, who had been walking backward along the second floor corridor so she could face Jimmy and Mim while she told them her idea, suddenly stopped talking and stood still.

"Good heavens," Mim said, "the air raid siren has ceased."

"Mim, you know that was no air raid siren, that was the air raid warden here, the one with the armband. She's been blinking her flashlight at us for the last block."

"Was that her flashlight, James? I thought it was a big red eye in the middle of her forehead."

"I see where you and I slipped up. The blinking effect was caused by light reflecting off her constantly moving tonsils, and mouth in general."

"You guys?"

"Tonsils or flashlight?" Mim and Jimmy looked at each other speculatively. "Would you mind opening up again?" they asked her.

"For God's SAKE!"

"Listen," Jimmy said, "even if you are an air raid warden you could get into a whole lot of trouble using language like that around here. The walls have ears. And eyes. And noses and throats."

"Bad breath, too. Ever notice it?" Mim held her nose. Deadpan, deadpan, deadpan, every bit of it, and Mary Kate loved it. They were teasing her about her brand new Student Council armband (official representative: Sophomore B), and about her idea for *The Flame*, the school news sheet. No horselaughs, no slaps on the back, none of the dirty garbage humor the Freshkill kids thought was so-o-o funny.

"Will you guys please . . ." she almost said *cut it out*, which would have been fatal. "A *Flame* series on the history of the Academy — you think Sister Alma would like the idea?"

"I think she'd flip," Jimmy said.

"Oh, I don't agree," Mim said. "I think she's flipped already."

"I didn't mean the air raid warden here, Mim. I meant Sister Alma. I predict her reaction will be generally favorable and that she'll throw in a philosophical bit or two about how people like to be part of an institution with a continuing history . . ."

"I should *think* so. What she means is, even the more illiterate among the social climbers will read it to find out who they have been. Does that make any sense?" Mim arched her brows questioningly.

It did and it didn't. That didn't matter, though. What she was saying was interesting: that kids would read it, not just out of idle curiosity, but to establish *them*selves as part of the Academy's history. Even if Mim were wrong, and Jimmy,

too, because she had been saying almost the same thing, it still
didn't matter; what mattered to her was that once again the
two of them had seen something from a different viewpoint
than hers, and you could learn a lot from people who didn't
always see things the same way you did. She knew, firsthand,
that all sorts of interesting conversations between the kids
and the grownups went on in the McNaughton and Shepard
households. At first she had been ashamed and embarrassed
that the only voices you could be sure of in her own flat were
the ones coming off the TV her dad had on, night and day.
Then she had just given up worrying about what *didn't* go on
in her house, and had jumped in, feet first, to all the talk in her
friends' houses. If she ever had kids, she would talk to them,
so that if *they* got an idea for something like this *Flame* series
she wanted to do, it would not be just because they had come
across, in an Academy closet, a box of ancient *Flame* cuts, it
would be because somebody at home had talked about how
alive people were part of history, too.

"I'm going to go see Sister Alma this afternoon after
school," Mary Kate said and soft-shoed around the still sta-
tionary Jimmy and Mim.

"Do you have any small change, James?"

"Yes. Why?"

"From the quality of her dancing, I'd say the air raid warden is collecting for the March of Dimes."

⌘

That afternoon, after a calm but minute-pinching study
period spent in the Academy library looking up and writing
down, Mary Kate presented herself at Sister Alma's room,

the Senior A homeroom. It was a wonderful place, stuffed
from floor to ceiling with bookcases and with pictures of authors and of characters from books and plays and with busts
of people and with green plants. There was even a model of
the Globe Theater, and the room had a river view. Sister Alma taught English III and IV and was considered by
everybody to be the best teacher in the Academy. She was
not a bit like Ev, who was teaching them English II (world
literature) this year. Just this morning Ev had introduced
the *Iliad:*

"The *Iliud* is a long famous poem about a war in Greece a
long time ago and the language is hard, like in Shakespeare,
and I don't want any complaining, you hear me? There's always a question about the *Iliud* on the Regents and you have
to pass the Regents to get your diploma!"

If Ev had ever had to describe Fred Astaire, she probably
would have made him sound like King Tut's mummy.

Sister Alma Maria looked up from her desk, where she
was correcting papers. Sister Alma was a medium-sized nun
who looked very tall only because she was about as skinny as
Mary Kate had ever seen a human being. If it hadn't been
for her habit, you'd probably have been able to see right
through her.

"What was it you wanted to see me about, Mary Catherine?"

It took a full ten minutes for Mary Kate to tell her,
between talking and showing her the outline she had made and
even going to *The Flame* closet to drag out the dusty box of
old cuts. In the end Sister Alma said:

"All right. Go ahead and prepare the first article, no more

than five hundred words, as a sample. Give me what
you've written up in, oh, about a week's time. I'll read it,
but that's all I promise. You understand that?"

"Yes, Sister. I'll have it for you a week from today."

"Don't forget you have schoolwork to do, too."

&

That afternoon, walking down all the hills to the ferry, by
herself because it was 4:15 and the Freshkill kids were long
gone, she had everything and nothing on her mind.

This year was going to be more exciting than last year, and
last year hadn't been a bad year at all, even taking Ev
and Akky into account. She remembered what Sister Alma
had told her about not forgetting her schoolwork. Well, she
wasn't going to! If good grades in grammar school could get
you a scholarship, then A's in high school might end up in a
college scholarship where you could study to be something.
And, if she learned to write really well for *The Flame*,
and then couldn't go to college after all, she might get a job
on a *real* newspaper. What's more, Miss Jantzen had given
her the hardest speech of anyone to work on this week, Hamlet's speech to the players, and it was a real tongue twister.

"Pay attention to the meaning as well as to the sound,"
Miss Jantzen had said. "There's a lot of good advice in there
for a young actor," she had said. No question, Miss Jantzen
was taking her seriously and, if you worked very hard, you
could learn a lot about acting from her in the three years left
at the Academy. Which meant, if she couldn't get to college
or get a job on a paper, then maybe she could get a job acting
on the stage, where you didn't have to be as beautiful as a
movie star to succeed.

She was so excited by all the possibilities suddenly facing her that she felt like dancing down the hills, past the Y.W.C.A. that had been somebody's Victorian town house with all its wrought iron and its bell pull, through the acres of geraniums around the city jail, up and down the porches of the old hotel that nobody used anymore because of the swanky new Holiday Inn out on Route 17. How could anybody want to eat or sleep in a chromium place like the Holiday Inn when there was a beautiful old building around with its name HOTEL AMSTERDAM 1868 spread out across the whole second floor in huge gilt letters?

"When I make my fortune, hotel, I will buy you and live in you and shine up your brass and everybody will flock to teas and *dansants* and banquets and receptions in your rooms and both of us will be famous, famous, famous!"

But first I have to arrange my time, set up my work, so that when opportunity knocks, I will have both ears open!

She went straight out onto the front deck of the ferryboat. The water was very still under the bright autumn sky. When the motors started up and the boat pushed out into the river, making busy little eddies in the calm, Mary Kate felt like an explorer setting out for unknown, exciting worlds.

She was so excited she almost forgot to ask God's blessing.

∞

When she showed her dad the third of her articles on the Academy's history — this one in the February issue was continued from page one and had several cuts from the olden days along with it — he said to her, "Mike seen any of these? I told you to show 'em to him."

"Sister Alma mails a copy directly to him."

"Well, I haven't heard nothing about 'em from Mike. No indi-cation from him whatso-ever."

That's probably because Rafferty can't read, Mary Kate thought viciously. And you probably can't read anymore, either, you're so busy doing your Pat and Mike imitation with your eyes glued to this damned TV set.

"Why . . ."

But he was busy working on the fine tuning so that the old movie would come in clear as well as loud.

Why can't *you* be my father, talk to me the way Jimmy's and Mim's fathers talk to them, instead of dumping me off on some stranger you're trying to impress. Even though Dr. Mc-Naughton's hardly ever home, he really, really pays attention to Jimmy and Alex, dear Alex, when he's home.

This year, Rafferty had even tried to tell her what courses to take, as if he were her father: "Do they give classical Greek, Mary Catherine? It makes a nice showing on your transcript when you're trying out for college. Only the bright-est lads were allowed to take classical Greek when I was a seminarian at Dunwoodie." "No, Father," she had said, laugh-ing on the inside, looking as serious as a tombstone on the out-side. And all her dad ever said to her, her *dad, not* her *mam,* was things like, "Comb your hair, for Christ's sake, you look like the Wild Man of Borneo," or "Stand up straight, you look like hell," or "Don't you ever press your clothes? You look like the back room of a Chink laundry!" as if he *were* her mam. And her mam, overconscientious, therefore worked off her feet as town clerk, hardly had anything at all to say except, "Why isn't supper ready?" Sometimes she didn't feel like a daughter at all. Sometimes she felt lonely as a stranger in the flat.

The only thing about her dad that hadn't changed was the confidential mail part of him. All those envelopes and bags were as complicated as a Solemn High Mass — well, at least he was still writing up his memoirs. It didn't seem to improve his disposition and he never talked to her about them, but sooner or later, for sure, he was going to say to her: "I want you to take all of those brown envelopes out of the safety box at the bank, Mary Catherine, because a fellow from Columbia University is coming up soon to turn them into a book for me so everybody'll get the real picture of what Reuther and the rest of us did. No fairy tales, no 'liberal' bushwa, just the straight stuff, the real thing."

When *that* happened, he would stop twiddling with this stupid TV the Rosary Society had bought Father Rafferty for his name day, even though he had already been given one by Freshkill Appliances, and his eyes would get snapping black with ideas again and he would say to her . . .

"WELL! What're you waiting for? Go right on over to the rectory with this thing, be sure he reads it."

"Now? I have to get supper started."

"NOW!"

How had it ever come to be that her dad made her feel like yesterday's newspaper?

⊗

She had to wait in Father Rafferty's office with its spooky picture of Pope Pius XII looking like a glow-in-the-dark skeleton. Mrs. Grady, the crippled housekeeper, had told her Himself is bazy with one of tha Pillars in tha front parlor.

He came in rubbing his hands together as if he had just pulled off a very shrewd deal.

"Mary Catherine? Ah, Mary Catherine. You've come upon me at a very joyous moment. And — " he debated with himself — "you might as well be the first to know."

He grinned at her that horrible grin that had scared the hell out of her in Holy Redeemer. She didn't bat an eyelash.

"That was Mrs. Sullivan I was just talking to in there." He pointed in the direction of the parlor. "You know, the widow of the lumberyard Sullivan so, therefore, a widow of substance. Well! Well!" He struck at his desk with his extended fingers. "Mrs. Sullivan is going to make come true a dream this parish has had for a long time. Can you guess? Can you guess?" But he didn't give her time to guess. "Mrs. Sullivan is going to pay for the machinery that will ring the Angelus automatically. Six A.M.! Noon! Six P.M.! No more relying on unreliable sextons and altar boys! All it took was the promise of a plaque with her husband's name on it placed prominently in the vestibule and, a masterstroke if I do say so myself, the name of her first son as well, you recall, ach! you're too young perhaps, the boy killed at Iwo Jima, I suggested *that*. The bells will ring out three times a day, morning, noon, and night, calling the faithful to prayer and — " his head dipped solemnly — "reminding all others of the emptiness of their lives outside the One True Faith."

Mary Kate wondered if anybody had bothered to ask the residents of Sycamore Street, Catholics as well as Protestants, about those bells ringing at six in the morning.

"Congratulations, Father."

"And what can I do for you, my dear? What little thing? You need funds for tennis shoes or extra books, just name it."

She-really-did-hate-Father-Rafferty.

"My dad wanted to be sure you saw this," she said, laying the copy of *The Flame* on his desk.

"Ah, nice quality of paper, this," he said, taking it up. "I like this shiny stock."

"There, on page one. It's one of a series of articles I'm doing on the history of the Academy." She might as well say all of it; that was what her dad wanted. "I'm the only sophomore with a by-line on the paper; usually by-lines are reserved for juniors and seniors."

"Very good, very good," he said, still glowing with his triumph over Mrs. Sullivan. He settled down, though, as he began to read the article. When he was done, he turned to her, his eyes very serious.

"Mary Catherine, I can hardly believe it, but do you know what has happened?" Again he didn't give her time to answer. "Twice in one afternoon Almighty God has seen fit to answer my humble prayers. First, with Mrs. Sullivan. Now, with . . . *you.*"

He sat back in his chair, letting his eyes go wide, pressing his fingers together in a church steeple.

"You," he said, very quietly, "are going to edit the church bulletin for me. You are capable of writing those little items of interest about the Holy Name and the Children of Mary and the CYO that I would wish to have in the bulletin to liven up the schedule of Masses and confessions and novenas. I'm a speaker, not a writer, so I'm not up to doing that sort of thing myself —" he shook his head sadly at his deficiency — "and Mrs. Alongi, kind as she is, is really only a typist. You can't, by any chance," he said suddenly, "cut a stencil? On a typewriter?"

"No, Father. I can't even type."

"Too bad. Too bad." He was nodding again. "But there are ways," he said. "There are ways."

๛

Her father hollered so she took the six typing lessons from Mrs. Alongi on the big rectory typewriter. As soon as Mary Kate knew where she was at on the keyboard, Mrs. Alongi swiftly resigned. Her father hollered about the noise when she practiced for an hour each day at home on the spare portable Rafferty had dug up somewhere. When she offered to give up typing altogether, he hollered at her even more for being a spite-ful child.

It didn't take any time at all to do the bulletin, even the part of cutting the stencil on the rectory typewrier. And Father Rafferty told her to keep the portable for her school-work, it would be a help. And it was.

What none of them knew was that she felt free of them all with those typewriter keys under her fingers. Maybe, was it possible? Maybe she could become an actress who wrote her own plays!

6. The Junior-Senior Prom

THERE WAS NO WAY of getting out of the Junior-Senior
Prom, even though she had spent most of the year trying to
figure out just how to do that. It didn't matter that she
couldn't afford a gown and all the trappings. It didn't even
matter that she had no one to ask. Neither did a lot of the
boarders, so, a week or two before any Academy prom, the
nuns counted noses and ordered that many boys, plus a few
extra, from Cardinal O'Halloran Military Academy up near
Poughkeepsie.

It didn't even matter that she didn't want to go. The junior
class was the sponsoring class; dead or alive, all juniors
attended.

But even if there *were* a way for her to get out of this dumb,
expensive dance, she was especially obliged to go because
Jimmy and Mim were the junior co-chairmen. They were
only friends, yet she felt as if they were her sisters, the "babbies" that had never come. In fact, she felt far more at home,
at ease, here in Jimmy's house, than she did at home. It was a
fact that worried her because it made her feel disloyal to her
father who was sick and to her mam who was overworked and
always tired. But it was a fact. Here at the McNaughtons',
all of them, Mrs. McNaughton, Dr. McNaughton if he was

home, Jimmy and her friends, Alex and his friends, anybody else who happened to have dropped in, would sometimes, most of the time, sit around the dinner table talking for hours after the meal had finished. There was no other time like it in Mary Kate's life. Maybe in the whole world.

This weekend, though, things would probably be different, for at least a couple of unavoidable reasons.

The three of them were together for this weekend at Jimmy's to make tentative plans for the prom (before committees met), but Jimmy was in no condition for prom logistics. Her boy friend, Justin Moriarity, a senior at Saint Bren's, had just broken off with her via a long letter filled with poetry and with quotations from *The Seven Storey Mountain*. He had decided to enter a monastery, instead of Notre Dame, in the fall.

Jimmy hadn't cried, at least in public. She had repaired to the upright piano in the McNaughton attic. The piano had been up there in the little room when the McNaughtons bought the pre-Revolutionary farmhouse. Nobody could guess how it had gotten there: the windows were too small, the stairway too narrow for it to have been lifted in either way. More than once Mrs. McNaughton, even though her name was Carlotta, had said she was glad it was up there because, if it had been downstairs for all to hear, between Jimmy in love and playing all the slushier Chopin and Tchaikovsky, and Alex, with his bad left hand, trying to imitate Thelonius Monk, she would have gone just plain raving nuts.

Mary Kate, deserting her role as unofficial prom adviser, was snugged away on the attic staircase looking at a book about Greece that Dr. McNaughton had brought back from

one of his more dangerous trips. It was up to Mim to distract
Jimmy from launching into, for the millionth time, the Chopin
etude that had been turned into a popular song called "No
Other Love." *Their* song. Justin would never have settled for
Rodgers and Hart or Cole Porter or even, for God's sake, the
Gershwins. Sometimes Mary Kate wondered about Justin.

"Oh, cripes! Not again!" Mim complained.

"I can't help it, Mim," Jimmy said. "If Jus were just interested in another girl, but my competition is *God*. I mean,
how would you like it if one day Zach left you for . . ."

There was an embarrassed silence, all of them thinking the
same thought at the same time. Zach was a yearling at West
Point. The only competition Mim had to worry about was
the war in Korea. He might not be able to get out of the
Point for an evening to take her to the prom but there, at
least, he was safe. Whether you wanted to admit it or not,
Mary Kate thought, you were old enough, practically, to be
a widow.

"Oh, crap!" Jimmy said. "I'm sorry, Mim. I'm sorry.
You know, if Jus weren't going into the service of the
Lord — " Jimmy tipped an imaginary hat to Heaven — "I'd
kill him."

Mary Kate shouted up the stairs to break the tension.

"Don't give her a drop of sympathy, Mim. If she can't nab
one of Justin's friends who walks upright, if there *is* one, she
can always nab one of Alex's friends."

"She does not speak with fork-ed tongue, you melancholic!"
Mim accused, and then forced Jimmy into a long conversation
about possible prom decorations. Dr. McNaughton was in
India for a long spell and had already sent home a trunkful

of exotics. That was why the theme "Pale hands, Shalimar, I have loved thee," or whatever it was, was under consideration.

Mary Kate closed the Greek book and thought, full of misery, about the prom. She had nobody to blame but herself. What she *should* have done was what she had *wanted* to do: ask Alex. Alex of the long and serious and delightful conversations.

But she had been afraid to.

She *had* made plans — first, feel out Jimmy about how Alex might respond to an invitation to a dance at that rotten Catholic girls' place, the Academy. She had never even got *that* far because . . . because she was afraid.

It was true that she and Jimmy were the closest of friends, that even if she had wanted to, Jimmy would never have burst out laughing at the thought of Mary Kate going to the prom with Alex, that Jimmy might even have tried to fix the two of them up on her own with no prompting . . .

The thing was.

The thing was that Mary Kate didn't know how to talk to Jimmy, who was not nervous or self-conscious around boys, about a boy, not even about Jimmy's own twin brother. It was like the other things: Jimmy and Mim already kicking around what they might major in in college, mentioning subjects she had never even *heard* of, and colleges she didn't even know *existed;* or Jimmy and Mim talking about Jacques Maritain, whom both their dads admired, or about editorials on civil liberties in the *New York Times* and she didn't even know what civil liberties were! They seemed so sure of themselves. She knew it came from the way they had been brought up . . .

The moment at the Waldorf-Astoria flashed before her eyes before she could stop it. Then she just gave in to it, that awful lesson of lessons . . .

She and Mim had been sent, last month, to the International Youth Forum at the Waldorf by the Academy (at great expense, young ladies, so make the most of it). They had split up to go to different sessions so that between the two of them they would hear most of the speakers, and be able to make a good report to the nuns. A session entitled *Culture: Tumbler of Walls* turned out to be as interesting as some of the best conversations she had heard at the McNaughtons'. The other kids in the audience were excited, too, and, even after the panel had left, some of the kids stayed behind, at the back of the meeting room, discussing the sorts of plays and movies America should be sending abroad. It was a mixed group, boys and girls, high school and college kids, and Mary Kate was standing next to two boys whose lapel tags said CCNY. One of them was getting fidgety to leave, but the other one had the floor: ". . . so if America really wants to make friends abroad, she oughta start getting honest about it and export movies that realistically show things like what it's like to be a Porto Rican in New York or a colored guy down South. Instead of all those crappy Technicolor musicals."

"But there *is* a place for . . ." Mary Kate interrupted and was almost instantly interrupted herself, but not by words. Words would have been kinder. The kid who had been talking looked briefly at her face, then his eyes dropped to her name tag. "Come on, Harry," he said to his friend, "we gotta go." The two of them leaving broke up the group and Mary Kate found herself alone in the meeting room with her unfinished thought and an identity tag that said on it Academy of Mount Saint Michael-on-the-Hudson. That was what had sent Harry's friend out of the door. What did some dumb convent school kid know?

Then, she had been mad. Now she wasn't sure. She *hadn't* been brought up in the way Jimmy and Mim had, although, if her dad had stayed well, maybe she would have. So, all these three years she had been thinking of the Academy as a place of constant challenge that would wake up in her all the things Freshkill had not. That when she was finished with the Academy, she would have caught up with kids like Jimmy and Mim. When Harry's friend had looked at her name tag, though, he had seen nothing more than girls in uniform and nuns and chapels and clouds of incense. And a party line that had to be toed. It was a harsh description, but one that had some truth in it. The Academy was a very small corner of the world that sometimes appeared not to belong to *this* world at all. For instance, when they had come to the Protestant Reformation in European History last month, Sister Edwina had spent fifteen minutes on it, fourteen of which involved criticizing the Jebbie who had written the history text as being far too Intellectual and generous to a whole lot of ignorant knownothings who had attacked the Church in the first place only because they were sunk in sins of the flesh and worse. She had gone on to say, wimple aquiver, that she had never wanted to use this text in the first place because the Jesuits were a worldly lot that delighted in sowing the seeds of confusion. Yet Mary Kate knew that the Catholic colleges considered absolutely first-rate were those run by the Jebbies.

She had begged God to let her get into the Academy. And

it had taken only a glance from Harry's friend to bring her
house of cards down around her head, to make her admit that
teachers like Ev and Akky and Edwina were figures of honor
at the Academy, that intramural sports and Chorister concerts
and Social Graces lessons were almost as highly regarded as
classes given by an exciting teacher like Sister Alma.

She had begged God, and He had given her what she wanted,
and now she was dissatisfied with it and wanted something
different and better. God must have tired of her greedy
prayers long ago. Maybe that was why what had happened
with Alex had happened.

Last Monday morning, Jimmy had roared into the dayhops'
cloakroom and she had hung up her coat as if she wanted to
cut its head off.

"My God, Jimmy, what's the matter? You look like a one-
man thunderstorm."

"Oh, nothing. Nothing at all, if you can call Greasy Joan
nothing!"

Greasy Joan was the adenoidal girl who lived up the road
from the McNaughtons. Her family kept horses and she was
going to be a vet even if it did take years and years. She had
just started college at Cornell last fall.

"What's with Joan?"

"Not a thing, if you can call Alex giving that creep his
Abba Dabba pin this weekend just nothing!"

"You're *kidding*." Abba Dabba was the fake fraternity
Alex and his friends had made up to ridicule the oh-so-serious
frats at W.F.A. You didn't give away your Abba Dabba pin
lightly.

"She *knows* how much he likes to ride and she and her

damned horse absolutely haunted our place this weekend. The creep."

"He's not a baby, Jimmy. He knows what he's doing."

"She's *two* years older than he is. Anyway, I thought he was going to give *you* his pin sooner or later, the way you two are always talking, oblivious to the en*tire* world."

All thoughts and words went out of Mary Kate for a terrifying second.

"Well, I haven't got a palomino," she said finally, trying to laugh.

"He's got his damned palomino and a colossal jackass to go along with it, payment *demanded!*" Jimmy's voice strangled and grew hoarse with anger.

"I have to go," Mary Kate had said and had run out of the cloakroom. When they had made something with sulfur in first period, chemistry, it had seemed so appropriate that Mary Kate had allowed her eyes to water noticeably.

But she had not allowed her eyes to water last night at dinner. Alex had sat at the table with them without his usual troop of friends. A reserved hi, another this morning at breakfast had been the entire extent of his conversation with her. The unavoidable thought of Greasy Joan had hung around the table like Banquo's ghost.

She missed talking to him. If he could get his grades in English and history up, he was planning to be a foreign correspondent and, by God, he was sure he had just the plan for cracking the secrets of the Kremlin; she knew it by heart. If, during one of his monologues, she broke in to talk about how she, too, might get a job on a paper or on the stage or about how she might write the definitive biography of George

Gershwin, he had never minded. He would stop talking and listen to her, and sometimes, if they were up in the attic, he would play one Gershwin song after another for her and make her sing the lyrics because she knew so many of them by heart. At first she had been afraid to sing because she knew what Sis thought of her voice, but then she had remembered that Fred Astaire and Gene Kelly weren't exactly professional singers, either, but that they had done all right by Ira Gershwin's lyrics and that glorious music. And sometimes, Alex had lifted his hands from the keyboard and applauded.

When she and Alex were talking or doing the songs together, sometimes she had wanted to stop and reach over and kiss him. Not a big messy kiss like in the movies, but not a dry little peck on the lips, either. A good straightforward kiss that could tell him better than words how much she liked him and how much she wanted him to succeed with his dreams. Only she never had, because doing that would be going against the rules.

She opened the book with its funny alphabet to a picture of the Parthenon.

A ruin, a ruin, she thought, just as the strains of "None but the Lonely Heart" penetrated her consciousness. Didn't Justin like *anything* but adaptations from the classics?

"Hey, Mim," she called out again, in the loudest voice she could manage, "who *are* you going with?"

"Who else? One of the paper tigers from O'Halloran."

Jimmy stopped playing abruptly. "You're kidding. You *know* the priests always send down the creepy ones just to be on the safe side."

"Jimmy. What difference does it make if it's not Zach? All

that's required is that I appear in a gown, *modest*, on the arm of something male. I'd go with my father if he could keep a straight face."

"I feel the same way myself," Mary Kate said from the stairs, a little more urgently than she meant to. "If I can't have Laurence Olivier in his Hamlet suit, just order me a *tall* paper tiger, Mother Adolphus."

Jimmy and Mim appeared at the top of the stairs.

"Come *on*, there must be some guy from Freshkill you can ask," Jimmy said. "Some compatriot from the ferryboat."

"The captain is married and eighty-two and the first mate spits his chaw. I did express some interest in Red Snyder," Mary Kate said, naming the Saint Bren's senior she did not know but had once seen carrying a copy of *Look Homeward, Angel* on the ferry, "but Bobbie Covetti rushed off and wagged her bosoms at him and that was the end of Red, the Intellectual. Anyway, why are you picking on *me?* You know yourself, Jimmy, you're going to end up with one of the toy soldiers, if worse comes to worst."

"Like hell! Justin may have me down but he hasn't got me out. Well, well," she said, "it seems to me that what we have here is a fraught situation. Definitely fraught. But, damn it, I'm going to see to it that we're all fixed up with respectable dates. And we'll have a party here, after the prom, with dimmed lights and everything and Justin can just go to hell as well as to the seminary!"

☙

Three weeks before the prom, Justin the Pious decided he would take his scholarship to Notre Dame, after all. There was a celebration dinner at the McNaughtons' and Jus brought along a short, shy blond boy from his class at Bren's.

"Here you are, Kev, the girl of your dreams. See how prettily she blushes. Mary Kate Mulligan, Kevin Little. He's tenor in the All-Irish Quartet, Mary Kate. Don't paralyze his vocal chords with your sharp wit."

Rubbing his hands together gleefully, Jus, the lead baritone, withdrew to let the chemistry he had arranged take.

Mary Kate was relieved to see Kev blushing, too. They were exactly the same height, therefore eye to eye.

"Uh," Mary Kate said nervously when Kevin didn't speak, "Jus . . . uh . . . I don't really think he means to sound like somebody's uncle in Dickens . . . I mean . . . well, I guess *you* probably know him better than I do . . . uh . . . well . . . hello?"

To her very great relief, he smiled, then said rather stiffly, "Hello, I'm pleased to meet you."

She doubted it but she could hardly give in to her impulse to run out of the McNaughtons' into the night. Without question, this boy knew he was being set up as her prom date; Jus had probably muscled him into coming; it was just too awful but she didn't have any right to make it worse.

"You must be awfully good to sing in the All-Irish."

"Oh, I don't know about that."

"There's a lot of competition . . ."

"Oh, well, I suppose so."

"It must be a lot of fun. Singing. All those concerts. You get your picture in the paper all the time."

"Yeah, it takes a lot of work, too, though. I've seen your picture in *The Flame*."

"And you still came?" She was mock-astonished.

He looked at her with alarm. Fortunately, Mrs. Mc-Naughton called them in to dinner at just that moment. She and Kev were seated side by side and, after a while, they stopped being scared of each other. Before dessert, he asked her for a date. Saturday night at the movies where he was an usher week-nights.

At the end of the date, she asked him to the prom. They both seemed relieved.

❦

Alex did go to the prom, after all. With Mim, who was Attached, so Greasy Joan, from her command post in Ithaca, didn't mind. Mary Kate had one dance with him. He held her so far away from him she felt sure he was trying to decide whether her problem was bad breath, leprosy, or just a short leg.

At the party at Jimmy's afterward, Kev kept his arm around her as the fire in the fireplace and the gardenias he had given her slowly died. He seemed to mean it, but she could not help feeling he was doing it because it was expected of him.

Kev and Jus were the last boys to leave the party. In the driveway, Jimmy and Jus disappeared under the trees, leaving the shadows around Jus's car free for Kev and Mary Kate.

"I had a swell time, Mary Kate. Thanks for asking me." He took her hand.

"It was very nice of you to come, Kev. And I had a good time at the movies, too. Imagine, getting in free!"

He took her other hand so they were face to face in the

moonlight. It was all very awkward and unromantic, still she was frightened.

"And it was a good picture, too. I really enjoyed . . ."

But he was already sliding his arms around her, his face coming toward her face, their exactly level lips meeting.

Sweet sixteen and finally kissed, she thought as their noses bumped and he pressed her up against Jus's car. His mouth was gentle and undemanding but the equally impersonal pressure of his body against hers was unnerving to her. Trying to keep her head, she became totally aware of the sweat on his upper lip and of the sweat on her palms against the wool of his suit jacket. She could smell her dead flowers and his Listerine. Maybe it would have been different with Alex. Maybe not. She didn't know anything about anything.

"Aha! Aha!" Justin trumpeted as he and Jimmy reappeared. "Desire under the swamp maples, I see."

"I'll call you," Kev whispered.

"No!" Mary Kate whispered back. "I mean my father's sick. The phone might disturb him."

"Okay . . . I'll give Jus a note for you. He can give it to Jimmy, okay?"

"What are you two little lovebirds twittering about?"

"Okay, Kev. And thanks again."

Jus's chuckle was startlingly like Father Rafferty's.

☙❧

Always, when they had dates, they had them in Westburgh. She had to admit there was practically no place to go in Freshkill, especially home. They went to record hops at Bren's or to the movie theater where Kev worked Sunday through

Thursday nights. Friday nights and all day Saturday, Kev sold shoes at Miles. He was saving up for college. If the draft didn't get him, he wanted to be an electrical engineer. He might be poor, and shy to the point of vanishing entirely from sight, but he knew what he wanted to do with his life and she didn't. So she began by respecting him, then grew to like him, successfully stopping herself from making comparisons between him and Alex.

A question arose about their dates, about his getting her home after their dates in Westburgh. Kev's family didn't have a car he could use, which made late night transportation between Westburgh and Freshkill a problem.

"Well," Mary Kate said, trying not to feel pushed into a corner, "I don't see *why* you have to come over the river with me. After eleven, the ferries run only once an hour and the Freshkill buses when they feel like it — it would take you *centuries* to see me all the way home, and then get back to Westburgh. And I probably couldn't even ask you in for a cup of coffee because of . . . my father's illness." This Kev understood only too well. His mother was in some kind of hospital, his father was a traveling salesman, and all the kids had been farmed out to relatives. Kev lived with his old grand-mother.

Still, when they were kissing good-night in the shadow of the Westburgh ferry-house, Mary Kate's mind was often occupied with the thought that if she missed the midnight ferry, she would have to take the one o'clock one and that was the one that was supposed to be full of drunks. And with one other thought: if time had not had to press on her so heavily, maybe she would have been excited, that was the

word Bobbie Covetti used, *excited,* by Kev's kisses. The way
things were, he meant his kisses but she only returned them.
Maybe she should be grateful that having a steady date was
not putting her in moral jeopardy, which was how the priest
in retreat had described some kinds of feelings between boys
and girls. But grateful was a word she associated with Father
Rafferty. Not a word, or a feeling, she liked.

❧

"I want you to be my girl, Mary Kate."
They were walking, almost running, down the hills to the
ferry in the dark, empty streets. He kept his voice low, even
though he could have shouted his request and no one would
have heard.
"*Me,* Kev?" she said, as if she were in the company of sixteen other girls from whom he might have chosen.
"*You,* who else!" He laughed and turned her around in
front of Cohen's Bootery, right under a streetlight, to give her
a lingering kiss. And still she felt nothing. Something must
have gone wrong with her feelings between Ronnie Ricatelli
and now. She had hoped to grow up; she must have just
withered on the vine. Probably she *would* end up an old maid
like Miss Verplanck. But, except for her painful arthritis,
there was nothing really wrong with Miss Verplanck that
she could see.
"Would you mind," she said, breaking away from their
second or third kiss there in the bright, deserted spot, "if I
think it over? My mind is all gummed up from cramming for
midterms."

"That's what I love about you, Mary Kate. You're so down to earth, not all silly and giggly. You take as long as you want to think it over."

⚜

"Kevin Little has asked me to go steady," she told her mam one night after her dad had gone to sleep. She wanted some womanly advice. After all, half the world had been in love with her mam when *she* was sixteen.

oh oh oh the in-visible man Kevin Little

"Do you want me to bring him home before I make up my mind?" Mary Kate asked sharply.

no need for that no need for that you're a sen-sible child only don't get preg-nant

Mary Kate bit her lip and said, "I won't, don't worry. He's not that kind of boy."

Pregnant. She probably knew more about it than either her mam or her dad, who had never seen fit to discuss the subject with her.

⚜

"I'd like to be your girl, Kev," she said (instead of "I'd like to be *some*body's *some*thing," which was closer to the truth), and he said, "Great!" and kissed her, bending her backward, almost off her feet.

He did not, however, offer her his class ring, which he had just gotten. She wouldn't even have thought of wanting it, except Bobbie had appeared, the week before, with Red's Bren's ring, banded with yards and yards of adhesive tape to show how infinitely dainty her finger was contrasted with his.

The pressure on, five other Freshkill juniors had shortly turned up with *their* Bren's rings. She understood why Kev didn't want to give up his ring: it had cost him so many hours of slave labor in the movies and at the shoe store that he was reluctant to let go of it, even to his girl. She understood that, clear as a bell, but she minded. She minded having her feelings hurt when she was trying so hard not to hurt his feelings. When she spoke severely to herself, she said, Why do you want his ring when you don't love him? Because, because, was her only answer. She really began to *despise* herself.

7. Joan-of-Arc-Saint-of-God

SHE WAS EXCITED beyond her wildest dreams when Miss Jantzen chose her as the single actress to represent the junior class in the final presentation of the year, the drama coach's highly publicized "Evening of Drama and Dahnce," a Friday evening.

Her mam couldn't come for the usual reasons and Rafferty was being kept in the dark about the whole thing in case he might decide to chauffeur the dead-tired mother of an accomplished parish graduate over the river to the actual scene of . . . And Kev was working tonight, fitting baby-doll pumps on the feet of ladies who had no other time but Friday nights for trying on shoes . . .

She would just have to be Joan of Arc on her own with nary a mother or a father or a sister or a brother or an aunt or an uncle or a boy friend . . .

Putting on her costume in the tiny dressing room that was ordinarily the Photography Club's darkroom, she worked hard to maintain the feeling of loss and abandonment that had come over her when she realized not even Kev would be here tonight to see her do, splendidly, Joan.

She couldn't, though, struggling with her gold tights. All along she had been expecting to do the monologue in a sort of gunny-sack costume, shapeless and gritty and brown, when, instead . . .

"Oh, Lord," Miss Jantzen had actually screeched this afternoon, "what *have* you done! Your lovely pageboy! Oh, the effect will be ruined, ruined!"

"This is how Joan of Arc wore her hair. I'm sure. I've seen pictures," Mary Kate said, ruffling her hair with her fingers to show the drama coach how efficiently Mr. Policelli had shingled it the afternoon before.

"But this, *this* is your costume," Miss Jantzen wailed, yanking it off the rack. A glistening white tunic, filigreed with gold braid, gold tights to match. It looked like the suit Columbus had discovered America in: "Hold it, guys, while I go below decks and change into my official Discovering-India outfit."

She bit her tongue to keep from laughing. There was even a hat, more shining white, with a sweeping gold plume.

"What counts," she admonished Miss Jantzen, "is how I essay the part, not how my hair is cut."

"Absolutely correct," the drama coach had said and had subsided.

Mary Kate looked at herself in the full-length mirror that had been dragged into the darkroom especially for her, and she laughed and laughed. The costume was wearing *her!* Her head, with practically no hair, seemed to vanish from sight. She pulled her shoulders back, stood with her spine straight. All was solved. But she felt giddy, very giddy.

The hat, in its nest of tissue in the Brooks' box, caught her eye.

"No hat," Miss Jantzen had decided. "You'll have enough to do managing your sword."

Mary Kate, neatly drawing her sword in the narrow room, lunged at her reflection.

"Have at you *now!*" she scowled, glaring at herself. "Have

at the whole damn bunch of you for not being here when I'm going to be good. I *know* it, I'm going to be good!"

In the distance she heard the record of Mendelssohn's *A Midsummer Night's Dream* music starting up. Millions and millions of freshmen and sophomores, dressed up in gauze and wings, were even now going into their incredible dance, trying not to step on each other on the tiny stage.

Mary Kate's eyes fell on the hat again. The seniors were busy in the regular dressing room getting ready for *Everyman*, probably painting their faces white and Looking Serious. She was alone, nobody would interrupt her.

She put on the hat.

It came down over her ears and eyes and she mimed a blind clown, jabbing her arms out in front of her, staggering around in circles. She could feel the storm of anger and nerves inside her beginning to melt away. She put the hat on sideways, causing the feather to rise up, languidly, from the back of her head. She crossed her arms over her chest.

"Me big chief Joan of Arcum . . ."

The hat down over one eye: "Darlings, zis is zee way zings are — " hand on hip, Corinne Calvet — "I am hearing voices and zings and they are telling me zat, wiz my leadairship, you boys of Notre Dame can cream . . . *crème* . . . Holy Cross zis day!"

She was getting too silly so she assumed a serious expression, put her hat on squarely, stood at attention, drew out her sword and, with the hat sliding slowly, majestically back down over her eyes, she did what she should have done all along.

"In the name of King Ferdinand and Queen Isabella of Spain, I claim . . ."

Someone was coming along the passageway like gangbusters. Mary Kate was calmly sheathing her sword when Janine, the senior who was stage manager, burst in.

"Listen, you ready? You got everything you need? Oh, you look great! It's almost time . . ." She began tugging at the bottom of Mary Kate's tunic to get it even all the way around, causing Mary Kate's teeth to bounce together painfully. From the stage they could hear the last part of the Mendelssohn, the wedding march, and the audience clapping as the bride and groom, Robin Hood and a milkmaid, appeared among all the fairies.

"Janine, Ja*nine!* You're killing me, this thing weighs a ton! Every time you yank it . . ."

"Oh, I'm sorry! I'm just a wreck of nerves trying to get everything straight. You must be a wreck of nerves, too. I'd die if I had to go on alone with nobody to feed me my lines. You must be a wreck of nerves!"

God, Mary Kate thought, I *am* a wreck of nerves. Her vision blurred, a rushing sound started in her ears, and the floor took on a life of its own.

"I'm all right," she squeezed out of her throat.

"Come on come on come on." Janine was propelling her toward Miss Jantzen in the wings for the final once-over. The fairies and the wedding party, all crushed up against each other, were taking their bows. A voice in the audience, it sounded like *Justin,* was yelling, "Bravo! Bravo!"

And suddenly it was quiet and dark, except for the spot picking her out on the stage.

"Look not upon me as a simple maid . . ."

The first words came out on their own. Her voice was

shaking and it sounded faint to her so she projected a little more but left the shaking in. The shaking was okay; it fit Joan trying to rally troops for the first time.

God! What *didn't* belong was this silly costume!

She was glad she had worked so hard on the speech, the words continued to flow out of her, because she realized somehow she had to incorporate this damned shining Holy Grail outfit into her Joan-the-Raggedy interpretation. Next time she did a part she would make damn sure she knew exactly what her costume was going to be like. In the meantime, she had to watch every gesture, every movement, keep the voice going, try to convince the audience she was only on her way to Orléans, not already there and dressed to the nines for Charles's coronation.

"It goes sore with you, defeat after defeat, but I tell you God has taken pity on France. His saints have spoken to me . . ."

She willed herself to see the grubby exhausted soldiers she was addressing, willed herself to smell the stink of men who had been living out-of-doors for a long time. She talked to them, looked into their faces, made them forget, ignore her absurd clothing. She argued, coaxed, accused, appealed; she *would* be taken seriously.

"We shall, we *shall*, with God's help, raise the siege at Orléans!"

She dropped down on one knee and, with both hands, held her sword out in front of her, using it as a cross.

"Blessed be the Lord, for he has heard the voice of my pleading, the Lord, my strength and my shield! Noble Father in Heaven, we soldiers of France are Yours!" Serious, serious words, full of valor and strength.

She tossed her sword a little way up into the air, leaped to her feet, caught the sword by its handle, swept her arms up into a big V. A shout, shattering the solemnity:

"ORLÉANS SHALL BE OURS!"

She stood there, arms still raised, not moving, not acknowledging the thunder of applause that intruded upon her, while sweat poured down the back of her neck and down her sides under the tunic.

"Bravo, bravo, bravo, bravo!" until finally the curtains closed and she was overrun by the *Everyman* spooks in their dark robes. She was trembling so she could hardly breathe. She didn't want to be congratulated; she wanted to stay who she was and where she had been: Joan of Arc alive and breathing in the fifteenth century.

As soon as she was clear of everybody, still in costume she dashed up the backstairs to the chapel. It wasn't that she wanted to pray; it wasn't even that she wanted to thank God for helping her with the part. If she could just sit there in the dim chapel with Someone who might understand, might help, perhaps she could figure out why the applause, the people slapping her on the back, all the things she had been looking forward to . . . didn't matter. Even annoyed her.

After a while, her thoughts slowed down.

For a few minutes downstairs on the stage, she had risen right out of her own skin, had forgotten everybody, everything. *Herself*, even!

She was changed; in some way she was different now from before, different even from the Mary Kate Mulligan who had stepped out onto the stage twenty minutes ago.

She didn't believe in voices or visions. But, looking at the big altar far away in the gloom, she wished Jesus on his cross

would say something to her, straight out, that would tell her
how her life was going to go, tell her how she was going to
survive going back to the ordinary routine of home and school.

He's right, she told the silent God, Thomas Wolfe is right.
You can't go home again.

✄

Kev was there, waiting for her with Jimmy and Justin.
His face was shining with astonishment and with Love.

No, no, Kev, she begged silently. Don't pick now to finally fall in love with me. I can't stay. I'm not going to stay
around here and get married and be your wife.

I just know it, Kev, there are different things I'm meant to
do with my life. It's like a religious vocation, there's nothing
I can do about it. I've got to get out of this valley, away from
all of you, away to somewhere where I can start being myself,
be with other people who have special . . . lives.

"A simply splendiferous spectacle, saintly star," Justin
bawled in her ear. Oh, he was nothing but a . . . stuffed
shirt!

She smiled at Kev and took his hand.

"I'm so glad you could come."

8. Akky

IT WAS ONE of the times her dad was on the verge of being dangerously ill, close enough to it that Dr. Kennedy didn't want him left alone in the flat. Mary Kate stayed home two days to sit with him. Her mam would have done it, except it was near the end of the tax quarter and the clerk's office was swamped with work. Her mother had sent a note to school carefully explaining Mary Kate's absence so close to final exams, and Mary Kate had handed the note, wordlessly, to Akky, who was the Junior B homeroom teacher.

The afternoon of the day she returned to school, there was the regular Thursday 1 P.M. Assembly. The kid who had to lay out the materials for the Oils class, which was held right after Assembly, was allowed to slip out of the auditorium early. Mary Kate went through the swing doors of the auditorium soundlessly and was halfway up the stairs on her way to the art room when she felt Akky's claw on her arm.

"Yes, Sister?"

"You've been absent from school for two whole days and you haven't said a word about it to me."

"It was all in the note from my mother that I gave to you, Sister."

"That's not the same as you telling me yourself. A matter of common courtesy."

"I saw the note, Sister. It explained very clearly . . ."

"You know, Mary Catherine, there's a certain coldness about you. I'm not the only one who's remarked on it."

Mary Kate stood silent.

"Others have put it down to a certain innate shyness you are trying to overcome."

Mary Kate still didn't say anything. It was finally happening. After all this time, Akky was finally closing in for the kill.

"I put it down to a certain . . . arrogance. Pride, my dear, as you may recall from your studies in philosophy with me, is one of the Seven Deadly Sins."

Mary Kate maintained her silence, even as the nun's fingers dug into her skin. If it meant her eternal damnation, she was not going to be baited into anger or any other kind of folly by this nun, especially since there was a very good chance that Mother Adolphus might come out of the auditorium at any moment and catch Akky red-handed.

"Certain persons who are good at run-of-the-mill activities sometimes think they are gifted . . . intellectually. They preen in their pride — " Akky had never been better at her parrot imitation — "and hold all others in contempt . . ."

"My father was seriously ill, Sister Aquinas. Since we cannot afford a nurse and my mother was obliged to remain at her job, I . . ."

"You loved it, didn't you? You loved the idea of being able to come back to the Academy and say your father was dying so people would feel sorry for you, pay attention to you, see you as Joan of Arc all over again."

Over Akky's shoulder, Mary Kate could see the kids coming out of the auditorium, starting up the curving staircase.

"I've seen your type before. Willful, self-centered lightweights, unable to bow to authority . . ."

"Oh, Sister," Mary Kate cried out in a loud voice, "why are you picking on me? I can't help it my father was so sick!"

She knew exactly what she was doing. She covered her face with her hands and turned toward the wall.

"Just a minute! Who do you think you are?"

Akky's angry voice suddenly lowered to a whisper when she realized they were no longer alone.

"Wah, wah," Mary Kate howled against the wall. "The doctor thought my dad was dying, and I had to be with him. I wasn't playing hooky. It's not my fault he didn't die after all!"

Her face hidden, she pinched her nose very hard to make tears start in her eyes. She hated what she was doing but it was her chance to get Akky for once and for all. Maybe expose Akky for all time so she would never again be able to terrorize the vulnerable.

The feet were shuffling by, not a yard away, and Akky was pulling at her, trying to get her to turn around: "Stop it! Stop it! Do you hear me? You're not fooling anybody!"

"Wah! Wa-a-ah!"

"What's going on here?"

Mother Adolphus' calm voice. The shuffling feet stopped.

"Get along with your business, young ladies," and the feet resumed.

"Calm down, Mary Catherine. Dear child, you're making a spectacle of yourself."

Gentle hands touching her shoulders. She allowed herself to be turned around, allowed all to witness her streaming eyes.

"I simply asked about her father," Akky said, "and she be-

came hysterical. I've told you before she's emotionally un-
stable."

"Hush now, Mary Catherine."

Looking into her face, still holding her arm in that kind
grasp, Mother Adolphus continued: "You've been under a
very great strain, I know that, Mary Catherine, but that is no
excuse for being undignified."

"I'm sorry," Mary Kate said, real tears supplanting the fake
ones. She wished she were far away from the eyes of the girls
filing past the nuns' backs. She did care about her dad being
near death, even if he didn't care about her anymore. Sometimes, these days, he called her Maureen.

Akky's eyes went from parrot to cobra.

"I think, Mother, that Mary Catherine is not quite so sincere
as she may seem."

"I think, Sister Aquinas, that it is time we had a little talk.
Can you be in my office at five?"

"Of course, Mother."

"Mary Catherine, go and wash your face. If you like, you
may stop in chapel for a moment. Then go to your class.
You're up to that, aren't you?"

"Yes, Mother. Thank you very much, Mother."

☙

"What happened? What happened?" the kids in Oils said
to her, the second she came in.

"I think," she said, still feeling weak in the knees, "I just
think Akky's been put on report."

"What is it? What is it?" the Art nun said, startled by the
loud Hooray! "Have those Dodger people won whatever
it is they're always trying for?"

9. Rory

"WAKE UP, WAKE UP, Mary Kate!" Somebody was shaking her very hard.

Mary Kate struggled up out of her dream. But it wasn't a dream, it was Bonnie Gravini, one of the other summer waitresses at Blount House sanitarium, standing by her bed.

"You've got to get up, Mary Kate. Monsignor Rafferty's on the phone!"

"My dad!" They had taken him to the hospital day before yesterday. The long August heat wave was affecting him badly and Dr. Kennedy wanted him in an air-conditioned room under a nurse's supervision: "Nothing to worry about, ladies, nothing to worry about," he had told them.

Not bothering with robe or slippers, Mary Kate dashed out to the pay phone in the living room of the waitresses' dorm.

"Monsignor Rafferty?" she said into the phone. Bonnie had switched on a light and she could see the wall clock: 2:11.

"Mary Catherine, you're a strong girl. I don't have to mince words with you. I'm here at the hospital and your dad's sinking fast. Father Gennaro is on his way to pick you up. Can you put on some kind of outside lights there so he'll be able to find his way?"

"Yes . . . yes!"

"Hurry up, then. Get dressed. He should be there in five
or ten minutes, there's no traffic this time of night. Good-bye.
God bless you. Good-bye."

"Is it your father?" Bonnie's face was filled with concern.

"Yes." Her voice had the shakes. "Would you run down
and put on the outside lights, Bon? Father G's coming for me
right away."

"Has your father . . ."

"No, no, not yet," she cried and raced off to get dressed.

∞

Monsignor Rafferty was standing outside the door of her
father's room.

"Has my dad . . ."

"No. Go straight in. He's still conscious." Even as he
spoke, Rafferty was gravely shaking his head from side to
side.

The sight of her dad stopped her just inside the door. He
was propped up in bed, his arms like sticks over the top of the
covers. His eyes were open, not staring, but expressionless,
as if he were concentrating on something very complicated.
The harsh sound of his breathing filled the room.

He is paying attention to his breathing, she thought. He is
putting all his strength and his thoughts into his breathing.
She found herself, as if hypnotized, holding her breath so that
he might have more air to breathe. If she didn't, he might
stop living and be dead. All the times she had wished him
dead, she had never thought of him actually passing from life
to death.

Her mam was there and Dr. Kennedy and a nurse. Nobody

seemed to have noticed her arrival. Rafferty touched her elbow and nodded toward Maureen.

Her mother was sitting in a chair pushed up to the edge of the bed. She was straining forward, holding Rory's limp hand.

"Ma," Mary Kate said softly and knelt beside the chair. Maureen slipped an arm around her, keeping her eyes on Rory's face.

Mary Kate stayed still under her mother's touch. She was not sure she could have moved if she wanted to.

I had forgotten about you, I had forgotten about both of you.

She quivered with alarm. Her thoughts had crashed so loud in the silence that for a moment she thought she must have spoken them out loud. But no one in the room moved, except her mam to give her an absent pat on the arm.

I have been so busy with plans and dreams for getting out of here that I never . . . I should have . . . I could have said to you Dad let me type up those labor notes for you so that . . .

Her dad let out a long shuddering breath as if in reply and then another and suddenly the room was full of sound and motion. With a cry, Maureen started up from her chair, causing it to fall over backward. Mary Kate leaped up and turned her mother away as Dr. Kennedy and the nurse bent over the bed.

oh dear oh dear oh dear oh dear, her mam wept, but so softly that Mary Kate could barely hear the words. She rocked her mother in her arms while the nurse took away the fallen chair.

oh dear oh dear

"Sh, sh," Mary Kate said gently. A silly sound but it seemed to help. Over her mother's head, she could see Rafferty, assisted by young Father Gennaro, starting to give her dad Extreme Unction for the final time. Her mam grew still so Mary Kate released her from her embrace and let her turn around. The two of them watched silently as the priest anointed Rory's body.

Mary Kate had never seen her mother look so old. Maureen was famous for looking a lot younger than her thirty-five years. But now her cheeks were sunken and there were deep semicircles under her eyes. Even the texture of her skin seemed to have changed: from peach to ash. The glorious red hair was a muddy copper color.

She took her mother's hand and was surprised to get a firm squeeze in return. All along she had thought that when the moment of her father's death came, her mam would fly off into a fit of proper Irish hysterics, absolutely and formally inconsolable. Hadn't she seen just that sort of thing happen often enough when she was a little kid singing funerals at Holy Redeemer? Everybody said it was Italians who made the most fuss at funerals, the Sicilians especially, but they were wrong. It was the old-fashioned Irish who howled like mad dogs, filling the church with terrifying echoes. The deathbed scenes must have been mind-boggling. Mary Kate pressed her mother's hand again, a new respect awakening in her.

"Maureen, Mary Catherine," Rafferty said when he was done and, following the others, left them alone in the room.

Her mam didn't say anything. Still crying quietly, she leaned over the bed and smoothed Rory's hair back from his damp forehead. Mary Kate had to move away because, out of

her control, her body had begun to shake with violent, sound-
less sobs.

Why was she weeping, why, why! Over and over she had
wished him dead. At first out of hate because he had
diminished their lives by not trying to be human, because he
had enshrined his illness as the household god that came before
everything else. But, as she had gotten older and run into
other wretched people, like Akky, she had come to understand that she didn't hate him, after all. Worse, she had come
to realize that, somewhere along the way, she had just stopped
caring about him: the Rory in his bed in the flat, because he
was not the real Rory. The other Rory, the impostor, was
not just a sick man, he was a sickness itself, like partial blind-
ness or a heart condition, that had to be taken into consideration, that had to be worked around, that was, plain and
simple, a hindrance in her life that would be removed only by
death.

And now he had been removed. It was a grievous shock.

The sight of her mother carefully arranging her father's
body so that he might at least look dignified in death calmed
her. She went around to the other side of the bed and helped
her mam plump the pillows and straighten the bedclothes.

"He looks very tired," Mary Kate said. She almost did not
recognize his face without its customary scowl.

he had a hard journey

"Yes." And for *what* reason? Mary Kate thought angrily.
What had he ever done that God should see fit to pluck him
out of a busy life and into an illness that was not so much an
illness as a ten-year-long torture? God damn God and the
exactly right cross He had given her dad to bear!

a hard journey, Maureen repeated and then just keeled over without any warning.

"Doctor Kennedy! Doctor Kennedy!" Mary Kate screamed.

The doctor burst into the room and went to Maureen, grabbing for her pulse.

"It's all right, Mary Kate. She's just fainted. She's worn out. She's been without sleep, that's all, and the shock of it. She wouldn't let us call you. Didn't want you worried.

"I'll take her," he said to the nurse. "Four-oh-four is empty. I'll put her in there and you stay with her."

"I'll stay with her, Doctor Kennedy," Mary Kate said.

"Good, good." The big man lifted Maureen up in his arms and Mary Kate suddenly remembered how, in the old days, her dad used to lift the two of them, squealing and giggling, high off the floor. She could feel Rafferty shepherding her out of the room behind the doctor but she stopped and looked past him at her dad. The nurse pressed the call button over the bed, then reached down and pulled the sheet over Rory's face.

Whether she wanted to believe it or not, it was over with her dad.

☙

Mary Kate and Maureen sat at the table in the stifling kitchen eating a delicatessen supper. They were too tired from the heat, missed sleep, and a day spent in making funeral arrangements to talk.

Mary Kate swept her fork in aimless circles around the plate she had filled to brimming as an example to her appetiteless mam, Maureen did not take the hint, just sat picking at her potato salad and cold cuts.

Her mam continued to amaze her. Mary Kate had expected that she and Rafferty would have to make all the arrangements at Sheehan's, the funeral parlor place, but it was Maureen who had done all that, who had remembered about flowers, the telegram to Auntie Kathleen, the telephone calls to friends, the death notice in the *Daily*. She had kept the two of them, who were trying to take care of her, make things easy for her, on the hop. Now she sat, quiet and self-possessed, across from Mary Kate. It was clear she was eating what little she could because it would be a nuisance if she fainted again.

whew, Maureen said, putting her fork down with finality, you think this heat is ever goin' to break I'm meltin' away

"Tell you what. You eat a dish of peach ice cream for me and I'll run a cool bath for you, okay?"

okay

"Then you're going to lie down for a little while, okay?" Mary Kate felt as if she were the mother and Maureen the exhausted child.

ach Mary Catherine it's much too hot for sleepin' but maybe we could sit out on the back steps and catch a breath of

There was the sound of people on the landing and then a knock on the door. A positive thump on the door, and the clamor of strange voices attacking each other: "Get outa me way, it's me she should see first, she'll hardly remember yer face!" "Settle down, settle down . . ." "Who are you to be handin' down orders at a time like this, you dried-up . . ."

Mary Kate opened the door to an elderly couple she didn't know.

"Well, now — " the woman's voice changed from anger to

melting sweetness — "and here we are and sorry I am that it's such a sad oc-casion bringin' us together for the first time." The old woman was middling tall but square with fat. Even her black dress with all its swags and draperies couldn't hide that. Sweat was pouring off her, some collecting in a drop on the end of her nose and transferring itself to the coarse veil hanging down from her big black hat. The man, smaller and trimmer, but with a fair-sized paunch, stood a little behind the woman, his hands clasped in front of him holding on to a dark fedora. He looked so neat it seemed he was in uniform.

Mary Kate looked questioningly at her mam, who had risen part way out of her chair.

"Here, now, woman, don't ye rec-ognize us? You've put on a little here and there," the old lady said, "but I'd recognize you anywhere. Tintin' yer hair these days, are you?"

Maureen was shaking her head, smiling, hurrying around the table.

Kathleen Blaise I didn't expect you'd be here this quick oh thanks for comin'

Mary Kate hastily slapped a smile on her face. Auntie Kathleen? Uncle Blaise? They looked *ancient*. Her dad had turned fifty-three this spring, that made Auntie Kathleen . . . sixty. She *looked* a million and one! She was swept into her aunt's embrace and given a sweaty, smelly kiss on each cheek. "Don't she feed you, ha,ha? Yer nothin' but skin and bones."

Mary Kate wiggled away and shook hands with her uncle.

"You're the very image of your dad," he said.

Whereupon Auntie Kathleen collapsed into loud sobs and a kitchen chair which creaked ominously. "Ah, me own babby

brother, fed and looked after him meself all those years after
the old folks died off so sudden, worried about him when he
went off to that Deetroit place, think of it, him dead and gone
with hardly a word of warnin', Blay'll tell you, I wept all the
way, *all* the way motorin' down from Boston over them
wicked fast roads, it's a good thin' he's the driver he is or you'd
have three funerals on your hands, steada one. Well, at least
he's up there in Heaven where he belongs, ooooooooooooh!
But think of it, the lesson of it, just a young man, struck down
in all his powers . . ." Kathleen began to roar with grief.

She doesn't care about my dad, Mary Kate thought, full of
disgust, she's only interested in *performing!*

there there Kathy dear take it easy now take it easy

Take it *easy?* What Mary Kate wanted to do was to throw
the old fraud down the stairs, nothing less. If she was behaving
this way *now*, God! she would make a shambles of the wake
and the funeral. Her poor mam had enough on her mind
without this.

"Why don't you wash up," Mary Kate suggested, pulling
herself together because chucking her auntie out on her back-
side was not permitted. "The bathroom's just around the
corner there, and I'll fix you something to eat. You must be
tired after your long trip."

Uncle Blaise smiled again, that careful smile of his that did
not involve his eyes yet was not a cold gesture. Where had
she seen that kind of smile before?

"Have you a drop of something?" he asked as soon as
Kathleen had gone off to the bathroom. "I haven't driven a
trip of that length in some years and with her bawling the
whole time . . ."

sure sure Mary Catherine get a glass for your uncle I'll just get the Irish out of the cupboard

Her uncle filled the glass half-full and drained it away in one gulp. The lines in his face eased. He pushed the glass away from him as he heard his wife open the bathroom door.

Auntie Kathleen had taken off her hat and Mary Kate could see her resemblance to Rory. The same high brow, the same proud Irish nose. But her mouth was fat and wet, not like his thin, compressed lips. Her cheeks were pasty and white where his had been lean and flushed.

"This is a min-gy place," the old lady said, looking around disapprovingly, "for all of that. Forgive me for speakin' out so plain, but I don't see no room for us to sleep. There's only the one bedroom, is there not?"

Mary Kate bit her tongue to keep from saying something nasty.

well the place suits three but not four that's why I've made some ar-rangements

"What do ye mean? Where does *she* sleep?" Kathleen pointed at Mary Kate.

that sofa out there in the livin' room it pulls out

"You mean to tell me all the years of her life that kid has been sleepin' on some kinda sofa bed con-traption?"

"Now just a minute . . ." Mary Kate started, but Maureen cut her off.

my dear friend Mrs. Sean O'Shaughnessy down the street just here is plannin' to put you up in her front bedroom big it is and empty since all her kids are married off now she's a good cook does a por-ridge you haven't had since you were a wee babe she came in all this year to look after Rory while I was at work and Mary Catherine was over the river at her Academy place and then at her waitressin' job live-in this summer

Auntie Kathleen's mouth was working.

"Yer askin' us to stay among strangers at a time like this? And how could you, a family needs to be to-gether, a time like this, for con-solation, you haven't changed a bit, I told Rory the first time he laid eyes on you . . ."

"Hush now, Kat, dear, your tongue is loose from your tiredness," Uncle Blaise cajoled.

"And I can smell the liquor off of you already, the curse of me life!" Kathleen's awful mouth turned down at the edges and Mary Kate prepared herself for another siege of that loathsome fake keening.

Siob O'Shaughnessy is the same as fa-mily Kath dear and grievin' over his death she is hard as any of us Rory was the one fought to get her a pension not only from the union but from the State of New York itself when Sean sickened then died from the fumes of the stuff they were usin' in his mill

"I want to stay here," Auntie Kathleen said, her voice as obstinate as a six-year-old's, and looked to her husband for support.

"Auntie Kathleen, darlin'," Mary Kate said, "with all the arrangements and such, the phone's liable to be ringin' at all hours of the day and the night you'd be better off down the way . . ." and stopped, appalled that she had dropped into the stage Irish of her aunt and of her dad at his worst. "I mean, gosh, you need your sleep and at Mrs. O'Shaughnessy's . . ."

"A so-fa bed, you say? I don't think the two of us ud be com-fortable on such a con-trivance. We'll take the bedroom."

"But . . ." Mary Kate said.

Blay dear why don't you bring up your va-lise I'll ring
Siob and tell her you need to stay here

"Ma!"

would you carry my night things out Mary Catherine to
the sittin' room so I won't have to go in later and dis-turb
your auntie and uncle

"*Ma!*"

"Ah, well, and I con-fess it," Kathleen said, nodding her
head piously, "you have that daughter of yours better in hand
than I ever had that former daughter of mine, Deirdre. Would
you believe it, they're livin' over there in Rome, Italy, these
days? That fellah she married got some kind of American
Academy Award, though it's nothin' to do with the movies.
She still writes to me in her pride, ex-pectin' an answer, well
how could I answer such a sin-ful person, I ask you, and livin'
there as they do, prac-tically in the lap of Our Holy Father,
they've never once gone to the Vati-can, and have no babbies
neither, married years and years, the sinnin' pair of them. I
can hardly lift up my head in the block from the shame of
them no matter how good the rest of the kids turned out, even
our little Blay with all his troubles at Boys' Catholic, I tell you
such a hand-some lad is sure to have de-tractors . . . you
don't mind if we take the bedroom, eh? I have a little back
trouble. I've always had a deli-cate con-stitution, you know
that. I find it easiest to sleep in a bed apart from Blay."

Blaise smiled his smile and Mary Kate recognized it. From
the movies, from the lay people who worked around the
Academy in menial jobs. A chauffeur's smile, a servant's smile.
The sort of smile her dad had worked so hard to abolish. Yet
not a smile to despise. Mary Kate decided to play along with
her mam.

in fact Kathleen I was plannin' to ask Mary Kate could I
share her sofa tonight I'm feelin' so lonely

⚜

The fact that the wake and the funeral Mass were crowded
with friends and acquaintances from all over Freshkill kept
Mary Kate from smashing her dear old auntie in the head
every time she let loose one of her theatrical yells, which was
about once a minute, depending on the audience. It poured
buckets during the interment, which caused auntie to hoot that
her ex-pensive mournin' clothes pur-chased for the oc-casion
was gettin' roooooned, but Mary Kate just paid attention to
the mahogany box going into the ground as Rafferty, his
voice breaking, said the sacred words over it.

"He shoulda bin berried in Boston with the old folks,"
Kathleen grumbled all the way back to the flat.

⚜

It was the morning after the funeral, crisp, clear, brilliantly
sunny. The heat wave had broken, giving Freshkill a taste
of the autumn to come. All along Main Street, the stores
were filled with mothers and kids buying back-to-school
clothes.

have a nice walk have a nice walk the day is near perfect,
Maureen called down the front stairs to Kathleen and Blaise.

"Ma," Mary Kate said as soon as the downstairs door
banged shut, "how *long* are they going to stay?"

only God Himself knows the answer to that one but come
now put on that dark dress of yours we've got busi-ness
to attend to that's why I got them off on a walk

"Business?"

Daniel Rothenberg the town attorney as well as other titles
made an appointment with us he's your dad's ex-ecutor

"Ex*e*cutor?"

well some things I should have told you about be-fore have
turned up hurry now child and dress in case they come back
Kathleen sus-pects somethin' that's clear as clear

        ❦

The Rothenbergs had been lawyers in Freshkill for almost
as long as there had been a Freshkill. Drawings and photographs of them lined the walls of the current Lawyer Rothenberg's office and Mary Kate knew that, in a couple of weeks,
yet another Rothenberg would enter Albany Law in the
proud tradition of his forebears.

Daniel Rothenberg, dignified and gray and smelling of
Pappas' coffee, hurried into his office where Maureen and
Mary Kate were waiting.

"There you are. I'm sorry to have kept you waiting." He
embraced Maureen, then shook hands with Mary Kate. "How
are you bearing up, Maureen? I'm sure it must have been a
shock to you, even after all these years." He slid into his chair
behind his massive oak desk.

fine I'm fine thanks to Mary Catherine who's been my good
help

"You're doing well at school, Mary Catherine, I can see
that from the papers. Next year you'll be off to college?"

"Thank you. Yes, I hope so."

forgive me for seemin' ab-rupt Daniel but we have relatives
back at the flat who may be waitin' on us per-haps you could
explain it all to my daughter it's a bit of a sur-prise even to me

if she has any questions you're the person to answer them

Mr. Rothenberg directed his words, slowly and carefully, to Mary Kate, causing her to feel both important and uneasy.

"Your father has left your mother the contents of his bank accounts and one half of the stocks registered in his name."

Bank accounts? *Stocks?* There must be some mistake. Poor people didn't have bank accounts or stocks. Or wills or executors, either.

"You are to receive the other half of his stocks and, in addition, the contents of the safe deposit boxes held in your name and his."

"But . . ."

all those brown paper bags Mary Catherine child his confidential mail I figured it out ages ago but his little in-trigues seemed im-portant to him

"I'm sorry, Mr. Rothenberg," Mary Kate said, "I don't understand." Her voice seemed to be coming from miles away. "There must be some sort of misunderstanding . . ."

what Daniel is sayin' darlin' don't look so alarmed is that your dad wanted to leave us a little somethin'

"It's all here, Mary Catherine." Mr. Rothenberg was holding up a handful of the red paper-covered account books she herself had bought for her dad at Woolworth's over the years. "His deposits, his stock transactions. Just at the end of the war he bought some stocks, very shrewdly, too, I'd say, and then got rid of all but the blue chips, selling high."

They might as well be talking Chinese to her.

when he found out about the emphy-sema you see he took some of our savins to buy the stocks an in-surance policy he called it

"What he's left isn't a great deal, but it's good steady stuff like GM, for instance."

and then when I got my job in the clerk's office he took to bankin' his pension checks and his divi-dends

"The estate amounts to a little less than fifteen thousand dollars," the lawyer continued. "Excluding the stocks, of course. I can have my secretary find out yesterday's closing quotations on that, if you wish."

won't you please explain the busi-ness with the safety boxes to Mary Catherine so she won't be alarmed

"I was just coming to that. First, when Miles Van Nostrand at the bank heard about your father's death, he was required by law to seal the boxes you held jointly with Rory. The boxes have to be opened, the law again, in the presence of a bank officer and a tax man, as well as us of course. That's next Tuesday morning at ten, by the way, Maureen."

so soon ach I thought matters like that took months

"Rory left a clear will, even though he did like things his own secret way, so there should be no complications. And he was very good about paying his taxes. However . . ."

he had me signin' forms, Maureen explained to Mary Kate, with them all covered over paid the taxes with money orders from the bank more of that con-fidential mail stuff he had you dealin' with

"However?" Mary Kate prompted, wanting to get done with all of this money business so that she could get away from this office, where she felt like a beetle trapped in a matchbox. Except beetles did not have fathers who were misers.

"Can you explain these notations? They appear to record dates and sums of money, and may have something to do with the contents of the safe deposit boxes."

"No, you're wrong," Mary Kate said, accepting one of the red notebooks from the lawyer. "The boxes are filled with notes about my father's experiences in the labor movement. He wanted them kept somewhere that was fireproof."

"Just have a look, all right?"

"All right," she said warily.

Right away she was sorry she had taken the notebook because written inside the front cover, in her dad's hand, were the initials MJR and BXS. She flipped a few pages into the book and read:

5/15/49   35.
5/28/49   15.
6/12/49   50.

6/12/49 was around the time of her graduation from Holy Redeemer. She went ahead a few pages.

11/15/51   25.
11/30/51   35.

She turned toward the end of the book, her eyes blurring with tears.

3/15/52   50.
3/31/52   50.
4/15/52   25.

She shut the notebook. The one thing in the world she wanted to do was go someplace private and throw up.

"I think maybe Monsignor Rafferty had been helping my dad out with presents of money. But that doesn't mean that's what's in the boxes. I mean, I saw him writing up the notes myself." But all those fat brown envelopes had felt just like packets of money, not like packets of notes. "I mean, if it's *money* in those boxes, why didn't he use it? We *needed* it!"

Daniel

"We *needed* it, mam!"

"Ladies, I have a pressing appointment up in Poughkeepsie," Mr. Rothenberg said hurriedly. "Why don't you stay here in the office as long as you like. If you have relatives at home, you may want a little privacy to discuss . . ." He gestured at the pile of notebooks on his desk.

thanks Daniel thanks a lot I'll telephone you later

hush child, Maureen said as the door shut, I can see you've had a bit of a shock it's a shock to me too

"I want to get out of here! I don't want to talk about him and his mattress full of money!"

hush now I tell you, Maureen's voice grew stern, you're behavin' like a proper babby instead of a grown girl I was married at your age on my way to bein' a mother

"Why did he do it? Why did he *rob* us all those years? We could have lived in a *house* . . . and all the rest of it! The nasty old bastard!"

Mary Kate's head jerked back from the force of her mother's slap. She wanted to scream and yell but the expression on her mother's face stopped all that.

now you just look me straight in the face and listen to what I have to say and then you can re-sume your hy-sterics

Her mother was bending over her, her face very close.

when he was fourteen years old he had everythin' taken away from him his home his com-fortable life his pros-pects for schoolin' and becomin' an architeck all because his father died so sudden in the car crash leavin' no pro-visions for his wife and kids and her your gran with no head for money spendin' like a queen then dead herself less than a year later you *look* at me this is no fairy tale I'm tellin' you no ro-mantical thing

in a book where everybody lives happy ever after he had the
whole thing happen to him again all over again when that
damned sick-ness came on him robbin' him of the job he loved
so much worked so hard at and all that these books here show

Maureen's voice was getting wilder and wilder, the reserve
of the last few days beginning to crack. Mary Kate stood up
suddenly, causing her mother to back off.

don't go yet you look awful I never meant to slap you but
you've got to understand this hoardin' of his he didn't want
us left high and dry the way

"What about us when he was alive — you a young woman,
me a little kid, always making do or doing without! What
about *that* if he cared so much about us?"

ask one of your psy-chi-atrical doctors out there at Blount
House not me oh oh oh no-o-ot me

All the tears Maureen had held back now came in a wild
and terrifying spasm of weeping. She looked as if she were
being torn apart. Frantic with concern and frustration, Mary
Kate began to cry again. The two of them stood facing each
other, not touching, isolated noisy islands of grief.

Finally Maureen sat down, her tears subsiding but her chest
still heaving. Mary Kate sat down, too.

it's done it's done, her mam repeated at uneven intervals
until she had once again become the dignified widow of the
past few days.

don't be cold-hearted don't be unforgivin' he was a mor-tal
man with a lotta good in him although God forgive me, she
sighed, I'm glad he's laid to rest and outa all of that

ach we'd better be gettin' back even though I left your
auntie a note she's li-able to be callin' out the po-lice

"Oh, *cripes!*" Mary Kate's fist hit the desk. She was glad to be able to turn her anger away from her mam. "I had forgotten about *her*. 'An wair have *you* bin, eh?' " she mimicked. " 'Slippin' out like that, sneakin' around . . .' "

that's her to the life no more of that though you make me want to laugh and I'm sore from weepin' shall we stop at Pappas' and get a cup of coffee before we go back

"Okay, but I'd like to go for a walk afterward, if it's okay with you. If I went back now, coffee or not, I'd just end up screaming at the old bat."

mind your tongue now she is your own flesh and blood you go ahead and take your walk oh Lord I almost forgot

She went out of the office and spoke to Mr. Rothenberg's secretary, then came back into where Mary Kate was sitting.

"What is it, Ma?" Mary Kate asked nervously. "I'm warning you, I'm not up to any more surprises."

no no there's a thin' in Rory's will leavin' a thousand to Kathy and a thousand to Blay and Daniel said he'd ar-range for me to give it to em straight-away

"Tell him to put some train tickets in with the money!"

on that subject I don't know about you but I'm goin' back to work tomorrow mornin' it's the only sen-sible thin' to do you should do the same

"You don't mind me going back out to Blount House and staying there? It'd mean you'd be alone . . ."

Her mother laughed a short, businesslike laugh.

"I've been alone a long time already."

☙

Mary Kate discovered that her aimless steps had carried her to the library end of Main Street where Main Street made a

right-angle turn and began to follow the course of the Freshkill Creek.

Looking down the embankment, she could see the ancient
iron ribs of the Stephanie Bridge, a "piece of engineering history" her dad had called it, crossing the rapids of the creek just
below the dye mills. Now, as in the days she had walked
around Freshkill with her dad, the whitecaps in the creek were
colored green and pink with the waste from the dye works.
There ought to be a law against such dumping.

There probably is, she told herself, but if you enforced it,
even more people would be put out of work than had been
laid off when so many mills closed after the war. The very
reason she had taken the job at Blount, which required living
in, was because there were no jobs for kids in town. The
counters of Woolworth's were staffed by widows who needed
the money to survive.

She had been terrified of the Stephanie Bridge when she was
little because it had seemed so perilously open, even the railings had very wide spaces between them, and there had been
no place, it had seemed, she, a tiny child, could hold on to
easily and she had been sure she would drop into the raging
waters below and be smashed to pieces on the rocks. But her
dad had liked the bridge so much, she had always followed
him out onto it, her knees knocking, her heart pounding.

She strode out onto the bridge now, unafraid, but she could
see why she had been afraid. The cars crossing the bridge
behind her were even noisier than they had been then because
nobody, then or now, was bothering to keep the boards of the
roadbed in decent repair. The town motto might as well be
Penny Wise, Pound Foolish.

One summer's noon, she and her dad had been standing on

this bridge when he pointed out to her a freight train crawling along the tracks on the creek bank.

"Look at the engineer of that train," he had said. "When he gets next to us, take a good look at him. He'll be eating his lunch, chewing on a sandwich or a chicken leg, driving his train at much less than half-speed. You know why, don't you?"

Desperately holding on to the bridge, she had looked up at her dad and had discovered he was asking her one of those questions he didn't expect her to answer.

"I've seen that guy driving his train lots of times," her dad said. "He always works it so he's pulling his train through here on his lunch hour. His own time, if you can call it that. The simple fact of the matter is that he inches his train along through here because it's the first place on his journey that gives him a clear view of the creek and of the town all at once. Which says a lot for him and about him because it's a sight to see. The library, the German church, the way Main Street makes its big bend carrying its shops with it and, at the same time, the creek rushing along, with trees on the other bank, as if it were out in the wilderness. Don't let anybody ever tell you that just because a man is a working man, uneducated, he hasn't got an eye for beauty. That train driver there . . . he loves the way these old buildings look lined up along the creek. Give him a wave now. You'll see what happens."

I'll fall in, she thought, but she trusted her dad, so she had let go and had taken her dad's big white handkerchief and waved to the trainman. And he had gone *Too-oot! Too-oot!* with his train whistle and waved back. Joy and fear had joined in her in such a glorious collision, she had started to bawl out

loud and her dad had laughed and carried her off the Stephanie
Bridge on his shoulders.

Mary Kate looked at the train tracks rusting and overgrown
with weeds. When she made her fortune, she would open up
all the mills this train track had served, give people jobs, get
this town back on its feet. But, first of all, she would buy that
track and shine it up and give that train engineer his old job
back, if he were still around. If he hadn't died.

The scene in the hospital flashed before her eyes in a sick-
ening rush: her dad passing from life to death.

Only, that had happened long ago, she told herself, long
before the official moment in the hospital. God just hadn't
seen fit to give her dad a decent burial, that's all. Had just
kept him around writing his own epitaph in a series of Woolworth account books.

All that money in the safety boxes, she thought. When the
tax man is through, I'll give what's left back to Rafferty. Only
I'll insist, maybe I'll get Mr. Rothenberg to help me, I'll insist that the money be given to somebody hard up who'll *use*
it to help out his kids.

Well, she thought, there is *still* a lot to be figured out. She
started back up the hill toward Main Street. Maybe she should
drop in and see Miss Verplanck, apologize for having to stop
being her assistant volunteer helper because of the waitressing
job. She had noticed, though, in her trips to the library this
summer, a startled-looking little kid, Italian to judge by her
coloring, self-consciously shelving books.

Maybe she would say to Miss Verplanck, "I see the torch
has been passed on."

Maybe not.

10. Seniors

ONE CARDBOARD FILE CASE in the Academy's library was devoted to college catalogues. Mim had its contents spread out on a table in the deserted reference room when Jimmy and Mary Kate came in after school.

"Will you look at this? Will you please look at this?" she said, shaking what looked like a fist at the catalogues.

They looked.

"What's the matter?" Jimmy said.

"Did you ever in your life see such an assortment of Sacred Hearts and Immaculate Hearts and Bleeding Hearts and Dripping Hearts as well as Our Ladys of This, That, and The Other *and* that's not counting the eleven dozen different Mount Saints *or* the absolute galaxy of places named after saints who are probably a*poc*ryphal! I mean, is Saint Proco-pius a name that pops into your head any old moment of the day or night?"

"*Who?*"

"Sounds Roman and obscene," Mary Kate pronounced. "Be careful or the Academy's Christian roof will fall on you."

"And if *it* doesn't, it sounds as if Saint What's-His-Name might. What's your problem, Mim?" Jimmy asked. "You're not yourself. You've lost your usual and characteristic condescending aplomb."

"Haven't you noticed anything about these catalogues?"

"You've already pointed out their variety of colorful names . . ."

"They're all *Catholic!*" Mim drew back with a well-what-do-you-think-of-that shudder.

Jimmy laughed out loud.

"Well, dopey, this is a Catholic school; you think it's going to advertise other brands in its very own library?"

"*Jimmy!*" Mim was genuinely shocked. "Don't tell me you ap*prove* of an attitude like that. I mean, the *old* 'If we just don't talk about it, it'll all go away'! That kind of thinking, that kind of provincialism doesn't *help* the Church — it just turns it into one big inbred family, getting stupider and stupider."

"Wow! Did you feel that earth tremor, Jimmy? The cardinal must have this place bugged."

"That's not as much of a joke as you seem to think, Mary Kate."

"Oh, come *on*, Mim. The cardinal has better things to do than eavesdrop on some dumb girls' school . . ."

"Yeah," Jimmy said, "he sticks strictly to seminaries!" She and Mary Kate burst out in horselaughs. Mim was not amused.

"You know what that implies, don't you? You're saying it your*self!* That to be a Catholic is to be somebody who can't always say what he thinks, and who isn't even sup*posed* to think about some things, for God's sake, because he might endanger his own faith or somebody else's, and don't give me that 'Does anybody have the right to yell Fire! in a crowded theater?' chestnut of Akky's, Jimmy, I see it coming."

"No, I wasn't going to say that. I was going to agree with you, that those kinds of attitudes *do* exist and they're *not* funny, but they're not the Church's *official* attitudes, they're sort of . . . informal interpretations of . . . what I *mean* is, you don't have to take seriously *every*thing some nun or parish priest or even the cardinal says. For instance, this whole thing of the Legion of Decency rating movies and everybody believing that if you see a movie on the Condemned list you commit a mortal sin, *well*, it's founded on *air*. Ozone. It's just a well-meaning bunch of . . ."

". . . priests and poops who are capable of insinuating that C pictures make mortal sins and you know it. And that's a Gestapo tactic they use — making everybody get up in church one Sunday at Mass and take an oath of loyalty to what's really a board of *cen*sors!"

"And you think that file there, filled up with nothing but Catholic catalogues, is part of the same thing?" Mary Kate was not sure whether she was asking a question or coming to a conclusion of her own. "Part of keeping us all in the family, so to speak." When she had thought of it before, which was practically never, she hadn't been too upset about things like the Legion of Decency or the Index; she had merely thought of them as handy guides that saved you from accidentally injuring yourself spiritually. But she could see what Mim meant. "You mean, they try to keep us cut off from the world, to protect us, and pretty soon we have no points of reference out *there* anymore, and we become . . . weaker, rather than stronger . . . weaker and more . . . manageable."

"Exactly. If after us having twelve years of Catholic school education, they *still* don't trust us to go off to some school where everybody isn't going to fall down on their knees at the mention of Pope Pius' name, then something's wrong. Something's very wrong."

And Mim is right, Mary Kate thought, amazed she hadn't figured it out for herself a long time ago.

Now that she didn't have to depend on scholarships for money for college, she had more of a pick. The only thing she wanted, for sure, about her college was that it be in New York City. If anything was ever going to happen to her in her life, it was going to happen in New York City. She had automatically assumed the college would be a Catholic one. In fact, she had been through that very file of catalogues Mim was now disgustedly jamming back in place and she had tentatively chosen a Mount Saint, out of the six Catholic women's colleges in the New York metropolitan area, because it was the shortest distance of them all from Times Square. She would have to start her search all over again. She grew excited at the thought of it.

". . . just don't agree with you, Mim," Jimmy was saying. "I think it's very important to go to a Catholic college, especially if you're going into something like nursing or medicine or journalism or social work where you're constantly faced with decisions of morals and ethics, because a Catholic college, a *good* one, pre*pares* you for the world — Alex and I have this argument all the time — *makes* you think about the problems of the world, but in the context of your religion. That's not cutting you off, that's kicking you the hell out of the nest."

"That looks great on paper, kiddo," Mim said, gathering up

her books, "but just make sure you read the fine print before you sign up at Saint Procopius'."

"Hey, Mim —" Mary Kate suddenly remembered — "what *was* the catalogue you were looking for and couldn't find?"

"Vassar. The *dog* ate mine, one of the babies fed it to him, so I guess I'll just have to go downtown to the Free Library to look up the list of Vassar scholarships. I'm going to prey on their consciences and get them to admit me as this year's Catholic but, with four other kids in the family plus that *dog*, I need money, too."

"I'll bet *that* little confidence blew out the cardinal's hearing aid."

"If it didn't, the tidal wave'll get him when it gets us for *her* blaspheming," Mary Kate said. "Who'd ever think in a nice quiet place like the Academy you could have such dangerous friends."

☙

Of the sixty of them who had started out together four years ago, only thirty were left. Transfers, vocations, expulsions, sudden marriages had thinned the ranks.

Mary Kate felt the warm June breeze flutter the wreath of red roses in her hair, smelled the heavy fragrance wafting up from the long-stemmed roses she held cradled in her left arm. Within the hour, she would be holding a diploma in her right hand.

No, that was wrong. She already had her diploma, had had it for six weeks: a letter of acceptance from Barnard College in New York City. Several times during the interview down there, she had just wanted to give up and say, "You don't want me; I'm just a dumb convent school kid; I don't know anything about anything." Funny thing was, *they* seemed to know that, and not to mind. Maybe all she was was this year's Catholic for Barnard. That was good enough for her, to begin with.

"Now if you young ladies will just take your places on the front steps of Main, we can get the class pictures done in no time at all, no time at all." The photographer was bustling from group to group, trying to separate his subjects from their well-wishers. "Parents, please, you'll be very disappointed with the results if the pictures have to be taken in a rush, please cooperate now, parents, let the girls assemble. Would you clear the steps, please?" Poor Mr. Dorati. He had been taking pictures at the Academy for years and years and it was always the same: talking when he wanted quiet, movement when he wanted repose, poker faces when he wanted smiles.

The girls strolled languidly toward the steps, and she did, too. It was the natural way to walk on a summery day when you were dressed up in a beautiful long white embroidered organdy gown and roses and roses and the sun was shining and the Hudson was sparkling and you were commencing your own life (and why did nuns think nobody knew why Commencement was called Commencement and keep telling you!) and Barnard College was not just Barnard College but also part of the gigantic Columbia University in the City of New York, and let Harry's friend at CCNY put *that* in his pipe and smoke it!

"Very good, young ladies. If the second row will just take one step to the left . . . good, good. I'm going to make several exposures — " she heard Bobbie Covetti's snort of a laugh — "so stand as still as possible and keep smiling, keep smiling," Mr. Dorati chirruped, "so you'll have a beautiful record of June nineteenth, nineteen fifty-three for your memory books."

A muscle in Mary Kate's temple twitched involuntarily, and she had the ominous feeling that the sky over the valley was about to gather itself together, turn black, and explode into a storm.

The Rosenbergs. She tried to shut them out of her mind and to concentrate on smiling but it was no good.

You couldn't go to Barnard without a social conscience like Eleanor Roosevelt's, Mim had said, so for the last six weeks Mary Kate had been slogging through the *New York Times*, cover to cover, every day. She didn't know yet whether she had developed a social conscience but she did know one thing. The world out there waiting for her was not all Fred Astaire and Ginger Rogers by a long shot. There were certain things you just couldn't ignore, like the irony of today, of this very moment.

After all, what was the opposite of commencement, except maybe death? That was what the Rosenbergs had been on the brink of yesterday until Justice Douglas' stay. And were on the brink of again today, if the rest of the Supreme Court disagreed with his reasons for the stay. The hearing was supposed to be at noon but nobody here had been near a radio since long before that.

Mary Kate had wanted the day to race along like a fast Viennese waltz or Gershwin's *Second Rhapsody* so she could get her diploma, her New York State scholarship, the other prizes, all that stuff, get all of that over, and be free of the Academy! But nobody decent could want to hurry along a day that might be the last day of somebody else's life.

Today, the string trio would pipe them aboard and the bishop would hand out the honors and the speaker, a Famous Catholic politician, would make appropriate, probably long, remarks, and the Choristers would do their four-part "Ecce Sacerdos" that laid 'em in the aisles and everybody would say how lovely it had all been.

While, down the Hudson, this very river, this ageless river, at Sing Sing, it would probably be very quiet, and not lovely at all.

Oh, *why* had they done it? They didn't look like spies — they looked like a pair of public school teachers. Why had they taken such risks when they had two little boys, one six, one ten, and she had seen a photograph of the kids picketing with their grandmother in front of the White House, and they had looked like *little* kids. Parents ought to know their kids *needed* them. Not take such chances, even if it was for something really important they really believed in.

And, why was it allowed that people could be officially legally killed for breaking *rules?* "An eye for an eye, a tooth for a tooth . . ." *That* was a whole lot of crap!

Oh God, she thought, if you *are* there, don't kill the Rosenbergs or any, any, *any*body else! They call you the Organizer of the Universe; well, for God's sake, *organize it for a change* and along *peace*ful lines.

"A little more of a smile, back there, Miss Mulligan, please?" The photographer's voice going up the scale.

"Oh, I'm sorry, Mr. Dorati," she said and then did concentrate on smiling.

The photographer took one more shot, then called out

girls, one after another, for the smaller photographs of class and club officers and of the senior staffs of *The Flame* and the yearbook. Mary Kate was kept busy moving from one group to another, smiling, smiling, smiling. Miss Jantzen had taught her well. She felt dead as a doornail inside, however she looked on the outside.

"Hey! You're a million miles away."

It was Jimmy.

"Gosh, Jimmy, you look beautiful." And she did. Transformed from her usual Tom Sawyer into Jo March, the best of all those simpy sisters she had cried over.

"Listen," Jimmy said, "you're going to hate this, but I want to say good-bye."

Mary Kate blinked hard, squeezing the Rosenberg tears out of all existence.

"Come *on*, Jimmy. That sounds C and D." Mim's shorthand for childish and dramatic.

"Come on, yourself. Me going out to Marquette, you going down to the city . . . we'll probably never see each other again. Both of us are ready to fly the coop and you know it."

"Okay."

"If you're ever home, and I doubt that with all the temptations of the city, and you want to come over for the weekend, call up my mother. She'll have my schedule."

A nun's voice sounded in the background, causing the girl graduates to scurry into proper position, carrying Jimmy and Mary Kate apart.

"Just don't get married to Justin, okay?"

"Mind your own business, okay?"

"You better believe it," Mary Kate shouted, absolutely sure of her words.

"Just save me a place in your memories when you're famous," Jimmy called.

"Jimmy!" She wanted to holler, Come back! Let's conquer New York together!

But there was that damned nun's voice interrupting, imperious, carrying with it the threat of excommunication and damnation if the young ladies did not im*med*iately get into single file, start their stately march up the front steps into Main, through the chapel vestibule, then down the stairs to the auditorium where All of It was about to happen.

All she could see of Jimmy was the back of her head, her crown of roses slipping slightly askew.

Wait a minute, she wanted to yell. I have to talk to you. I should have talked to you, much, much more honestly, all these years but I was afrai—

She saw Jimmy's face suddenly turn around, strained to hear her words.

" 'Adieu, adieu, remember me . . .' " Jimmy had played Horatio to her Hamlet in the Senior Production and she knew all the words, *all* the words.

Mary Kate stood on her toes and shouted Hamlet's words:
" 'I HAVE SWORN'T!' "

"Miss Mulligan!"

Mary Kate knifed a look at the bossy nun, one from the convent side whose name she didn't know. Then, it came as a surprise to her, too, she burst into the biggest smile of her entire life. Having to say good-bye to Jimmy, and Jimmy was right, was more proof than a million diplomas or letters from

Barnard that her life was commencing, that — the song flooded through her —

> There's a boat that's leavin' sooooon for New York
> Come with me
> That's where we belong, sis-tuh!

The nun was visibly taken aback. My *God*, Mary Kate thought, did I sing it out loud?

Then the nun smiled back.

"Congratulations," she said. "Good luck and God bless you."

God. God is beginning to be a problem, Mary Kate thought, but said to the nun, "Thank you, Sister. I'm so nervous I could die," which caused the nun to *tsk tsk* at her. And rightly so.

No, not die. If the Justices have said no, the Rosenbergs will be killed tonight and the papers said before sunset because the Jewish Sabbath begins at sunset and the Rosenbergs are Jewish. And it was the Jews who had written down "an eye for an eye . . ." Maybe, instead of commencing, she just ought to run someplace and lock herself in a closet and never, ever come out. The world was a good, exciting place, but it was also a mean, dangerous place.

The line had slowed down, almost to a halt, as the girls ahead of her negotiated all those steps in their long skirts. She was the last one in line, and the bossy nun had disappeared; she turned around and looked at the river and its valley.

She hadn't been born here, like Miss Verplanck, but, true enough, here was where her roots were sunk, no matter if, in the life ahead of her, she traveled the world. Over there,

Freshkill snored in the sun. On the river, the ferry-boats crossed like sleepwalkers in the shimmering heat. All of it was her Catawba.

Probably none of it would ever change. She would come back and she would say, It's so good to be back; nothing ever seems to change.

There was a rustle of movement and she turned around, once more the graduating senior, parent and friends awaiting within.

You dumbbell! Think how much it's changed over there just in your lifetime. Gone from that wonderful brawling Labor Day, nobody who was there will ever forget it, to a set of rusty railroad tracks running past empty mills. And it'll probably go downhill from there. There will always be bad, unhappy things going on in the world. Her mam had said.

She had the impulse to say a prayer for the Rosenberg kids. Ever since her dad's death, though, she had grown self-conscious about praying. Until she had time to make up her mind, one way or the other, about praying and God and all that, and that would be during the long, sleepy breaks between waitressing shifts at Blount House this summer, she was just going to try to get along by going through the motions of her religion. She wasn't the first Catholic this sort of thing had happened to. She would just go through the motions, the way she had done, in the beginning, with field hockey and the Choristers and Social Graces and even, sometimes, with Miss Jantzen, and maybe, as then, she would come to know something she hadn't known before, that would be a help to her in living her life.

Her *life! Her* life! *Her life!*

She was in the cool marble chapel lobby now. Already it seemed less familiar, *past*. Good, good! She had *miles* to go and promises to keep she hadn't even found out about yet.

As she solemnly paced down the stairs to the auditorium, she could hear the music of the string trio and a low, but real, murmur of laughter in the auditorium. Had some elegant graduate tripped on her skirts and fallen flat on her face in a hurricane of drying rose petals? But, no, the line was moving steadily.

Then she recognized the music. Schubert's *March Militaire*, a sprightly tune, one that Jimmy had often played while she and Mim racketed around the McNaughtons' attic, doing their own versions of silent movies. Schubert's *March Militaire*, known to every lay member of the audience as the music sparkplugs and headlights and car batteries precision-marched to on a television commercial once a week in prime time.

Maybe God was up there, after all, putting graduates of the Academy in proper perspective.

Like a bride going down the aisle, she smiled and nodded at the people she knew along the way.

Good-bye, good-bye, she was saying inside.